D0973940

A COMPROMISING POSITION

If Charmaine hadn't been wearing a darn corset, she would have been able to right herself in time, but as it was she fell stiffly forward and into the stranger's ill-prepared arms. The boot he'd been holding in one hand went flying, and as he caught her around the waist they went tumbling over the side of the gazebo. Strong arms tightened around her, and when they fell, his body cushioned the blow for her.

He landed flat on his back, and she landed atop him with a knee on either side of his waist and her skirts bunched around her thighs. Her heart was pounding, her hair was falling in disarray about her face, and her expensive gown was falling off of one shoulder.

His hand found her face; long fingers touched her cheek briefly and then moved to the back of her head, and after a pause where taking a breath was impossible, the stranger pulled her face to his and kissed her again. She had never been so close to any man before, never had her body pressed to his and her mouth joined in this impossible way. The rush of longing that coursed through her body was unexpected and unwanted and much too powerful for her to ignore.

"I'll kill you."

It took Charmaine a moment to realize that the husky voice had not come from the man beneath her.

Cinderfella

Linda Jones

LOVE SPELL BOOKS NEW YORK CITY

*This book is dedicated to my middle baby, Brian,
the only one of my three sons who will read a
book without the dreaded threat of his mother's singing.
Here's to happy endings.*

LOVE SPELL®

September 1998

Published by

Dorchester Publishing Co., Inc.
276 Fifth Avenue
New York, NY 10001

ISBN 0-505-52275-6

Cinderfella

Prologue

Kansas, 1895

It wasn't just a ranch, it was an empire. It wasn't just land, it was his kingdom.

Stuart Haley shoved his hands into his pockets and squinted against the golden sunset's radiance that poured through the window. The setting sun shone on this fine house, lit the study that was his domain in this, his castle.

What would become of his empire when he was gone? Felicity, the eldest and most practical of his three daughters, was firmly settled in Boston with that physician husband of hers and a little girl of her own. Jeanette, who had been flighty all her life, was now content to make a home in Philadelphia with her husband, a lawyer for God's sake! They had their own lives, families of their own. It seemed neither of his older daughters had any concern for their childhood home.

He never should've allowed them to go East. His wife, Maureen, had been so insistent on seeing her daughters properly educated, and one after another his girls had headed from home for a so-called better life. Hogwash! He should've insisted that *one* of them stay here and marry a local boy who would become the son he'd never had, but he'd never had the heart to deny Maureen anything.

Charmaine was his last chance. If he was to see this kingdom passed on to his own blood, it would be through her. His youngest daughter was his last chance to save this empire.

"Where are your thoughts, Stuart?"

Maureen's soft question wiped the frown from his face, and when he turned to see her standing in the doorway of his study his heart beat a little faster. She was nearly forty-five years old, he was just past forty-eight, they'd been married twenty-seven years—and the sight of her still took his breath away.

"I was just thinking about Charmaine. She'll be here in three days."

Maureen's smile was brilliant. If anything, she was more beautiful today than she'd been at seventeen, when he'd met her and fallen instantly in love. Her hair was no longer a pale blond, but was a light brown streaked with touches of gray. Her body had matured with the birth of three children and the passing years, but she was slender and graceful as ever. "I'm excited, too."

He'd never uttered a word of displeasure to Maureen about not having sons. He'd rather have her than a dozen sons to follow in his footsteps. The girls had come not much more than a year apart, each more beautiful than the last, and then—nothing. Not because they hadn't tried. The doctor had no answers, and Maureen had finally accepted her inability to have more children as the will of God. It had rarely been mentioned in the past fifteen years.

"Maybe she'll decide to stay," he said hopefully.

Maureen crossed the room, gliding gracefully across the thick carpet and stepping past his polished walnut desk until she stood beside him. She slipped a slender arm around his waist and leaned against his side. "She might not, you know," she said softly. "This is just a visit, and she agreed only because your letters have been so insistent. She'd just as soon wait to see us when we can make the trip to Boston."

"She does like the city, doesn't she?"

Maureen nodded. "Remember her last letter? It was three pages long and exclusively about that masked ball she attended. Felicity and Howard evidently thought it much too fool-hardy, but Charmaine had a grand time."

Charmaine was his only hope. Somehow he had to convince her that there was nothing in Boston that she couldn't have in Salley Creek. "We could throw a masked ball right here."

Maureen laughed lightly. "Here? Why, there's never been such a thing in Salley Creek."

"There's got to be a first time for everything." He would show Charmaine that Salley Creek could be just as exciting as Boston. There would be music, food, people from miles around. Men, lots of good, solid, Kansans who would be happy to marry into the Haley family.

"I don't know. . . ."

"Let's do it." It was the perfect solution, and his mind was made up. Maureen would try to change it, but the decision had already been made. "Why, Charmaine might even meet a man who can convince her to stay here where she belongs."

"Stuart!" Maureen stepped away from him and stared up with shock in those big blue eyes of hers. "You're not thinking . . ."

He couldn't stop the grin that spread across his face.

"You *are!*"

"And why not?" He pulled her back into his embrace. "If I put out the word that I'm looking for a husband for Charmaine, every eligible

man for a hundred miles will be here. There's
bound to be *one*—"

"Stuart!"

"One man who can convince Charmaine to
stay here where she belongs." It was a chance
he had to take. "Dammit, Maureen, what have
I worked for all my life, if not for my family?
What's going to become of this place when
we're gone?"

Those blue eyes softened. "I should have
given you a son."

He placed a finger over Maureen's lips to
gently silence her. "You know I wouldn't trade
any one of my girls for a son. I have no regrets
about my life, and goodness knows there's nothing like having four beautiful women in the
house to keep a man on his toes."

His finger slid away, and he bent to kiss her.
Her lips were welcoming, tender, and anxious.
She pulled her mouth away from his, but con-
tinued to hold on tight.

"Don't get your hopes up about Charmaine
staying. She's been away eight years, and not
once in her letters or during our visits East has
she expressed a desire to come back to Kansas
to live. She's building a new life for herself in
Boston, with the help of Felicity and Howard."

"You don't know," he began, turning with
Maureen in his arms and heading for the door,
"that there's nothing and no one who can con-

13

vince her to stay. We'll have that masked ball, and just see what happens."

"But Stuart," Maureen protested weakly.

"We'll talk about it later," he said, propelling her toward the stairs and their bedroom.

Chapter One

Odd, this flutter in her chest that could only be called excitement. She hadn't expected it at all, but the closer the train came to Salley Creek the more decidedly eager Charmaine felt.

"Isn't it beautiful?" she breathed, turning from the window to her traveling companion.

Ruth looked less than impressed, but then the poor girl had been sour since their departure from Boston, even though Felicity had promised a nice bonus for this service that was above and beyond that of a ladies' maid. Charmaine would have been quite content to travel alone but Howard would have none of that, so Charmaine found herself saddled with a young and

15

inexperienced ladies' maid who evidently didn't like her job *or* traveling.

Ruth glanced beyond Charmaine's shoulder, as if perhaps she'd missed something in her earlier perusal of the landscape. "It's lovely, in its own simple way," she said tactfully.

Lovely. Charmaine ignored the hint of reservation in Ruth's voice. Green, rolling hills as far as she could see, the tall grasses swaying in the wind. Sunshine touching it all with a gentle golden light. Sky so wide and so bright a blue it nearly hurt her eyes to look at it. Lovely, and she hadn't missed it until this very moment.

Her homecoming was spoiled by the certainty of her father's plans. Yes, she knew exactly what he wanted, what he *expected* of her. He tried to be subtle, the poor dear, but it simply wasn't in his nature. A few loudly mumbled sentences on his last visit to Boston, terse lines scribbled at the bottoms of her mother's letters—his intentions were quite clear. He wanted her to come home and stay, marry a man who would follow in his footsteps, and have a baby every year until the Haley land— all 720 acres—was bursting with them.

How could she make her father see that she was a modern woman, with ideas and plans of her own? She would forever be the baby in his eyes, she feared, and he would never approve of her plan to stay in Boston and assist Howard by giving lectures and distributing manuals to educate women. Charmaine was certain she was meant for greater things than domesticity, and working with Howard gave her such a sense of purpose. Still, Stuart Haley would never understand why one of his daughters might choose to never marry.

They were almost there. She could see the buildings at the edge of Salley Creek. Goodness, it had grown in eight years, but it was still such a small town. The buildings were rough and low, and only one rose above two stories. The entire tiny town was dusty and crude, in a charming way, and was utterly isolated. How could she convince her father that she could never be happy here, except on an occasional visit?

Charmaine nervously smoothed the skirt of her blue serge traveling suit. Why, she just wouldn't mention it. When he brought up the subject she would be vague and pretend not to understand. She could do that, couldn't she? Pretend not to understand and keep her opinions to herself. Keeping her opinions to herself had never been her strong suit, but in this case she would make the effort. And when her father gave up, as he finally must, she would visit and rest, spend time with her mother, and see old friends.

In spite of her nervousness, she smiled widely. Eula was still in Salley Creek, married to the owner of the mercantile, and the mother of two. Delia was teaching school now, unmarried and living with her brother, since their folks had given up the farm and moved back to St. Louis. Those were the only two she was sure of. So many of her old chums had moved on, searching, as she was herself, for a better life.

Ash Coleman was still there, she was sure, even though her mother never mentioned him in her letters. Maureen Haley had never approved of her youngest daughter's childish infatuation with the son of the farmer whose land adjoined theirs to the west, and Charmaine remembered still that the very idea had made her father livid.

Ash was firmly planted in her mind, an indelible part of her memories, but in the past few years the clarity of his features had faded. Sometimes, for a fleeting moment, she could picture him so distinctly, and then he'd be gone. Ash had been beautiful at seventeen, when she'd last seen him, and for all of her life in Kansas the sight of him had made her heart beat a little faster. She'd even declared—to Felicity and Jeanette more than once and on one mortifying occasion to Ash himself—that one day she was going to marry him.

Goodness, why was she wasting her thoughts on such childish memories? Ash Coleman was probably already married and raising a brood on his father's farm. After all, he was twenty-five years old.

They were slowing down, approaching the station at last. Charmaine fluffed the oversized bow at her throat and checked her fashionably small felt hat to see that it was seated properly. She couldn't believe that she was so excited about a two-week visit in a town where nothing ever happened. There would be no seminars, no heated discussions of the latest manuals over coffee and cake, no theater, no concerts. Why, if she were to discuss the latest thoughts on women's rights, she would likely shock all of Salley Creek. If she were to discuss the latest findings on the more intimate aspects of marital relations, she'd likely be run out of town on a rail. This was, after all, a sleepy town where nothing ever happened and time stood still while the rest of the world marched forward.

Oh well, in her heart it would always be home. And it was, after all, just for two weeks.

She saw her father's head towering above the rest as she stepped down onto the platform. He was wearing a great smile, a grin that deepened the wrinkles on his weathered face. Less than a minute later she was lifted from her feet in a great bear hug.

"I can't believe you're finally home," he said as he set Charmaine on her feet.

It sounded so permanent, *finally home*, but she wouldn't argue with him now and ruin this homecoming. Her mother's hug was gentler, but no less loving.

After Ruth was introduced and arrangements were made for the luggage to be delivered, they all walked from the depot to the house. Charmaine was positioned comfortably and closely between her parents.

"You're too durn skinny," her father said as he slipped his arm over her shoulder.

"She is not," her mother said with a despairing sigh. "She's perfectly lovely and looks very grown up."

Charmaine didn't correct her father with the admission that she was far from skinny, nor did she tell her mother that at twenty-one she *was* grown up. She was too busy looking past her parents to the bustling town that was familiar and at the same time very *un*familiar. There were two mercantiles *and* a feed store, and with customers coming and going they all seemed to flourish. The bank had doubled in size, and there was a restaurant right next door. The post office now had its own building, leaving the funeral parlor the lone occupant of a building they had once shared.

The boarding house, the single three-story building in town, had expanded and was freshly painted. Right next door to the boarding house was a small pharmacy, and there was a sign in the window that advertised ice cream. At the end of the street stood the newly built stone schoolhouse, a building that had recently replaced the log cabin where the children of Salley Creek had attended school for thirty years.

There were lots of people out and about, most of them strangers to Charmaine. Some of the faces that turned her way were vaguely familiar, but names eluded her. Eight years hadn't seemed like such a long time until this very moment.

Ruth was evidently unimpressed. She kept her eyes on the boardwalk and followed silently.

Memories flooded Charmaine as she walked down the boardwalk, sandwiched between her parents who were chattering happily. The move from the original ranch cabin to the big house at the edge of town, when she was six years old. That crotchety old schoolmaster, Mr. Warren. Her first heartbreak at the age of ten, when Zachary Middleton had told her he didn't play with *girls*. She could almost taste the lemon drops her father had always bought for her when he purchased his tobacco from the mercantile.

She remembered Ash Coleman laughing at her when she declared she was going to marry him one day, and how well she recalled watching him ride away with his father, laughing still, a man at sixteen while she was still a puny and unformed twelve.

He'd called her Runt, after hearing Jeanette use that dreaded nickname once as they left church. It had always been the bane of Charmaine's existence that she wasn't tall and willowy like her sisters. She'd always been short, and though she'd been a late bloomer, her breasts and hips had rounded quickly. Even now, she wished for a leaner and taller frame, a more austere silhouette. There were some people who simply refused to take you seriously if you were short, and rounded in the wrong places.

A squeal that was uncannily familiar after all these years made Charmaine stop in her tracks. She whirled around in time to catch the woman who hurled herself forward.

"I can't believe you're really here!" Eula said as she squeezed once and then stepped back, her hands resting comfortably on Charmaine's arms.

The voice hadn't changed, but Charmaine was sure she wouldn't have recognized Eula if she'd passed her on a Boston street. Not only was the dark-haired woman considerably taller than she'd been at thirteen, but she'd put on several pounds with each of the two children she'd given birth to, a fact she'd complained about in her frequent letters. Charmaine, to her own dismay, had barely grown an inch in height since leaving Salley Creek. She stood a mere five-feet-one-inch tall, if she stretched out as much as possible. She had to look up into Eula's face.

"Neither can I. Can you come home with me now? Talk to me while I settle in? We have so much to catch up on." A visit with Eula would also postpone the inevitable confrontation with her father.

Eula shook her head quickly. "I can't. This is a busy time of the day for us. The only reason Winston allowed me to run out here and greet you is so I can give a message to Mrs. Haley."

Eula straighted her spine and turned to face Charmaine's mother. "Winston is certain he can have those supplies for you in two weeks, and Mrs. O'Neal is going to help me with the masks."

"Two weeks?" Maureen Haley repeated, obviously disappointed.

"Masks?" Charmaine looked to her mother for an answer.

"Two weeks, ma'am, and that's paying extra freight costs for the materials that are coming in from San Francisco."

Maureen Haley had always been unfailingly practical, and she was calm now. "That doesn't leave us much time for preparation, does it? Oh well, we'll just have the party in three weeks."

"Party?"

Eula turned her smiling face back to Charmaine. "Why, everyone's so excited they're about to bust. Just think of it, a masked ball right here in Salley Creek. I've already started working on my gown."

"I'm supposed to return to Boston in two weeks." Charmaine directed this statement to her mother, who continued to smile serenely.

"Another week or two won't make all that much difference, now will it?" she replied.

"Not a bit," Stuart Haley thundered.

Charmaine rolled her eyes at her father's hearty and much too jolly interruption. Fortunately, no one saw but Eula, and her only reaction was a slight lifting of dark eyebrows.

"There's nothing in Boston," he declared with finality, "that won't still be there in a month or two."

Charmaine sighed. Had her two weeks already turned into a month or two?

Eula hurried back to the mercantile and to her husband, Winston, and Charmaine was physically turned about by her father's big hands on her shoulders.

The air that drifted through the open window was cool, almost cold, but Ash didn't make a move to close it. Fall was a busy time of the year for him, though he always enjoyed it while it lasted. Winter was close behind, and that meant bouts of snow and ice, and wind that was truly cold.

In the moonlight, the farm was peaceful. The barnyard was quiet, the fields beyond were perfection in the soft light of the moon. In the house all was quiet as well. No one stirred but him. He was the restless one, the one who roamed the house or stood at an open window long after dark.

He heard it, a soft peal that carried on the wind. Midnight, struck on the Salley Creek clock that old Randall Salley had erected before his death. His gift to the town, he said, a monster of a clock that sounded each hour of the day. Ash couldn't always hear the chimes from miles away, but when the air and the wind were right, the sound carried to his window like a soft and plaintive cry in the night.

The peal of midnight reminded him that another day had begun, another day that promised to be just like the one that had passed.

He closed the window softly.

She'd been home five days, and already she was beginning to feel like the child her parents treated her as. They refused to accept that she was no longer thirteen, that she had thoughts and plans of her own.

There wasn't a single ally in this house, not even the one person who shared her predicament. Ruth was quite unhappy with the change of plans. An extended visit to Salley Creek, Kansas, was not on her agenda, but like Charmaine she saw no way out. Instead of joining forces and commiserating, Ruth preferred to take her frustration out on Charmaine.

These evening meals were becoming a tedious routine. Her father went on and on about how wonderfully the ranch was doing, and how great some man or another was, and how splendid it was to have his baby home.

After the first three nights, she'd quit trying to tell him that she was *not* his baby any more.

She wanted to go home. Home to Boston. It wasn't just her father who had her distressed. Eula, her oldest and dearest friend, was so changed. She had become everything Charmaine had preached against in the past two years. How could poor Eula be truly happy? She was a virtual slave to her husband's whims, working in his store, keeping his house, bearing and raising his children. And yet she seemed to be happy, poor thing.

Charmaine had at first had such hope for her other friend, Delia. She was a schoolteacher, a dedicated professional, and an independent woman . . . but a brief visit had quickly revealed that Delia had one desire in life. To find a man, get married, and settle down into the same drudgery Eula groveled in.

It had been Eula who'd shared the news about Ash Coleman, remembering that Charmaine had once been smitten. John Coleman, Ash's father, had passed on last year, and Ash was sharing the ranch with his stepmother—a woman Charmaine had never met or heard about—and two stepbrothers.

It occurred to Charmaine, then and now, that she really should stop by the Coleman farm to pay her respects to Ash and perhaps meet the rest of the family. That would be, certainly, the civilized and proper thing to do.

Her father was going on again, as he speared a large chunk of beef, about the plans for the masked ball. He really seemed to think that if he threw a party she would stay. Goodness, he didn't understand her at all.

"Stuart, you should see the dress we're making for Charmaine," her mother said between delicate bites of beef. "It's the most gorgeous creation, snow-white with just a touch of peach in the bodice and skirt ornamentation. Seed pearls are sewn into the neckline and into a floral motif on the full skirt."

Her father winked at her and smiled widely. "Sounds like a wedding dress to me."

Charmaine took her napkin from her lap and placed it, slowly and gently, on the table by her plate. She couldn't go on this way, not for better than another two weeks. Her father had to understand who she was and what she wanted. Now was as good a time as any to get this over with.

"I've made a very important decision, recently." Charmaine's voice was low and composed, but the calm was all an act. Her heart pounded, and her palms began to sweat. "I do hope you'll understand and support me." She straightened her spine and took a deep breath before continuing. "I'll probably never marry."

"What?" her father leaned forward, head

tilted to bring one ear closer to this unthinkable statement.

If she explained, surely he would understand. "Women are meant for more than breeding and submission to a man's pleasure, and what other reasons—"

"Charmaine Haley!" Her father shot to his feet, and his face turned an alarming shade of red.

"Now, now." Maureen Haley patted the hand her husband had placed on the table and now leaned against. "I'm sure Charmaine didn't mean what she said." A censuring look that was surely meant to convey an order to agree shot from Maureen to her daughter.

"I *did* mean what I said," Charmaine insisted gently. "There's an entire world outside Salley Creek, and it's growing and changing every day. There's more to life for an educated woman than a sorry existence of emotional servitude and physical subservience."

Stuart Haley narrowed his eyes as if he couldn't believe that this was his daughter he was looking at. "Howard filled your head with this nonsense, didn't he, that puny little pompous ass."

"Now, Stuart—"

Charmaine interrupted her mother. "Howard is an intelligent and well-respected physician, your son-in-law, and the father of your granddaughter. I think it's inappropriate for you to call him a pompous ass."

"What has he done to you?" With a sigh, her father took his seat.

If only she could make him see that what she was doing was important, necessary, and *right*, she could enjoy her visit here and then return home to Boston with a clear conscience. And perhaps in the future they could avoid these awkward moments. "I've assisted him in several seminars, distributed educational manuals, and spoken with those women who were uncomfortable discussing personal matters with a man, even one who is a physician."

"Personal matters?" he asked dully, as if he didn't really want to know. "Personal matters such as what?"

"Marital continence, for one." She tried not to blush, but this was, after all, her father. "Contraception, if the more desirable self-restraint is impossible. The unhealthy influence of the bicycle and romantic novels on young women, for another. Then there's the physical detriment of the corset, and the—"

"Marital continence?" he repeated in a monotone. "Does that mean what I think it means?"

"Of course. Healthy marriages don't depend on a physical relationship." She forgot, for a moment, that these were her parents. "Once a married couple has all the children they desire, abstinence is the healthiest course of action for everyone involved. The myth that the marital embrace is necessary—"

"Maureen, make her stop."

Charmaine bit her lower lip as she studied her father's unnaturally pale face. "I didn't mean to embarrass you, Daddy."

His shock gave way to anger. She could see it, as the color came back to his face all at once, his jaw hardened, and his gray eyes glinted like steel. She could see it, as the hands that had been flat on the tablecloth slowly balled into fists.

"Boston!" he spat. "I never should have sent you there, and you're not going back!"

"Daddy!" Charmaine shot to her feet as her father had. They stood at opposite ends of the long table and faced one another defiantly. "You can't—"

"This discussion is over," he said as he turned away. "I think I'll skip dessert tonight, Maureen. I've lost my appetite."

After her father stormed from the room, Charmaine slowly and gracefully took her seat. He'd change his mind in a day or two. After all, she was twenty-one years old, and he couldn't force her to stay here. He couldn't keep her prisoner.

"Well, Charmaine." The slightly edgy voice reminded Charmaine that she was not alone. Of course, her mother would understand. Her mother wouldn't force her stay here when the time to leave came. "That was a scene I could have done without."

It *had* turned rather ugly, there at the end. Charmaine hadn't meant to embarrass her father, not really, she'd just said what was on her mind as she usually did. If he would simply accept the fact that she was a grown woman and treat her as such, they wouldn't have a problem at all.

"I did think Daddy was more open-minded than this," she declared sensibly.

"And whatever gave you that idea?"

There was a sharpness Charmaine had never heard in Maureen Haley's voice, and she realized again that she had not a single ally in this house. Not even her own mother.

Chapter Two

Ash hurried through the morning chores, taking the time to say a few soothing words to the dairy cows and the horses as he saw them fed and watered. It was Elmo's job, supposedly, but Elmo was feeling poorly this morning. Again. Ash was certain that his youngest stepbrother would be feeling fine as soon as the chores were done.

This was a bad morning for Elmo to lie in bed and moan about his aching rounded stomach and his pounding ugly head. It was time to plant the winter wheat, and Ash had his hands full. When the animals were taken care of, he'd grab a bite to eat and a glass of milk and head out to the fields. Oswald was supposed to help, but he'd no doubt have his head stuck in a book and be too engrossed to leave the comfort of the house. It was just as well. Oswald usually ended up making more work for Ash, when he should have been helping.

When he had time to daydream, which wasn't often, Ash wondered what his life would be like if his father had never married Verna March and brought her and her two boys to the farm. It was a nice thought, one that had intruded into his thoughts often in the past two years and with increasing regularity in the ten months since his father's death.

In his daydream he worked the farm alone—though that was pretty much the way it was now. The way things were, Elmo and Oswald were no help at all, and Verna would never get her lily-white hands dirty. But with very little effort, Ash could imagine stepping into the house at the end of the day and finding everything peaceful and quiet.

Without his stepbrothers and stepmother in the house, he could finally think about getting married. As it was, he couldn't imagine bringing any decent woman here to endure life with Verna and Elmo and Oswald.

Ash had very definite ideas about what he wanted in a wife. Someone quiet and even-tempered—a quality his father had evidently forgotten to look for when he'd chosen his

33

wives—someone who could cook and sew and wouldn't mind helping with the animals during planting and harvesting season. Someone who was healthy enough to bear several children. He didn't really care if she was especially pretty. There were other, more important qualities he'd look for in a wife when the time came. A good healthy dose of common sense would be necessary, that and a love of the simple life. Not every woman was cut out to be a farm wife.

He stepped into the house and was assaulted by the pleasant smell of bacon and eggs. A smile crept across his face and his mouth watered as he walked toward the kitchen. Verna must be in one of her rare domestic moods today, and he wasn't going to complain.

The deserted kitchen contained the warmth of the stove on this chilly autumn morning, and the odor of breakfast hung in the air—but there was no food on the table save a few biscuits left over from dinner last night, and the skillet on the stove was empty.

He stroked his thick beard with one thumb and then hooked a long strand of hair behind his ear. When John Coleman had first brought his second wife home, she'd been a fireball. Cooking fairly decent meals, cleaning, doing the laundry. That was the reason, after all, that his father had remarried. A working farm needed a woman's touch, and two hardworking farmers needed someone to take care of the house.

It hadn't lasted long. As soon as Verna had settled in and sent for her grown sons, she had changed. Meals were whatever she could throw together quickly, the laundry was poorly done, if at all, and the house was no cleaner than when John and Ash Coleman had lived there alone. In fact, with three new residents it was often worse.

His father had never complained about the boys. It was a big house, after all, with four bedrooms upstairs and a sitting room downstairs that Verna had converted into a bedroom when John had become ill.

If only they would occasionally make themselves useful. If only they would pitch in and do their share—a child's share—anything.

Verna stepped into the kitchen with a tarnished silver tray and two plates that looked as if they'd been licked clean. "Oh, Ash, you're still here," she said, placing the tray on the table that sat in the middle of the large, square room.

Verna March Coleman had probably once been a real beauty and she was still attractive, for an older woman. She was tall and trim, and had very little gray in her dark hair, even though she had to be approaching fifty. She refused to reveal her age to anyone, but Oswald was twenty-six and Elmo was twenty-one.

Attractive or not she was, to Ash, the ugliest

woman on earth. He was sure she'd made his father miserable in his last year of life, with her nagging and her barbs, and she'd always treated Ash as if he were less than nothing. As a farmhand, at best; as a nuisance, most of the time. Never mind that she and her boys would likely starve without him.

"Just grabbing some breakfast," he said simply, "before I head out to the fields."

Verna flashed a smile that was so cold it made the hairs on the back of Ash's neck stand up. "I made bacon and scrambled eggs, but Elmo was so hungry I'm afraid he ate it all. Since he's not feeling well, I thought it might help. There are biscuits."

Ash grabbed a couple of the cold biscuits and poured himself a glass of milk.

If he could leave this place, he would be tempted. If he could throw Verna and her good-for-nothing boys out of this house and off this farm, he would do it in a heartbeat and without regret. But the woman had been his father's wife, and when the pneumonia that had taken John Coleman's life had taken a turn for the worse, he'd made Ash promise to take care of this woman he had, for some reason Ash couldn't fathom, come to care for.

Oswald came into the kitchen with a book in one hand and a strip of crispy bacon in the other. The book was held high, shielding his face, and he moved the nearly black bacon before him as if it were a schoolmaster's baton.

"We've got to finish planting the wheat today," Ash said as he finished off his cold breakfast.

Oswald lowered his book slowly, revealing a face that was clean shaven, well formed, and almost pretty. Pale hair, more blond than brown, had been slicked straight back. "I must finish this chapter before I even think about *work*. This is the most mesmerizing novel I have ever read, and I can't possibly put it down now."

Just as well. "I thought that book you read last week was the most mesmerizing."

Oswald raised a finely shaped eyebrow. It was the left one, arching up in a way he had surely studied before the mirror. "I shouldn't expect *you* to understand. Have you ever read a novel? A book of any kind? Have you ever read anything but the Farmer's Almanac?" He shared an amused smile with his mother. "Can you even imagine it, Ash Coleman reading a *book?*"

Ash was certain that this was an insult, but he let it slide by without comment. He'd rather work alone, anyway, than listen to Oswald's inane chatter all day. And no matter what Oswald said about finishing a chapter, Ash knew that if he walked out of here alone he'd not see Oswald again until dinnertime. He pocketed two more of the cold biscuits and an apple so that he wouldn't have to return for the noontime meal.

*   *   *

Stuart stared at the figures scribbled in the accounting books that lay open on the desk before him, but he didn't see the numbers. They blurred and ran together, danced before his eyes.

Howard Stillwell, that worthless son-in-law of his, had ruined his youngest daughter. Marital continence. Physical servitude! What had happened to Charmaine's common sense? Howard had filled her head with nonsense, and she believed it. *She believed it!*

He'd made his ranch a success, he had more money than he would ever need, but it was Maureen and their daughters who made his life worthwhile. He didn't want Charmaine to become an old maid, to live her life without knowing the joys of love and a family, but that's where she was headed. Thanks to Howard.

Maureen came into the room so quietly, he didn't know she was there until she placed a hand on his shoulder. The touch was familiar, gentle, and soothing. Even though she surprised him, he didn't so much as flinch.

"Worrying about Charmaine again?" she asked, and the fingers of that hand began to knead his tense muscles.

"Of course," he muttered.

Her other hand fell upon his other shoulder, and the long fingers massaged.

"It is distressing," she said softly.

"Distressing! That's an understatement. It's downright terrifying."

If he wasn't mistaken, she laughed lightly. "She'll come around."

"I wish I could be sure." He grabbed the wrist of one of those gentle hands, and pulled his wife to his side and then onto his lap. Immediately, he felt better, soothed somehow because Maureen was with him. "Did you hear her last night? Good God."

Maureen perched on his thigh, and the comfort he'd thought impossible a few minutes ago grew and settled in his heart. She always did this to him.

Her hands settled gently on his shoulders. "You needn't worry, darling. Charmaine's our daughter," Maureen said sensibly. "She's smart and pretty and still so very young. I'll agree that Boston and its modern ways have had a disturbing influence on her, but when the right man comes along, she'll change her mind about all that nonsense."

"Do you really think so?"

After all these years, his wife's smile still had the power to soothe him, to make him forget, for a while, about bad market prices, rustlers, storms, and even, she proved to him now, a disobedient and disgustingly *modern* daughter.

"I do."

The right man.

* * *

39

Ash sat by the fire, his back to Verna and the boys. A dinner of burnt steak and nearly raw potatoes sat heavy in his stomach, and his muscles—every muscle in his body—ached. It was a good ache, one that confirmed a hard day's work.

Elmo was complaining about his neurasthenia, an invisible ailment he blamed for everything from exhaustion and headaches to bad dreams, regaling his mother with the details of his aches and pains. Truth of the matter was, Elmo March was a lazy bum, a big baby, and the king of whiners. If he'd move that fat behind of his a little more often, he'd likely not be so troubled by this malady. He was telling Verna about some electric treatments he'd read about, and he was just sure that if he had sufficient funds, those treatments would cure him.

There was a moment of silence as they waited—Ash was certain—for him to offer to raise the cash to send Elmo to Kansas City.

Only if he'd stay there.

Ash said nothing, and eventually the conversation resumed.

Oswald had his nose in a book, as usual, there in a rocking chair very near the brightest kerosene lantern in the room. At least Oswald was quiet, when he was reading. He lived in his own world, a world of fiction that didn't include anything so common as milking cows or feeding chickens or working in the fields.

Why didn't they just leave? Oswald and Elmo didn't want to be farmers, why the hell were they still here? There was an entire world out there, full of possibilities. Didn't they want lives of their own? Were they truly so lazy that they wanted nothing more than to be taken care of? Ash shook his head. He didn't understand these stepbrothers of his at all.

Ash wondered if he'd rest tonight. He should sleep like the dead every night the way he worked, but he usually slept only a few hours, and that came in bits and pieces. He closed his eyes at night but his mind wouldn't be still. Even in the softest bed he couldn't quite get comfortable; the dreams that came were usually unremembered and never restful.

"You know her, don't you, Ash?"

It was the sound of his name that grabbed his attention. Verna chose to ignore him, whenever possible, especially in the evenings. Ash was never a part of the conversation, and didn't want to be.

"I know who?" He twisted to face his stepmother.

"Charmaine Haley," Verna snapped. "Haven't you been paying attention to a word I say?"

"What about her?"

Verna rolled her eyes and clasped her hands in her lap. "I saw her in town today. Eula Markam at the mercantile pointed her out to me, but she was headed home and we weren't introduced."

The Runt was home. Charmaine Haley had always been a little bundle of energy, a nervy kid who had said exactly what was on her mind. He'd watched Mrs. Haley cringe when Charmaine, all of six years old, had asked the preacher how he knew God was real. He'd been there a year or so later, in the old general store with his father, when she'd told old Mr. Whitman that he needed a bath. It was the truth, but everyone else had simply turned their heads or held their breath. She'd eventually learned to be more tactful, but she had always been an insistent and frequent voice in school, questioning everything from literature to history, and asking aloud what every other kid wanted to know. Exactly why did they need to be proficient in arithmetic?

"When did she get back?"

"Last week, but that's not important." Verna obviously had something on her mind, but she was having a difficult time getting it out. "Do you think she'll remember you?"

"I don't know. It's been a long time."

Verna squirmed in her chair, and Ash noticed that Elmo and Oswald were both staring at him; Elmo with his hands settled over a rounded stomach, Oswald with his book cradled in his lap. *They* knew what was on Verna's mind.

"What's going on here?" It was bad enough

when they ignored him. The three of them staring at him as if they expected something was much worse.

"Stuart Haley is giving a party," Verna said quickly. "A masked ball, to be precise."

"A *what?*"

"A masked ball," she repeated slowly. "It's to be very fancy, elegant, the finest party ever thrown in Salley Creek, and perhaps in the entire state of Kansas. Word is, he's looking for a husband for his daughter."

Little Charmaine Haley? In his mind she was still a kid, the little girl who'd followed him around town every chance she got. It was hard to believe she was all grown up and looking for a husband. But years had passed since he'd seen or thought of her. "She would be about that age."

Verna leaned forward in her chair, and the firelight on her normally even features gave her face an evil cast. "I want to go, and I want Elmo and Oswald to go. Why, either of my boys would make a fine husband for Miss Haley."

Ash almost laughed, but he didn't. It was a ridiculous thought—but a fine one. If Charmaine were to marry Elmo or Oswald they'd surely move out, probably to Haley's ranch. Maybe the whole bunch of them would go. It was a heavenly prospect

"I'm sure you'll all be invited," he assured her.

Verna was not convinced. "That Maureen Haley doesn't like me, I just know it. She's never *said* anything, but the way she looks at me I can tell."

Ash refrained from saying that Maureen Haley had too much class to convey in any way her dislike for another human being. Even Verna. "Well, what do you want me to do?"

"Next time you go to town, drop by the Haley house and say hello, and I'm sure she'll invite the entire family."

This time Ash did laugh. It had been so long since he'd actually smiled that his face almost hurt with the effort. "I'd more likely get shot. The Haleys and the Colemans haven't gotten along since Dad put barbed wire up to keep Haley's cattle out of his wheat, and that was some twenty years ago."

Verna harumphed and leaned back in her chair, Oswald returned to his reading, and Elmo headed for the kitchen and a bit of bread and milk to ease his stomachache.

Ash turned his back on the lot of them, and a smile crept across his face. He couldn't imagine any sane woman willingly marrying Elmo, but Oswald had potential—for a city girl. He'd never make a farmhand or a rancher, that's for sure, but Haley didn't have to know that until after the wedding.

He remembered, in a flash of deeply buried memory, that as a child Charmaine had declared that one day they would marry. She'd been a little thing, a kid who was mad at her sisters over some slight, and he'd told her they were just jealous because she was the pretty one, and then he'd wiped the tears from her eyes with his sleeve. He'd just been trying to make her stop crying, but she'd taken him very seriously. Her response had been to declare him the most wonderful and handsome man in the world, and to swear that when she was grown she would marry him. She'd stated it, in her usual way, as a fact, a foregone conclusion.

He'd laughed, which hadn't been a very tactful response, he now realized. But shoot, she'd been a skinny kid at the time and the very idea had been startling and ridiculous. He hadn't meant to hurt her feelings, but a sniffling marriage proposal had been the *last* response he'd expected from the Runt.

Well, she likely wasn't a runt any more. She was a fully grown woman of marriageable age, and Oswald would make a right fine Haley son-in-law. And when Oswald left the farm to move into the big Haley house, he could take his mother and his brother with him.

She'd never seen anyone do so many things at once. Charmaine watched in horrified fascination as her friend Eula bounced a baby on her knee, scolded the one at her feet, sipped a cup of tea, glanced over the mercantile books, and planned what she'd prepare for supper.

They were seated in the small office at the rear of the Markam mercantile, and Winston was up front behind the counter for a change.

"There it is, another error. I swear, Win never was good at math." Eula brought the tea to her mouth and then set it beside the open accounting book. "Sarah Elizabeth, take that out of your mouth right this minute," she snapped at the two-year-old who sat on the floor with a collection of odds and ends as playthings.

Eula smiled brightly as she turned her attention to her guest. "Sarah's a handful, I can tell you that. From the day she was born she was demanding and ornery. Now Little Win, on the other hand, is an absolute angel." She presented her angel with a crinkled nose and a "gootchy-goo."

"They're beautiful children," Charmaine said as she tasted her own tea. "But I don't know how you have time to do all that you do. With the store and the children and the household . . ." She refrained, with some difficulty, from jumping into a speech on the unrealistic demands placed on women.

"You make time for the things that have to be done," Eula said sensibly, and with an air of contentment. "Oh," she said sharply, and her eyes widened slightly. "Now, that's an idea. I have to use those apples anyway, I might as well make a pie. That will go nicely with the ham and the beans, don't you think? Win loves my apple pie."

Charmaine sighed, unable to help herself. "Don't you think Winston could occasionally prepare his own meal, and perhaps even yours? You work so—"

Eula interrupted with a laugh. "Win in my kitchen? Oh, no. He'd only make a mess, and he'd likely burn the place down in the process."

"But you work so hard," Charmaine said insistently. "He demands too much of you."

"Nonsense," Eula said, her smile fading but not disappearing entirely. "I like taking care of my husband and my children, and working in the store give me a chance to meet new people and visit with old friends."

Proving Charmaine's point, Winston Markam opened the door and leaned in. He was a thin man, relatively handsome with his neatly groomed auburn hair and startling blue eyes and neat, sensible clothing befitting a merchant. A white shirt Eula had washed and starched and ironed. Brown trousers with a sharp crease—also courtesy of Eula. "Where's that new ribbon?" he asked without preamble. "Mrs. Provost is having a conniption trying to find what she wants."

With that out of the way, he nodded politely to Charmaine and smiled widely at Sarah Elizabeth.

"Mrs. Provost always pitches a fit," Eula said,

and she stood with Little Win on her hip. Then, without warning, she placed the baby on Charmaine's lap. "I'll be right back."

The door closed, and Charmaine found herself alone with Eula's children. Little Win immediately grabbed her ear and squealed with delight. Charmaine's left ear stung with the grip of those strong little fingers and rang from the surprisingly high pitch of the screech. Before she had time to recover, Sarah Elizabeth went in search of trouble. The tot stood, nose barely even with the desk, and reached for her mother's tea.

"No!" Charmaine said, coming out of her seat with Little Win—who still grasped her ear with all his might—in one arm. She reached the teacup just in time, and moved it safely out of reach. Sarah Elizabeth didn't even pause to take a breath. She reached a chubby hand to the accounting book and pulled it to the floor before Charmaine could stop her.

"Now, now," Charmaine said, stooping down with Little Win on one hip and a delighted Sarah Elizabeth tugging on her skirt. Still, she managed to pick up the book and return it to Winston's desk. "You musn't touch your mother's things. You have your own toys to play with," she said sensibly, pointing to the collection of dolls and brightly painted wooden blocks on the floor.

Little Win released Charmaine's ear, and she

sighed with relief. Then he grabbed her hair.

"Ouch!" She tried to pry his fingers loose, but that chubby little fist held tight and pulled, and he squeaked a delighted proclamation directly into her ear.

At least Sarah Elizabeth was settling down. She sat on the floor amidst her wooden blocks and picked one up. Charmaine was somewhat mollified to be assured that children *could* be reasoned with.

And then Sarah Elizabeth drew back her arm and let a red block fly. It bounced off the side of the desk with a resounding thud.

"Stop that right this minute," Charmaine said in her most stern yet reasonable voice.

The little girl smiled sweetly, and picked up another block. This one came directly at Charmaine, but with a quick hand she deflected it so that it fell to the floor. Little Win, perhaps distressed by the excitement, pulled on his handful of hair and squealed loudly.

"Sarah Elizabeth," Charmaine said calmly, "would you build me a house with your blocks?"

The little girl looked at the blocks before her, stacked one on top of another, and smiled widely. Win relaxed, and instead of pulling on Charmaine's hair and screaming, he simply gnawed quietly on her shoulder.

It was just as well that she'd decided never to marry. Having a husband to answer to was bad enough, but children! A few minutes with

Eula's "angels" and she was doubly glad she'd decided to remain unmarried and chaste.

"There now," Eula cooed as she swept through the door. "Did you miss your mommy?" She scooped Little Win into her embrace and retook her seat.

Sarah Elizabeth was innocently stacking blocks, and Charmaine sighed in relief. *Yes, it was just as well.*

Chapter Three

"No, no, *no!*" Ash hurried across the grassy yard that separated him from the wagon Oswald was struggling to hitch up. Elmo turned to see what the commotion was about, after he tossed another bucket of water into the pigsty. That big old boar was already rolling in the mud, delighted with the cool treat.

The horses were prancing, pulling away from one another and whinnying softly.

"What have I done now?" Oswald asked tiredly.

"You've hitched them up on the wrong sides again," Ash said, as he began to undo Oswald's work.

"The wrong side, the wrong side," Oswald moaned. Ash cut a biting glance at his stepbrother just in time to see Oswald roll his eyes in despair. "They're horses, dumb animals, what possible difference does it make?"

"Betsy on the right," Ash said through gritted teeth, keeping to himself the conviction that these dumb animals were a lot smarter than the man who couldn't remember the simplest instruction. "Lady on the left. Always. It's what they're used to. They get skittish when you change their routine."

It was Saturday, and Verna was going to town. She used shopping as an excuse, but this was a ritual more social than practical. Oswald and Elmo usually accompanied her, which made Saturday afternoons Ash's favorite time of the week. Oswald would visit the small Salley Creek library, and Elmo would find the doctor and casually bring up his aches and pains, his imagined illnesses. Poor Doc Whitfield. Even when he tried to hide, Elmo managed to find him.

Ash switched the horses, whispering soothing words as he hitched them up correctly. It didn't take long. If Oswald could remember this one little detail, life would be so much simpler. It didn't take a genius to remember how to hitch a pair of horses to a wagon, but half the time Oswald managed to botch the job. By the time Ash was finished, the mares were settled.

Elmo carried a couple more buckets of water from the well to the pigsty, complaining constantly about his throbbing back and cramping hands. He was sure he'd done himself serious injury by carrying the heavy buckets. By the time Verna emerged from the house, Oswald and Elmo were waiting for her in the wagon.

"Are you sure you won't come with us?" Verna asked again as Ash assisted her into the seat of the wagon. She'd never asked him to ride to town with her before. Never. And this was the third time she'd asked this morning.

"I'm sure. There's work to be done around here."

"There always is," Verna sighed. "You work much too hard, Ash. You need to expand your horizons, to look beyond this farm now and again. Why," she said as if the thought had just occurred to her, "you should come to town and pay a call on that nice Charmaine Haley." She looked him up and down critically, taking in the dark beard, the hair that desperately needed to be cut, the worn and dirty work shirt and the faded Levis. "Well, perhaps another time would be best."

Ash watched them ride away, and when he could no longer see the wagon along the winding road, he closed his eyes for a moment. Peace. Quiet.

When he opened his eyes he saw that Elmo had left the gate to the pigsty wide open. The ornery old boar had stepped into the barnyard, his beady eyes intent upon an unsuspecting chicken.

Ash stepped forward. "Back where you belong, old man," he said, waving his hands at the boar. "Let's go."

In answer, the boar rushed past, his big body brushing against Ash's leg. The hen squawked, flapped her wings, and headed for the safety of the chicken house. With his prey out of sight the boar stopped in his tracks, suddenly aloof as he surveyed his surroundings.

Ash held the gate to the pigsty open in invitation. "Come on. The food's in here, and this nice cool mud is just waiting for you. What do you want with a scrawny old hen, anyway?"

The boar headed for the open gate, lumbering, his big body moving ponderously toward the pigsty. And then he stopped. He looked at Ash as if there was something he all of a sudden found offensive. He snorted, shook his big head, and rushed forward before Ash knew what the nasty old boar was thinking.

Ash stepped back as the boar charged him, ready to sidestep the big, low body and slip out the gate. But the boar changed directions without warning, and knocked Ash's legs out from under him. His arms automatically extended to break the fall, finding the slick mud and causing the muck to splash into his face. Ash's hands slipped forward, and he landed face down in the pigsty.

He snapped his head up quickly, but not before he got a good dose of cool mud up his nose.

Once that was done, the boar was perfectly satisfied to roll happily in the mud beside the newest resident of the pigsty.

"Ham," Ash muttered as he sat up and wiped the worst of the mud from his face. "If you weren't such a tough old bastard, that's just what you'd be." The boar was not insulted. Now that the excitement was over, the other pigs joined in the fun, wallowing in the mud to their hearts' content.

Ash shook his hands and arms vigorously as he left the pigsty, closing the gate securely behind him and reminding himself that this was another strike against Elmo. Was it possible that he'd done this on purpose? That he'd known exactly what would happen?

No. That required thinking a few minutes into the future, a task Elmo was incapable of.

He lifted his head and saw her coming toward him. Before he knew she was there, she was almost upon him. For a moment he thought she was a vision—a ghost or an angel. Her horse was creamy white, her dress the same. Her hair was gold, the color of wheat, and she had a small hat perched on top. A white feather danced there with each step of her horse.

It seemed the sunlight was drawn to her, and

everything around her paled. As she came closer he saw that her eyes were brilliant blue, her features so delicate and fine they were surely not real. A strand of pale, straight hair brushed one cheek, there where it had fallen from its bun; an imperfection that made her all the more perfect. This was not a ghost or an angel, but a woman. The most extraordinary woman he had ever seen.

She leaned slightly forward. "Hello," she said in a pure, sweet greeting. "I'm looking for Ash Coleman." It was the voice that gave her away, some inflection still there even though she was a woman now and not a child.

"Charmaine Haley," he said, and when he tasted mud he brushed his face and his mouth again. Mud fell in clumps small and large.

She straightened quickly, obviously a little frightened. "Do I know you, sir? Are you one of Ash's stepbrothers? As I said, I'm looking for Ash."

"You found him."

It was impossible. This filthy, unshaven man was *not* Ash Coleman! Why, her Ash was beautiful. Smart and witty and handsome. He had to be. That was the way she had remembered him all these years. *This* man had done battle with a pig and lost, ending up face down in the mud. She'd seen a portion of the undignified contest as she'd approached the farm, but it hadn't occurred to her, not once, that the man she watched might be Ash.

Eight years *was* a very long time.

"I can't stay long," she began cautiously, having no choice but to accept this man's claim that he was, indeed, Ash Coleman. "I heard about your father, and I just wanted to pay my respects."

Ash nodded his head in acknowledgment, but his eyes never left her, didn't drop to the ground or stray to the side.

"Your father was," she said softly, "a wonderful man."

He stepped forward. "Yes, he was." There was a huskiness in his voice that hadn't been there eight years ago, another reminder that Ash Coleman was a man, now, and not a boy. "He always liked you, Runt, better than those prissy sisters of yours. He said you had sand."

When he grinned, his smile was startlingly white against a mud-splattered face and heavy dark beard. Another step, and he stood beside her. He placed a soothing, muddy hand on the horse's neck.

"Did he really?"

Ash lifted his arms to assist her from the saddle. Long, muddy, wet arms. Impossibly long, impossibly muddy. When she'd left Salley Creek he'd been lanky and perhaps a trifle awkward, but he'd grown into his height in the past eight years. Ash's legs were long but not too long, and

Linda Jones

he seemed comfortable in his tall body, graceful in a way that was impossible for growing boys. He was lean still, but there was nothing skinny about him. The shoulders were wide, the arms muscular, and the legs filled those denim trousers almost obscenely. His hands were big and strong and dirty, a working man's hands offered to her. Goodness, if she thought about this a moment longer she was going to blush and stammer like a silly girl, and that would never do.

She hesitated, looking down critically. "You seem to have stepped into something."

He glanced down at the big battered boots that had recently been dragged through the mud and otherwise befouled.

"Well," he drawled. "This is a farm. It happens."

Charmaine had no intention of leaving her safe and relatively clean perch. Obviously Ash realized this, and he let his arms fall. The mare pranced anxiously, and Ash reached out to soothe her once again, this time with a few soft words as well as his muddy hand against the mare's neck.

"We're having a big party in two weeks," she blurted out, deciding to proceed with the other purpose of her visit. "A masked ball, actually," she sighed. "I know it's ridiculous, but my father is bound and determined to prove to me

58

that there's nothing I can have in Boston that I can't have here."

"Stuart Haley always was a stubborn man," Ash said softly.

Charmaine didn't attempt to defend her father against the all-too-true charge. "You're invited, of course," she said brightly. Perhaps too brightly. "It should be fun. Everyone will be there."

"I'm not much for parties," Ash said. His eyes were no longer locked on her, they were on the horse's fine, creamy neck. "But I appreciate the invitation."

It was a very nice refusal, and Charmaine found she was ungraciously relieved. Perhaps some things from childhood shouldn't be revisited. They didn't always stand up to expectations. "Well, if you change your mind . . ."

"Now, my stepmother and my stepbrothers, I'm sure they'd enjoy a masked ball," he said with a hint of amusement.

"By all means, I'd love for them to come, also. I look forward to meeting them."

Was that a laugh? She couldn't be sure. Either that, or Ash had very quickly cleared his throat. "I'll pass the invitation along. Verna will be pleased."

He was staring at her again, silent and a bit too attentive, those mossy green eyes locked boldly to hers. It was quite unnerving.

"Is she here? I could meet her and deliver the invitation personally."

Ash shook his head. "They've all gone to town. You probably passed them on the road." His voice was gritty and soft. "A wagon pulled by two grays, with an older woman and two men."

"I took a short cut." She smiled in spite of her unease. "Through the pasture and the trees that line your property. There's a small break in the fence, by the way." She shifted in her seat to look over her shoulder. "Right about there." She lifted a hand and pointed in the direction she'd come from.

Ash shook his head. "I had Oswald check that section of fence just two days ago."

"Oswald. That's one of your stepbrothers, I assume."

Ash lifted his eyes to her again. Good heavens, how very brazenly he stared at her. She ignored her consternation and gave Ash an audacious stare of her own. He looked as if he had something to say. His chest rose and fell, his fingers twitched. Finally, he answered with a simple and inadequate "Yes."

"Well, I really should be getting back," she said cheerfully, trying not to show her desire for escape. What had she expected, that she'd arrive and find Ash Coleman waiting anxiously for her? Dressed in a fine suit, unchanged by the time that had passed, a gentleman farmer who would make her feel like a happy child again?

"I guess you should," he agreed.

"Please reconsider coming to the party," she said, the new invitation an impulse she couldn't contain. Why, she wasn't quite sure. It was the polite thing to say, and so was most likely her mother's influence coming to the surface. "There will be so many strangers there, a few friendly faces would be a comfort to me."

She thought he might actually smile again. The muscles at the corners of his mouth twitched, and there was a pleasant softening of his features. "A masked ball. Well, if I'm going to step foot in the Haley house I reckon it had better be in disguise."

Charmaine found herself smiling down at the muddy, dirty, hairy man who had disappointed her by not being a beautiful seventeen-year-old boy. How silly she was! Time had passed for Ash just as it had for her, and he was no more a child than she was. "Surely you don't think my father holds a grudge?"

"He mutters and grumbles and spits whenever I happen to see him in town, and the only words I can ever make out are 'barbed wire.'"

"That was an awfully long time ago," Charmaine said. "I'm sure you misunderstood."

She expected a smile and a shrug of those broad shoulders, but Ash's eyes were perfectly serious, and he didn't smile. "I don't think so, Runt. He wouldn't like you being here."

Charmaine didn't agree or disagree, but it

was the truth. Her father had been furious with John Coleman for putting up that barbed wire, and Stuart Haley was not what anyone would call a forgiving man.

"Think about the party, would you?" Charmaine asked as she turned her horse about to head for home. "And don't forget to extend the invitation to your family."

Your family. Ash suppressed an unnatural chill as he watched Charmaine Haley ride away from the farm. He never thought of the people he lived with as his *family.* They were strangers who had been forced upon him, his father's responsibilities that had become his. When he thought of one day having a family of his own, Verna, Elmo, and Oswald were not included.

Charmaine Haley had grown up nicely. More than nicely, he conceded, she had grown up beautifully. After she disappeared into the tree line, Ash's eyes fell to his mud-encrusted hands and arms. What a fool he'd been to lift those arms to her, but for a moment he had forgotten about his fall in the mud, the manure on his boots. He had forgotten—for a moment—who he was.

Oswald would probably suit Charmaine Haley just fine. She'd turned her nose up at his offered hands the same way Oswald turned his nose up a dozen times a day.

He forgot about Charmaine Haley and headed for the barn and his tools. Apparently, there was a section of fence that needed to be repaired.

Stuart enjoyed his last cigar of the day, savoring every puff. He'd had another long, hard day, but there was great satisfaction in ending it here, in his comfortable study in his fine house with his family around him. Part of his family, anyway.

Maureen had gone to bed early, and Charmaine was sulking in her room about one thing or another, but they were *here* and that was enough.

His youngest daughter was being more difficult than he'd imagined. She visited with her friends, she helped her mother with the plans for the ball, she rode that mare he'd bought just for her . . . but there was an air of defiance in everything she did. Where did she get that quality from? Not from her mother. Maureen had always been sweet and rational and forgiving.

It was Howard, he was sure, who had influenced her.

"Smells divine," the daughter in question said sweetly as she waltzed into his study with a deceptive smile on her face. Just a couple of hours ago she'd been sullen and silent. "May I?"

She reached for the cigars he kept handy, there on his desk.

"You may *not!*" he said, and her hand stilled

and hovered above the engraved mahogany box.

"Are you being selfish, Daddy, or is this simply another of your double standards?"

She was trying to get his goat, and doing a fine job of it. "Proper young ladies don't smoke," he said with relative calm.

Charmaine turned to face him and leaned against the desk. She didn't want a cigar and never had. She was just being ornery. Where *did* she get that trait from? "You'll never guess who I saw today," she said with a wicked gleam in her eye.

"Then you'll have to tell me." He leaned back in his chair and took another long draw on the cigar.

"Ash Coleman."

The name Coleman still brought a bubble of bad temper to the surface. "At the mercantile? You've been spending an awful lot of time there."

"Not at the mercantile. I rode out to the farm to say hello." Her voice and her pose were nonchalant, but he was sure this was a trick to get a rise out of him.

"That's nice."

It was clear she was a little disappointed that he hadn't bounded out of his chair with a demand that she stay away from the Coleman farm.

"Yes, we had a very nice visit." Her smile

faded, and for a moment she didn't look like his little girl at all. She looked like a woman who had an awful lot on her mind. "Why didn't you tell me about Mr. Coleman passing on?"

He shrugged his shoulders. "Didn't think of it, I suppose."

"He was a good man," she insisted.

"For a sodbuster."

Charmaine sighed dramatically. "You're such a snob, Daddy. Just because Mr. Coleman was a farmer and not a cattleman, that doesn't mean he doesn't deserve just as much respect as any other man."

"I didn't know you'd taken up defense of the common man as one of your crusades."

She pouted, actually puffing out her lower lip just a little bit. "He bought me lemon drops, just like you did, and told me riddles."

If she knew what a picture she made she would surely be devastated. Maureen was right. Charmaine was still a child, in many ways, spoiled and unreasonable and occasionally intolerant. For all her education and damned seminars, she still had so much to learn.

"Then I apologize," he conceded. "I should have passed the news along."

The apology seemed to appease her, as he'd hoped it would. Damnation, she was beautiful, so much like her mother, and while he couldn't say he cared for this sort of fierce independence in a female of any age, there was something special about Charmaine. A spark, a brightness. When she turned her devotion in the right direction—her family, her home—she was going to be quite a woman.

But for now, for the moment, she was still his little girl.

Chapter Four

Ash was headed in for the day when he was stopped by the sound of squeaking wheels and slow, tired hoofbeats on the road. The sun was setting, and it was the middle of the week. Who would be paying a call at this time?

A friend of Verna's, he imagined with a sigh. One of those high-hat women from town she occasionally invited for dinner. But on a Wednesday? He had a stray and unwanted thought that perhaps it was Charmaine Haley, come to torment him as she had just four days earlier. But of course if Charmaine were to come again it would be on a fast white horse by the bright light of day, not in a lumbering wagon at sunset.

When the wagon came into view, Ash's dismay disappeared.

The conveyance that crept toward the barn with an occasional lurch was a boxy enclosed wagon with the words "Sweet's Traveling Thespians" painted on the side in fading red paint. The wagon had seen better days. There were large sections of rotting wood on the side Ash could see, and a good-sized hole in the roof; and the entire conveyance canted oddly to one side. The nag that pulled the wagon, Pumpkin by name, was a red roan the unfortunate color of the vegetable she was named for. And the man driving the wagon looked as run-down as Pumpkin.

"I'll be damned," Ash said as the lumbering wagon came to a halt. It had been three years since he'd seen his godfather, the eccentric actor Nathan Sweet, though they had corresponded by mail sporadically. There was more gray in Nathan's hair, a little more meat on his tiny bones, but other than that he was unchanged. Five-foot-four standing ramrod straight, he'd always been given to expensive clothes that had no place on a farm. His traveling ensemble consisted of a bowler, fancy shoes, and a gray Easterner's suit given a splash of color by a bright yellow scarf.

The years had left their mark, but Nathan's

aristocratic features were the same, as was the drooping and well-groomed moustache.

"After all this time," Nathan said wearily as Ash assisted him to the ground, "that's the greeting I get?"

Ash gave his godfather a hearty hug that lifted the older man from the ground. "It's good to see you."

When Ash stepped away, Nathan smiled and smoothed back his mussed hair. "Much better."

There was no movement from the wagon, no sound but the labored breathing of Pumpkin.

"You alone this time?" Ash asked, and Nathan nodded once.

"It's just Pumpkin and I, this visit," he said. "Two weary travelers in search of solace and the occasional adventure. I hope you don't mind if we stay for a while. I felt the need for the simplicity of the country—fresh air, wide skies, honest people."

"Mind? Of course I don't mind. How often have I asked you to visit?"

"I wanted to come earlier, really I did, but the troupe's been busy," Nathan said grandly. "San Francisco, Denver, St. Louis, and everywhere in between." He gave a grandiose sweep of his hand. "Sold-out performances across the West, standing ovations, extensive newspaper coverage in every town."

Always the actor. "Then what are you doing here?"

"I told you, fresh air, wide skies . . ." Nathan's arm dropped heavily and his face fell. "My leading man quit, unfortunately taking my leading lady with him, the bastard. Shows were canceled, money refunded, and before the week was out the rest of my troupe deserted me like the seditious cowards they are."

"Broke again?" Ash asked, sure already of the answer.

"Completely."

They unhitched Pumpkin, and Ash offered to see to the animal while Nathan sat and rested for a few minutes. There was no need to face Verna any sooner than was absolutely necessary.

He led Pumpkin to the barn, and Nathan followed. "So," the refined voice broke the rapidly chilling air. "How have you been?"

"Fine," Ash answered, the word a habitual response to almost any such question. *How's the wheat, Ash? Fine. How's the family, Ash? Fine. How's life treating you, Ash? Fine.*

"Well, that's a barefaced lie," Nathan said as he plopped his small body on a stool and leaned against the rough wall of the barn. "Fine. Hah! You're tired and unhappy and there are circles under your eyes. You haven't been sleeping, have you?"

Ash turned from the horse to stare at the little man on the stool. Just like that, Nathan saw what no one else did. "Not too well," he confessed.

Nathan's face was lightened by a coy smile. "You're much like your father, you know. Your mother Lila, bless her departed soul, told me that when John was tense he would roam through the house half the night. She'd find him in your room one night, on the porch the next, in the kitchen perhaps . . . just wandering. She said she was never sure exactly what he was searching for."

"I didn't know that." Ash turned back to Pumpkin and began to brush her coat.

Lila Montgomery, before her marriage, had been one of Nathan's leading ladies. John Coleman had taken one look at her and fallen head over heels in love. She'd been playing Juliet at the time, in Lawrence. Used to such attentions, she had spurned the persistent man. Ah, but she didn't know just how persistent this particular man could be. It had taken some courting, on John's part, but Lila had finally fallen deeply in love with the quiet farmer. Many times Ash had heard this story, from his mother and then from his father and on occasion from Nathan, who still smarted over losing his favorite leading lady.

All those years ago Lila Montgomery Coleman had given up the stage to come here, to this farm, but she hadn't left her thespian friends behind. They had visited the Coleman farm over the years, for a few days or a few weeks at a time. Ash could remember his father grumbling over the odd people who'd regularly show up without warning at his door, but he would never think of turning away one of his beloved wife's friends.

"So," Nathan said brightly. "Before I meet this woman who was foolish enough to try to take Lila's place, why don't you tell me a little bit about her?"

Charmaine watched her mother finger the trimmings of the ballgown they'd worked on for the past week. White satin was spread across her bed, and the lights sparkled on its elaborate ornamentation.

The gown was frivolous, most likely sinful, surely made for nothing but attracting a man and appealing to his lower instincts. Howard would despise it.

Still, Charmaine couldn't help but be just a little bit excited at the prospect of wearing such a beautiful garment. All her life, she'd had the best—the best clothes, the best education. The best of everything. But she'd never owned a fine gown like this one.

She felt a little guilty for allowing herself to get giddy over something as frivolous as a gown. She had to learn to still her excitement, if she was ever to truly become the woman she wanted to be.

She'd felt a similar guilt after the masked ball she'd attended with Felicity and Howard. It had been thrilling! Bright and beautiful and vibrant. The music, the dancing, the laughter, it was all intoxicating. She'd prattled on for days, until Howard had pulled her aside and explained to her how debasing such an event was, that the waltz was nothing more than a mating dance and that the finery was donned solely to appeal to the baser nature of the opposite sex. That a masked ball, any such grand entertainment, was an unnecessary frivolity, sure to lead to the fall of many a weak soul. He told her the only reason he'd attended, with his wife and sister-in-law in tow, was to appease a generous contributor to his current cause.

Guilt. She'd had fun at that masked ball, and she was actually beginning to look forward to this one.

What harm could it possibly do to humor her father?

"The musicians will arrive from Kansas City on Thursday morning," her mother said as she turned away from the gown that was spread across Charmaine's bed, "and your father's ordered the old cabin aired out and scrubbed down for them, so they'll have their own place away from the house. Several of your father's cronies will be spending the night, so every guest room in the house will be filled."

"This is too much work for you." Charmaine

took her mother's hands and squeezed. "You've been tired, and don't tell me I'm wrong. I can always tell."

Maureen Haley smiled softly. "You could always see right through me, more easily than your father, more easily than either of your sisters. Yes, I'm tired, but I'm also having great fun. Ruth has been a tremendous help, and I've hired two new girls to help Jane full-time until after the ball. Now that everything's in motion and your gown is finished, I'll have a few days to sit back and relax."

Charmaine knew her mother too well to believe that she would sit back and relax while there was work to be done. Maureen Haley always had to have a finger in every pie. Even if she didn't do the actual work, she would be there to make certain it was done correctly.

Her mother didn't stay much longer, but excused herself and headed for bed. When she was alone, Charmaine sat on the edge of the bed and fingered the heavy white satin and the peach trim, much as her mother had done. A strong wind rocked the limbs of the maple tree that grew just outside her window. Brilliant red leaves brushed against the window, dancing and whispering against the glass.

In the past week, since her visit to the Coleman farm, she'd found herself often thinking of Ash. Out of the blue there he would be, a mud-encrusted hairy man with big rough hands and still, clear eyes.

Like now, as she fingered the white satin. His face was just *there*, in her mind, as clear and true as if he stood before her. Not Ash the boy she remembered, but Ash the man, whose bearded cheeks and wide shoulders held no resemblance to the smooth skin and lithe frame of the young man she recalled so distinctly.

Had time changed him so much, or did her memories lie? Of all her childhood memories, the heartbreaking moments with Ash Coleman were the strongest. Especially the day he'd dried her tears and she'd declared that one day she would be his wife. She'd had a lemon drop in her mouth, and the sun had been shining very brightly. Her dress had been a blue gingham, and Ash had been wearing a new hat.

Ridiculous! She wasn't a silly child anymore, she was a grown woman with very definite ideas of her own, and there was no call for her to get sentimental and weepy over a memory that was probably as much false as true. People had a tendency to remember only what they wanted to, and she was sure it was the same with Ash.

This dose of realism was for the best, she was certain. She could return to Boston after the masked ball and resume her work with Howard. No illusions remained, no childish fantasy. If she ever thought of Ash Coleman again, she would remember him as he really was, a common farmer.

There was a seminar planned for next month, and she should be back in time to assist. At one time, Felicity had been the one to stand at Howard's side and support him. It had been Felicity who had handed out manuals and spoken privately with those women who were too embarrassed to discuss such delicate matters as marital relations and contraception with a man. But that had been before Hester's birth. Motherhood was demanding, and it seemed that Felicity had lost interest in Howard's important work.

And so it had fallen to Charmaine to stand at Howard's side and do her part to convince the uneducated that a woman had more to offer this world than servitude to a man. That a pure marriage was a higher calling, and that baser impulses could and should be ignored.

Howard and Felicity had a pure marriage. They loved one another deeply, but unless and until they decided to have more children there was no physical relationship. They even had separate bedrooms to avoid the possible excitement of shared quarters. Charmaine knew her parents would be shocked to hear this, and would be even more shocked to learn of Charmaine's knowledge of such personal matters.

They should understand. Surely they didn't have a physical relationship, not at their age.

They'd settled into married life comfortably, with respect and honor and pure love. If not, there would have been other children.

Charmaine knew she would likely never marry. Her work with Howard was too important, her beliefs too strong. How could she throw it all aside to become no better than a man's slave? To offer herself up to his demands and expectations? She couldn't do it. Wouldn't.

Besides, deep down she was a little afraid. Felicity had suffered a difficult pregnancy and an even more difficult childbirth. She didn't only agree to Howard's insistence on marital continence, she seemed relieved by it. The sexual embrace, Felicity had confided on one cold Boston evening nearly a year ago, was solely for the man's benefit. It was an act to be endured, to be suffered through.

Charmaine had never been one for suffering, if she could help it.

So it was definitely a relief to find that she had no tender feelings for the *real* Ash Coleman, that her fanciful imaginings were just that. Imaginings.

Elmo leaned forward in his chair, as anxious as a child. Since their dinner of burned fried chicken and nearly raw corn, Nathan had been entertaining with stories of his travels. Ash listened with interest, Verna was coolly attentive,

Oswald was bored . . . but Elmo was fascinated. "You've been to San Francisco?"

Nathan's demeanor was apathetic, as he looked past Ash and into the fire. "Many times. Lovely city. It was there that my troupe performed for a Russian prince, and it was there that I met Lily Langtry."

"Lily Langtry?" Elmo shook his head in wonder.

Oswald didn't even lower his book. "Don't be such a rube, Elmo. That's Ash's job."

"You can't blame me for being interested." Elmo defended himself. "Shoot, nothing ever happens around here."

"That's why I love it here so very much," Nathan said with a smile.

Verna was quite put out to have a guest in the house. While her cooking was wretched, and often offensive, she *did* have to prepare meals when there was company.

Nathan was comfortably settled in the spare room upstairs, the one Verna had been using to store her seldom used sewing supplies. She had actually suggested that he stay in the tack room in the barn, the room where Ash put up the drifters he hired to help with the wheat harvest in the summertime. Ash didn't often put his foot down, but he wouldn't have his godfather sleeping in the barn.

Nathan was telling his story about the Russian prince, a story Ash had heard a number of times. On occasion the Russian in question was a duke rather than a prince, but Ash believed the story was mostly true. He half-listened, allowing his bones to relax, allowing his mind to wander. It was nice to listen to a voice that wasn't harping, whining, or insulting.

"You should've seen Lila in those days." Nathan shook his head in wonder. "She was a beauty, she was, perhaps the greatest of this century."

The harumph that came from Verna's direction was soft but unmistakable.

"Why, that Russian prince did his best to sweep her off her feet," Nathan continued undaunted. "Flowers, confections, jewels . . . she refused them all."

Ash loved hearing Nathan's stories about his mother. All he knew of her was the woman who had kept this house and raised her only child and delighted in her small family. He remembered just as well her heartbreak and her illness, her last days on this earth.

But when Nathan spoke, Ash saw his mother as she'd been before coming to this place in her life. Talented and sought after, surprisingly adventurous, and wise enough to spurn her many admirers . . . until John Coleman came along.

"What a foolish woman," Verna snapped, "to refuse a prince and then turn around and marry a farmer."

Nathan's smile vanished. So did Ash's rare good mood.

It wasn't long before Verna excused herself and took to her downstairs bedchamber. Elmo yawned and climbed the stairs, and even Oswald eventually closed his book and headed for bed. They'd been gone for several minutes before Nathan spoke.

"How *do* you stand it?" he asked softly.

It was a question Ash had asked himself many times. "I have no choice."

"I suppose multiple murder is out of the question," Nathan said dryly.

Ash smiled. "I'm afraid so."

Nathan stood and stretched short arms over his head, yawning with theatrical flair. "Well," he said as his arms dropped. "If you change your mind and need an accomplice, you know where to turn."

"Why, thank you, Nathan, but I think that's above and beyond your duties as a godfather."

After Nathan climbed the stairs, Ash doused the lamps and made sure all the downstairs windows were closed securely. This time of the year it could get mighty cold at night, and icy wind through an open window could make for a chilly morning.

He didn't imagine Charmaine Haley had ever been cold in her life. The Haley house probably had a fireplace in every room, and she'd surely have a wardrobe of warm wool and fur wraps and earmuffs. She'd certainly never awakened in the morning and been forced to place her bare feet on a cold floor.

Oswald would love her lifestyle. Not only was life on the farm distasteful to Verna's oldest boy, he seemed to think he'd been cheated because he hadn't been pampered all his life. While Ash dreamed of the simple pleasure of living alone, Oswald probably dreamed of discovering that he was a long-lost prince switched at birth and that his real parents would arrive any day to whisk him away to a life of luxury.

Ash had thought, often as of late, that Oswald and the Runt would make quite a pair. Pretty and spoiled, they were surely two of a kind. But when he tried to picture them together, when he tried to imagine Charmaine and Oswald standing side by side as a couple—he couldn't quite make it work.

She was too good for him. Hell, no woman deserved Oswald March as her husband, not even Charmaine Haley.

Chapter Five

The last-minute preparations for the masked ball had taken the better part of the week. Charmaine did what she could to help her mother, taking care of the details that inevitably came up when organizing an affair of this size. Making certain that there was a sufficient amount of good silverware and china, hiring extra help for the evening, checking to see that the cabin was prepared for the musicians who would arrive on tomorrow's morning train.

Eula, an excellent seamstress since the age of twelve, had taken a hand in preparing the masks that would be handed out at the door. Goodness knows when she'd had the time! All the guests would be in disguise, and if they arrived without a mask, one would be provided.

Charmaine looked in wonder over the array of fancy masks in the box on the counter. There were feathers and beads of every color, silver and gold thread, the finest silks and velvets.

"You've done a magnificent job, Eula," Charmaine said as she lifted the mask nearest her hand, of royal blue velvet with a silver feather and blue silk ribbons in varying shades. Beneath the royal blue was a jumble of colors both bright and muted, masks elegantly plain and frivolously extravagant. The sunlight that came through the mercantile window shone on strands of gold. "How will I ever decide?"

Eula smiled proudly. "You'll not have to decide at all. Yours was special-made, to your mother's specifications, and it's by far the most beautiful of them all. Mrs. Haley had very definite ideas about what she wanted for you." With that, Eula reached beneath the counter and removed a bundle of brown paper. She handled it carefully, as if what was hidden inside were of the finest and most fragile crystal, and her smile widened as she placed the oddly shaped package on the counter and waited for Charmaine to unwrap it.

The plain string that held the package together came undone first, the knot plucked loose with anxious fingers. If the look on Eula's face was any indication of what waited inside, it was sure to be a treasure.

The brown paper fell back to reveal a white satin mask. There was a touch of peach lace at one corner, resting on a triangular bed of a darker peach silk that would surely match the trim of her ball gown perfectly. And there were pearls everywhere. Seed pearls were sewn around the exotically slanted eyeholes and planted carefully amid the peach lace, and there were larger, oddly elongated pearls that literally dripped from the bottom edge.

It was decadently beautiful. "Oh, this is magnificent." Charmaine lifted the mask, carefully and with both hands, and held it against her face. She peeked through the eyeholes at a grinning Eula, squealed with undignified glee, and spun around just in time to watch Ash Coleman come sauntering through the door.

He stopped dead in his tracks. Goodness, he filled the doorway, blocking the sunlight and evidently the air as well, for all of a sudden there wasn't quite enough to take in a good deep breath.

"Hello," she said softly. The mask fell, still protected by two cautious hands.

Ash simply nodded, to her and then to Eula, and walked to the back of the store to do his shopping.

He looked a little better today, without the mud covering his face. There was still the bushy beard, though, and the dark hair that was unfashionably long and untended, and while Ash hadn't recently taken a plunge into the pigsty, he was wearing more than his share of plain Kansas dirt.

The glee she'd felt upon unwrapping her mask vanished. How silly and unproductive it was to get carried away with plans for this inappropriate masked ball. To become breathless at the very appearance of a *man*. A man entirely inappropriate for her, in any case. Howard and Felicity would be mortified by her reckless behavior.

"Can I help you find something, Ash?" Eula stepped from behind the counter and down the center aisle to the rear of the store. Charmaine carefully rewrapped the mask and listened intently to the soft conversation drifting to her from the back of the store. Something about salt and flour and tobacco, evidently forgotten by Verna on her last visit to town.

The voices came closer, and they were accompanied by Eula's soft step and Ash's heavier footfall. Charmaine directed all her attention to the string she was retying. She needed to tie the string quickly, place her mask in the box with the others, and mutter a quick and gracious farewell to Eula and her customer. Her suddenly clumsy fingers refused to cooperate.

"Here, let me do that," Eula said as she stepped behind the counter and took the package that was much the worse for wear. The brown paper was crumpled, and the string was in knots. In a flash, Eula had unknotted the string and fastened it securely around the covered mask.

Charmaine was well aware that Ash stood behind her. He didn't say a word, she couldn't hear him breathing or moving, but he was there. She could *feel* it, as if the air around him was agitated.

She jumped when a cheerful voice called from the doorway. "My, this charming town has changed since I was here last."

The man standing in the doorway wasn't much taller than she was, and he wasn't dressed like any farmer or rancher she'd ever seen. His clothes were, in fact, very up to date, very Eastern, from the bowler hat that was perched atop a graying head to the brown checked frock suit to the shiny shoes that were marred with more than a touch of dust. The smile on his face was brilliant as he stepped toward the counter.

"Ash, you must introduce me to these lovely ladies," the man said as he removed his bowler with a gentlemanly flourish.

Ash cleared his throat. "Mrs. Eula Markam," he said softly, "this is Nathan Sweet, an old friend of the family. Mrs. Markam and her husband own this mercantile."

Eula nodded and muttered a friendly "How do you do." In answer, Nathan Sweet bowed deeply. And then he faced Charmaine.

"And this is Miss Charmaine Haley," Ash said, his voice dropping to a lower note.

"Mr. Sweet," Charmaine said as she offered her hand. "It's a pleasure to meet you."

The little man beamed at her. "The pleasure is all mine, Miss. I swear, Ash, this young woman is every bit as ravishing as your mother, and I never thought I'd hear myself say that about anyone." His eyes twinkled. "Have you ever given thought, Miss Haley, to stepping upon the stage? You would make a fabulous Juliet."

Charmaine felt the heat rising to her face. Blushing! She was much too old to blush at a compliment, no matter how outrageous it might be. "I have no aspirations to the stage, Mr. Sweet."

"Pity," he said, and he seemed to mean it.

"I must be going," Charmaine said with a weak smile, nodding first to Eula and then to the gentleman before her. "There are a thousand errands to be taken care of this afternoon. It was very nice to meet you, Mr. Sweet."

She wrapped her arms around the box of masks, anxious to escape into the sunlight. A few minutes ago she'd been laughing, but right now she felt uncommonly uncomfortable. No one else seemed to be affected by the change of mood. Eula was smiling brightly, Mr. Sweet was grinning, and Ash . . . well, she hadn't turned to face Ash, not once.

"Good heavens, Ash, you're not going to allow this lovely creature to carry this cumbersome load." Mr. Sweet's voice was faintly outraged, and still he smiled.

"It's not heavy . . ." Charmaine began, but before she could finish her sentence Mr. Sweet swept the box from her grasp and deposited it into Ash's arms.

"It's all right, really it is," Charmaine insisted as she attempted—and failed—to take the box from Ash.

"I'll get the supplies loaded into the wagon," Mr. Sweet said to Ash. "By the time you return from assisting the lovely Miss Charmaine Haley with her errand, we'll be ready to go."

Mr. Sweet immediately struck up a conversation with Eula, leaving no room for an argument from either Ash or Charmaine.

He was going to have Nathan's hide when they got back to the farm.

Charmaine walked silently beside him, her eyes straight ahead. When Ash glanced down he saw sunlight on golden hair, squared shoulders encased in a gray muslin that looked almost silver, a profile as delicate as that of a porcelain figurine.

Below that fragile face Charmaine Haley had the body of a woman, pure and simple. She was curvaceous and delicate, and with one glimpse at that body his mind was filled with all sorts of indecent thoughts. Thoughts he couldn't afford to entertain.

The box Ash carried was ridiculously light—a child could have carried it for miles without tiring.

He was definitely going to have Nathan's hide.

The big Haley house was situated at the edge of town, a good walk from the Markam mercantile but not much of a trip. They passed people on the boardwalk and on the street, people they'd known all their lives and those recently come to Salley Creek. Those people, friends and strangers alike, nodded and stared.

As they passed a window, a glimpse of their reflection made Ash realize what a ridiculous sight they made—Charmaine in her prim and proper gown, hair perfectly styled, skin like silk, and him in his work clothes, his hair hanging nearly to his shoulders, his beard rough, his skin tough as old leather.

As they stepped from the boardwalk for the last leg of their walk Charmaine cleared her throat, a soft murmur from deep inside that slender throat that made Ash's own insides tighten.

"Thank you for your help, but I can manage from here." She tried to take the box from him, as she had in the mercantile, but he didn't let go. Not yet.

He could see the Haley house from here, that landmark at the end of the street. Big, white, majestic—it was an imposing structure. "I've come this far, might as well go all the way."

She squirmed, so slightly she might not have realized that he could see the feeble rotation of her gently rounded shoulders, the ruffling of pale, dainty fingers. "It's not necessary . . ."

"I take it Daddy's home." He couldn't help the wide smile that crossed his face. Charmaine was becoming more and more anxious, and they both knew why. Stuart Haley would dearly hate to see his precious daughter in the company of Ash Coleman.

"Well, yes, I suppose he is, but it's really not necessary . . ." she began again.

"I insist."

She sighed in resignation and stepped toward the house at the end of the street. Now that the silence had been broken, Ash decided he'd like this conversation to continue. "Fancy masks," he said, glancing into the box he held and past the brown paper package atop it all. Bright colors, sparkles and spangles, fluffy feathers.

"Yes, they are. Beautiful but frivolous," she said sharply, but Ash didn't quite buy it. He'd heard her squeal with her own mask on her face, seen her twirl around in pure delight.

"Your Daddy sure is going to a lot of trouble

just to find you a husband," he said casually. "What, there weren't any Easterners who suited you?"

Charmaine stopped in her tracks, and Ash had to take a step backwards to stand beside her.

Her face went white, her blue eyes widened, and her mouth fell slightly open. It was a mesmerizing sight. "*A husband*. I should have known," she whispered.

"You didn't know?" Well, wasn't he the fool. "Maybe I'm wrong. It's just a rumor I heard from Verna, that you were looking to get married and this party was a chance to meet the men from hereabouts. Verna's not a reliable gossip, not at all dependable."

Charmaine's mouth snapped shut, her eyes hardened until they were positively frosty, and the color rushed to her face. "No. It makes perfect sense. My father is bound and determined that one of his daughters stay here and since Felicity and Jeanette are married, well, that leaves me. Gullible, dim-witted Charmaine."

She took a long step forward. "Every fortune hunter for three hundred miles will be at this dratted masked ball. Every man who ever dreamed of having a ranch the size of Daddy's, every *man* in East Kansas!"

Ash definitely didn't like the way she said *man*, as if she wouldn't give two cents for any one of them. "Well, you're bound to get married sooner or later, so you might as well—"

"I'm not getting married, not sooner *or* later," she snapped forcefully. "Daddy just refuses to accept that as fact."

He wanted to ask her why, but decided he was better off keeping his mouth shut. It looked like he'd done enough damage already.

As they reached the walkway to the Haley house, Charmaine snatched the box from him, muttered a curt and very ungracious thanks, and stormed toward the front door. That gray skirt moved as ominously as any storm cloud he'd ever seen, and this one was definitely dangerous.

When she reached the steps she turned to face him. Some of the anger had faded from her face, but her eyes were still like ice.

"Are you coming to the party?"

Ash shook his head slowly. This was as close to the Haley house as he wanted to be. Ever.

"I wish you would."

For a second, a brief and ridiculously wonderful moment in time, he believed her. *I wish you would.* And then she shattered his belief.

"That would show Daddy, wouldn't it," she said, more thoughtful than angry, "if I spent the entire evening dancing with a Coleman." She thanked him again, turned her back, and blazed through the front door and into the house.

The walk back to the mercantile was quick, since his long stride was unchecked and his speed steadily increased until he was practically running. People got out of his way, and this time there were no friendly greetings. They took one look at him and knew better.

"That would show Daddy . . ."

Nathan was waiting in the wagon, and the supplies were loaded into the bed. All Ash had to do was jump aboard and head for home. The next time Verna forgot supplies she would damn well make another trip to town herself.

He didn't so much as look at Nathan as he set the wagon in motion.

"Oh, dear," Nathan said as they headed at a quick clip out of town. "I'm guessing things didn't go well."

Ash didn't respond, didn't so much as glance to the side.

"Too bad. She is fabulously gorgeous, with that fair hair and those magnificently elegant features, and those striking blue eyes. Forgive me for interfering, but it was just so *obvious*. She likes you, you like her—"

Nathan shut his mouth quickly as Ash turned a cold glare his way. "That's the dumbest notion I ever heard."

"I knew it the moment I walked into the mercantile." For some reason there was a wide smile on Nathan's face. "She wasn't breathing, you weren't breathing, you both jumped out of your skin when I said hello." The smile widened to a ridiculously broad grin. "I could have lit all of Kansas if I could've harnessed the electricity in the room."

Ash snorted and turned his eyes to the road. "You were mistaken."

"But—"

Ash gave Nathan one more cold glare. "You were mistaken," he said again, and with a sigh Nathan was blessedly silent.

If her father had been home when she'd returned with the masks, Charmaine would've certainly let him have a piece of her mind. How dare he presume to find a husband for her, when she had very plainly told him she didn't want one? He might as well be done with the formalities and auction her off like a prize mare.

But an emergency had taken him out to the range, and it had been late when he'd returned to the house. Charmaine had been very aware of and concerned about her mother's exhaustion, and had decided to refrain from bringing the subject up until she was alone with her father. Then she could let him have it without restraint.

In spite of her fury and indignation, she'd fallen asleep early, weary herself from all the preparations for this now-dreaded ball and somewhat disturbed by the unexpected encounter with Ash.

By breakfast her father had gone for the day,

and her mother was preparing to meet the musicians and get them settled in the cabin. Charmaine's anger had cooled by then, and it no longer seemed so terribly important that she confront her father head-on with this bit of news. It was at least in part her fault as much as his. She should've realized from the start what his intent was in throwing this ball. He was so transparent, she should have known from that first day.

Besides, just because Stuart Haley had spread the word that he was looking for a husband for his youngest daughter, that didn't mean she had to cooperate. She didn't have to actually accept any one of the louts who dared to present himself with that intent.

Her father had already shown her that most men had no tolerance for a woman who dared to speak her mind. She had no doubt that any man he seriously presented to her as a potential husband would be of like temper. A discourse on the inadvisability of the corset, the way the romantic novel was leading young women and young men astray, or the impure influence of the bicycle, perhaps even a lecture on the appalling lack of independence afforded women in this country, and any man bearing a hair of resemblance to Stuart Haley would go running into the night.

By the morning of the ball, Charmaine was able to give her father a true, wide smile over breakfast.

Chapter Six

He'd never seen Verna in such a state, and she'd been this way since morning. It was not a pleasant sight, Verna Coleman in a dither.

She'd convinced herself that Charmaine Haley would fall madly in love with one of her boys, and they would all move into the big Haley house and be set for life. She was so adamant, so eager, that she was well on her way to convincing Oswald and Elmo of that possibility.

If only it were true. Ash could close his eyes and see it, the house without Verna and her boys in it. What a soothing and pleasant thought it was. With the three of them gone, he could finally give serious thought to getting married and having a family of his own and making this farm truly his home once again. It was time.

Charmaine and Oswald would make quite a pair, of that Ash was certain, but Verna seemed certain that Elmo had an equal chance of attracting the beautiful and spoiled Charmaine. Only a mother could look at Elmo and see anything of value.

Ash's chores kept him close to the house today, and he'd watched the day's progress with silent amusement. Verna and the boys were alternately giddy and nervous, and displayed more energy than he'd seen from the lot of them in some time. Nathan had slept until quite late, but since rising he'd watched the proceedings with an apparent interest of his own.

The boys were finally bathed and shaved and dressed in their Sunday best. Verna was not quite pleased with Oswald's hair. Each time she passed him she fussed with it a little more, until he'd had enough and drew back to gently slap her hand away.

All Elmo had to do was move and his once neat appearance was altered. The lapels of his navy blue coat fell askew, his shirt came untucked and poked forward, his tie scooted to one side. Verna righted her younger son's clothing every five minutes or so, for all the good it did.

And Elmo already had a headache.

Verna readied herself in bits and spurts. Bathing behind the curtain in the kitchen while the boys dressed, fussing with her hair from her ground floor bedroom while she shouted instructions on manners and dress. Finally, she had no choice but to retreat to her room, behind a closed door, to dress herself.

It was while Verna was safely and quietly in her room that Nathan pulled Ash aside.

"When are you going to get ready?" he hissed. "You haven't much time!"

Ash looked Nathan up and down as if he were a demented stranger. "I'm not going anywhere."

"You must go," Nathan insisted, as strident as Verna ever was.

Ash shook his head and headed for the door. Nathan followed closely.

"An event of this kind might never come again to Salley Creek," Nathan said, his voice rising to a new high. "You can't miss it."

"I can."

"But that lovely Miss Haley will be there in her fanciest gown. Wouldn't you like to dance with her, just once?"

Ash snorted as he headed for the pigsty, certain that Nathan wouldn't follow him there. "She's not interested in dancing with a Coleman." *That would show Daddy* . . .

"Don't be ridiculous." Nathan stopped outside the closed pigsty gate. "I'd say she's *very* interested."

. . . wouldn't it, if I spent the entire evening dancing with a Coleman. "You're wrong."

Nathan leaned against the fence casually and he didn't say another word, but his eyes remained intent on Ash as he went about his chores. The older man, who was intelligent and witty and at home in any situation, would never understand Ash's misgivings, hell, his fears, about stepping into the Haley house with the intention of *courting* Charmaine.

Verna and the boys came bustling out of the house, a chattering explosion through the front door. Verna was dressed in a lavender gown that was heavy with lace and ruffles and just a bit too snug, and the boys were as spiffy as they were likely to get.

"Ash!" Verna snapped. "Hitch up the wagon! I expected it to be ready by now."

There was no speed in his step or his movements, but Ash did as Verna demanded, hitching up the grays while his stepmother waited impatiently. "Sorry you had to wait, but I didn't expect you to leave quite this early," he said as he assisted Verna into her seat.

"Sarah Lewis has invited us to stop by and freshen up before the party begins. She and I will probably go to the Haleys' together."

Nathan pushed away from the fence. "Maybe you'll see Ash at the party."

Oswald laughed out loud, and Elmo snickered. Verna just looked horrified. "He can't possibly attend."

"Why not?" Nathan asked.

"Why, he's . . ." Verna looked Ash up and down, and the disdain in her eyes was as telling as the boys' continuing laughter. ". . . it wouldn't be . . . just look at him!"

"Besides." Elmo leaned forward to see past his mother and meet Ash's glare. "I didn't have time to milk the cows, so you'll have to do it. And I meant to tell you yesterday that there's a break in the fence on the east edge of the property. It really should be repaired."

"I fixed that break last week," Ash said tonelessly.

"This is a new one," Elmo said with a smile.

"Oh, and I left a pile of dishes in the kitchen. Be a dear and wash them up for me," Verna said with a smile of her own. "Don't wait up for us. We'll probably spend the night at the Lewises'."

With that they were gone. Wonderfully, blessedly gone. His peaceful moment didn't last long.

"Are you going to let her do this to you?" Nathan snapped as the wagon disappeared.

"Do what?"

Nathan sighed and threw his hands into the air. "Leave you here with all the work while they go off to dance and court Miss Haley!"

Ash shrugged his shoulders. "I don't mind." He started toward the barn to get the tools necessary to repair the fence. He really didn't mind.

He was just grateful for an entire evening without Verna and her boys in the house. It was all he wanted. It was enough.

Nathan was silent for a moment, and Ash almost allowed himself to believe that his godfather had given up. How very foolish.

"Can't you just see it, my boy?" Nathan said in a purposely enticing voice. "Charmaine Haley, dressed in her fanciest gown. I imagine she'll go in for the French fashion, a low-cut bodice to reveal white skin that will positively gleam in the bright lights of a ballroom. That golden hair, piled atop her beautiful head in the most fashionable style, soft curls of silken tresses to catch the light. And to top it all off, a dazzling smile to tempt any red-blooded man. What a vision she'll surely be. She'll dance with everyone I suppose, even those oafish stepbrothers of yours, but she'll be incredibly bored." Nathan lowered his voice. "Unless, of course, a mysterious stranger comes in to sweep her off her feet."

Ash stilled with his hands on the hammer he needed. Nathan was too good at this. He *could* see it, in agonizing detail, and it was tempting as hell. "I'm no mysterious stranger."

"You can be." Nathan said with a touch of humor. "This is a masked ball, after all."

"I've still got the cows to milk and the fence to repair and the dishes to wash . . ."

"I can milk the cows and wash the dishes, and

I suppose the fence can wait one more day."

It was tempting, not just because he wanted to dance with Charmaine Haley in his arms, just once, but because he wanted to see the look on her face when she discovered it was him. She might not believe it was possible, but Ash's mother had taught him to dance well. He wanted to dance with Charmaine, he wanted to dazzle her, to make her laugh. He wanted to sweep her off her feet . . . and then he wanted to watch those blue eyes widen in horror when he took off his mask.

"I suppose it can," he said as he put the hammer back in its proper place.

"I never wear a corset," Charmaine insisted again, as she glared at the contraption on the bed. "It's an instrument of ruin, the greatest cause of female troubles . . ."

"Just for tonight," her mother said tiredly. "The gown won't look right without a properly laced corset."

Charmaine grimaced at the laces and buckles on the apparatus that was placed beside her gown. As a physician, Howard railed against the corset. Of course, Howard railed against many things.

"Please." It was her mother's simply uttered *please* that convinced Charmaine to comply.

Ruth was there to assist with the torturous device that would push Charmaine's breasts high and force her waist to an unnaturally small circumference. Charmaine gripped the bedpost while Ruth tightened.

After tonight, she would be her own woman. An opinion voiced with certainty over a cup of punch, an unbending criticism of this backward lifestyle . . . she'd make sure that there wouldn't be a man for a hundred miles who would have her.

After tonight, she would be free. Her father would surely despair of ever finding her a proper Kansan husband, and allow her to return to Boston.

Her thoughts were interrupted by a vigorous yank. Ruth was especially strong and evidently dedicated to her chore this evening. Charmaine took a deep breath, and the pressure around her torso tightened.

"That's too tight," she insisted, casting a glance to her mother. Maureen sat on the edge of a chaise, dressed already for the evening ahead.

"It's properly tightened, Miss," Ruth said in a clipped voice.

"I can't breathe!" Charmaine cast an angry glance over her shoulder.

There was no visible reaction from the ladies' maid. No chagrin or triumph. Still, Charmaine was sure this was some sort of punishment for dragging the unwilling servant to the wilderness.

"Take shallow breaths," her mother advised. "From here." She patted high on her own chest.

Charmaine did as her mother directed, taking a series of shallow breaths that felt unnatural and were too much of an effort. But she *could* breathe.

After tonight, she would never wear a corset again.

Her mother waited until Ruth had assisted Charmaine into the magnificent white gown and arranged her hair atop her head with a spray of white and peach flowers artfully placed in the soft knot.

When Ruth was finished, Charmaine stepped back to study her reflection in the cheval glass. This wasn't her, not really. But the gown was magnificent, and her hair was perfect, and the torturous corset did give her a tiny waist. Of course, it also forced her breasts up and into an unnatural state. There was much too much skin revealed above the peach trim. Howard would be mortified.

Still, Charmaine smiled. After tonight, she'd never again be this beautiful.

"My baby." In the mirror, past her shoulders, Charmaine saw a smile grow on her mother's face. "You look very little like my baby girl at this moment."

Charmaine returned her mother's smile.

After tonight.

*   *   *

"Stop squirming!" Nathan ordered, and Ash was immediately still. The scissors snipped quickly, and another strand of damp, dark hair fell over Ash's shoulder and onto the floor. "You won't be very dashing if you're missing an ear."

This was a mistake, and Ash knew it already. Nathan had insisted that a pitcher of water and a bar of soap wouldn't do. A full tub bath with Nathan's own special soap was called for. Ash had mumbled to himself constantly as he scrubbed in the tin tub that sat in the middle of the kitchen. He did *not* think it was a good idea to walk into the Haley house smelling like a flower, but Nathan had insisted.

A close shave followed, and now the haircut. Sitting before the fire in nothing but his underwear, Ash allowed the old man to snip and shave.

"You have a wonderfully thick head of hair," Nathan said with apparent joy. "What I wouldn't give for such a crowning glory." Another long strand fell to the floor.

Ash felt naked, vulnerable, as the chilly air touched his neck. This was a terrible mistake. He wasn't going to fool anyone with a haircut and a shave. Charmaine Haley would laugh him out of her house and out of town for pretending to be something he wasn't.

With fingers cradling his scalp, Nathan turned Ash's head this way and that, studying his work carefully. A few careful snips, and he declared the job finished.

"And now for the clothes," Nathan said with a flourish. "I've placed an outfit on your bed."

Ash looked over his shoulder as he rose. "I'll wear my own clothes."

Nathan shook his head, short quick bursts of negativity. "Even your Sunday best won't do, not for tonight. I have trunks full of costumes in that old wagon, and Richard was about your size." Nathan's smile disappeared. "That traitorous ne'er-do-well."

"Costumes?"

"Well, this *is* a masked ball."

"A masked ball, not a costume party," Ash snapped. "You want me to make a fool of myself?"

Nathan gave Ash a shove toward the stairs. "Of course not. Just have a look at what I laid out for you."

Ash climbed the stairs with a dread he usually reserved for Verna and her boys. This was a mistake. He'd allowed Nathan to push and cajole and tempt him to this point, but he could call it all off right now. . . .

But then he had the vision again. Dancing with Charmaine Haley in his arms, her hair spun-gold in the bright lights of the Haley house, her body close to his, her smile just for him.

And then, of course, unmasking himself at

the end of the evening, preferably with Stuart Haley close by.

The clothes across his bed made him forget even those pleasant thoughts.

"What is this?" Ash shouted from the top of the stairs.

Nathan stood at the foot of the stairs and frowned. "You don't like it?"

Ash shook the red coat toward the stubborn old man. "I can't wear this! And what are these?" He waved the bright blue breeches before him like a flag.

"Too much?" Nathan asked softly. "I did think that crushed crimson velvet would look wonderful on you with your coloring . . ." He stopped his protests, the words trailing into nothing.

"I'll wear my gray suit," Ash said as he turned away.

"No!" Nathan shouted. "Give me one more chance. I promise I'll be more conservative this time."

Ash glared down the staircase. "No red."

Nathan nodded somberly.

"No crushed velvet."

This time Nathan sighed. "If you insist."

"And I couldn't even get my big toe in those shoes you put on the bed. I'll have to wear my boots."

Nathan brought a hand to his chest and struck a pose of revulsion and alarm. "Not those horrid things you wear to slop the pigs and wallow in the dirt."

Ash was ready to call this off here and now, when he remembered what Charmaine Haley had looked like when she'd ridden to the farm on her white horse. He'd likely never see anything to compare with the way she'd look tonight. Maybe it would be an image to lull himself to sleep with on restless nights. "I have a pair of good boots," he said softly. "And just because I'm a farmer, that doesn't mean I *wallow* in the dirt."

"Sorry, this is just very stressful for me." Nathan spun on his heel and made his way quickly out the front door, mumbling something lowly. All Ash could hear, as he lowered himself to the top step, was the single word *conservative*. He gripped the ridiculous outfit in one hand and waited to see what Nathan would come up with this time.

The house had been transformed. The largest rooms on the ground floor had been cleared of furniture, but for the chairs placed along the wall in the dining room. Every room was brightly lit, and decorated with flowers and expertly placed swags of fabric shot with gold. The orchestra was warming up, the dining room was bustling with servants who added last-minute hot foods to the long table, and Maureen was directing it all.

She was always beautiful, but tonight she looked like a girl again. The girl he had married twenty-seven years ago. It was the sparkle in her eyes and the color in her cheeks that did the trick, not the fancy gown and the new emerald necklace.

"You're not wearing your mask, Stuart," she said as she passed him on her way from the dining room to the newly transformed ballroom.

"Neither are you," he said, falling into step behind her. "Besides, no one's arrived yet."

"The first guest will be here any minute. I think everything's ready. Goodness, I hope I didn't forget anything! The masks are in a basket by the front door, and Jane's niece will pass them out as the guests arrive." Her voice was a little high and excited, as she started one by one to list the foods that would be served.

Stuart grabbed her arm gently, turned her around before she entered the ballroom, and kissed her.

"Stuart!" she said as she pulled slightly away. "What on the earth . . ."

"A man can't kiss his wife?"

"Not right now," she scolded, but she was wearing a smile and she didn't step away.

He kissed her again, deeper this time, and she relaxed in his embrace and returned the kiss.

"Have I told you today that I love you?" he asked as he broke the kiss.

"No, you haven't," Maureen answered with a

complacent smile. "I love you too, you know, in spite of the fact that you're a man who will go to extreme measures to get what he wants."

"That's what you love about me," he said huskily. "Admit it, darling."

She laughed, a clear peal that warmed his heart.

Chapter Seven

What an oaf! Charmaine smiled as her dance partner prattled on, but only because her father was watching closely. Let him imagine, for a few minutes, what it would be like to have this fool as his son-in-law. *That* would teach him to meddle.

She hadn't gotten in a single word since this dance had begun, because her partner—one of Ash Coleman's inept stepbrothers—had complained constantly about his head and his back and his infected toenail that made dancing so difficult.

Surely she had danced with every man in East Kansas tonight, and the evening was young. Her father had introduced his obvious favorites with a transparently satisfied wide smile, and there were a number of cowboys from neighboring ranches who'd crashed the party. Old acquaintances, her father's friends' sons, complete strangers, she'd danced with them all.

On more than one occasion she'd tried to voice her opinion—a modern and shocking conviction that would scare off even the most persistent suitor—but it was a waste of time. Not a one of the men even bothered to listen to her.

Their eyes glazed over, and they stared at her exposed cleavage or the other dancers or the lavishly appointed room that had been cleared for dancing. That's what they were interested in, she reminded herself. The Haley house, the Haley Ranch . . . not her and her opinions. She could be a raving lunatic and they'd continue to dance and smile like the louts they were. What a fool she'd been to think she could spoil her father's plans!

She practiced the art of not listening herself as Elmo March went on and on about his disgusting infected toenail.

Apparently assured that she was behaving herself, her father stepped into the dining room where the food was laid out. There beef, chicken, and pork weighed the tables down, and there were potatoes prepared in several different ways, as well as soft rolls and corn pudding. A separate dessert table was crowded with pies and cakes and cookies. The fare wasn't as fancy as what was normally served at a society affair in Boston, but it was good food and there was plenty of it.

At least it *smelled* good. Charmaine hadn't been able to take so much as a bite, this darn corset was tied so tight. All evening she'd breathed as her mother instructed, shallow breaths that caused her exposed cleavage to rise and fall softly. Elmo with the infected toenail was staring down at that cleavage as he prattled on. Ninny.

If the intent of the masked ball was to disguise the appearance of the dancers, it was a dismal failure. A mask covering half of someone's face didn't disguise their identity. It was ridiculously simple to spot the townspeople. Doc Whitfield with his potbelly and canted walk. Eula, with her dark hair in sculpted curls. Delia, smiling and flirting shamelessly. Every unmarried man for miles, doing their best to be charming.

A small mask was a poor disguise, but there were moments when Charmaine felt as if she were actually hiding behind hers, the white creation resplendent with pearls and lace. She smiled and spoke and danced, but behind the mask her thoughts were her own.

This particular song had to be nearing its end.

Surely she had been dancing with this dolt for hours. He was already red-faced and huffing, and she wondered if he might not drop to the floor without warning, blessedly dead from exhaustion and his infected toe.

At last, the music ended. Gratefully, Charmaine stepped away and gave a small curtsey to her partner. She would not dance with Elmo March again. If he presented himself she would come up with some excuse.

"May I have this dance?" The voice came from close behind her, a husky whisper near her ear, and she spun around with every intention of begging off. She was hungry, she could barely breathe, she was tired of having her feet stepped on. . . .

But no excuse left her parted lips as she stared up at the tall man who was dressed entirely in black but for the stark white shirt beneath his frock coat. He was bareheaded, thick dark brown hair gleaming in the bright lights of the ballroom. The coat was finely cut, and the trousers were tucked into tall boots. His silk necktie was as coal-black as the rest, and was adorned with a very small diamond stickpin. Even his mask was black, a plain, soft leather mask that covered three-quarters of his face.

She hadn't noticed him earlier, which meant he surely hadn't been here. Even in the most crushing crowd, she would never have overlooked such a striking figure.

"Of course."

Who was he? She studied the small part of his face she could see beneath the mask, a strong and sharp jaw, a finely shaped chin not too prominent or too weak, lips full and perfectly sculpted—not too firm or too soft. She tried to look past the small holes in his mask to his eyes, but there was nothing familiar in what little she could see beyond the shadows of the leather mask.

"I don't believe we were introduced," she said as he spun her around. At last, a competent dancer. This man moved gracefully, and he hadn't stepped on her toes once. "I'm Charmaine Haley."

"I know." Those finely shaped lips almost smiled.

"And you are . . ." she pressed.

"A stranger passing through town," he whispered.

A tremor passed through her body, a deep and surely imperceptible trembling she immediately attributed to hunger and exhaustion and the darn corset.

Charmaine quivered in his arms, a quiver so soft it couldn't be seen—only felt. She was gorgeous, more beautiful than in his wildest fantasy. Her white mask didn't hide much. It wrapped around the upper half of her face, and dripping pearls danced against her pale cheeks as she moved. There was a strand of pearls at her throat, and more tiny pearls sewn into her gown. The lustrous gems suited her.

"The waltz is a decadent and barbaric ritual," she said sharply, and his eyes snapped up from the pearls at her throat to blue eyes that flashed behind the mask.

"Is it really? And you waltz so well." He smiled at the surprise on her face. "I always thought the waltz was just a bit of harmless fun."

"Harmless fun?" Her lips twitched, as if she might smile herself but was trying very hard not to. "Look around you, sir. What do you see?"

Ash glanced quickly across the room. Verna was standing between Elmo and Oswald, and she was staring at him with pursed lips while fanning herself furiously and looking as if she might burst from that too-snug lavender gown. Did she recognize him? Surely not. Stuart Haley stepped into the room and watched with a frown on his face. Dancers passed between them, so that he came in and out of view.

"I see a lot of happy faces, dancers laughing, smiling, enjoying themselves," he said as he returned his attention to Charmaine.

"They're entirely too excited," she said primly.

Ash leaned in close, as close as he dared. Charmaine had no idea who he was and he could pretend, for a while, that he was someone else entirely. It was a game, purely an escape. "Are you getting excited, Charmaine Haley?"

There was a sharp intake of breath, but she didn't pull away, as he'd expected she might. "What an improper question that is."

He laughed softly. She might pretend to be shocked, but there was new color in her cheeks, and fire in the eyes he glimpsed behind the mask. "Improper? What do you care about propriety? You say the waltz is improper, but you're dancing with me. Proper or not, you've been dancing all night, haven't you?"

The music stopped and the dance was stilled, but Ash didn't release his tenuous hold on Charmaine and she didn't back away. They stood in the center of the dance floor, poised for another decadent waltz. Was she breathing as she waited? He didn't think so.

Oswald was making his way across the dance floor. When the music began again, and the dancers began to move, Oswald came to an awkward halt. Unsure. Angry. And then he stepped forward to tap Ash on the shoulder.

"This dance was promised to me," he said as primly as any old maid.

"Too bad," Ash whispered.

"But Miss Haley . . ." Oswald began. He shut his mouth quickly as Ash turned his head to stare at his lazy stepbrother.

"Go away," he ordered softly, and Oswald did.

When he looked down at Charmaine, she had a wide grin on her face. It was the kind of smile that might visit a man's dreams for the rest of his life.

"Thank you, sir."

"For what?"

"I've already endured one dance with that gentleman this evening, and believe me, one was enough."

"Why's that?"

"He talked about nothing but some boring book he was reading. Why, novels are a terrible influence on young men and women. Romantic nonsense that leads to the physical and spiritual downfall of many."

"Is that so?"

"Yes, it is. And besides," her smile widened, "he stepped on my toes four times in one dance."

He spun Charmaine around, once, twice, again. "Clumsy lout."

It had been years since he'd danced, but it all came back to him easily. His mother's insistence that every man needed to know how to dance and to recite at least one poem had met some resistance from the sensible John Coleman, but he'd never denied his wife anything. The dancing Ash remembered. The poem was another matter.

"Who are you?" Charmaine asked as they whirled past brightly dressed dancers.

"No one," he whispered.

*   *   *

"I'm going out there to stop this nonsense," Stuart whispered hoarsely.

"No." Maureen placed her hand on her husband's arm, and he was immediately still. Charmaine and the man she danced with—had been dancing with for some time now—made quite an arresting picture. Startling black and white amid a sea of color, they moved with grace and harmony.

"People are beginning to talk," Stuart hissed angrily. "Every time someone goes out there to ask Charmaine to dance, that . . . that man warns them off. And who the hell *is* he, anyway?"

Maureen kept her hand on Stuart's arm and he didn't move away, even though he obviously wanted to storm across the dance floor to his youngest daughter. "You wanted Charmaine to meet someone here tonight, didn't you?"

"Yes," he conceded softly.

"Look at her, Stuart," Maureen whispered. "Has there been any other man here tonight who's been able to light up her face like that?"

He hesitated, watching his daughter dance with the tall dark stranger. For the first time tonight, for the first time since her arrival in Salley Creek, she looked truly happy. "No."

"And have you seen another man here who'd make Charmaine a suitable husband? One of those idiot March brothers, or Doc Whitfield's nephew William from Emporia? Jake Rogers, who's old enough to be Charmaine's father, by the way? Perhaps one of those crude cowboys from the Goodman ranch. Why, did you see what that one young man—"

"I get your point," Stuart grumbled.

"Good." Maureen smiled brightly as Stuart turned his face to hers. "Now, on to other matters. I'm positively starving. Would you kindly escort me to the dining room for a bite of supper?"

"Again? You just ate an hour ago."

"I've been dreadfully hungry lately," she said as she led Stuart into the dining room. "Throwing a party is hard work."

"Evidently," he grumbled as they left the dance floor.

It was amazing. No matter what she said he didn't seem to mind. And he was actually listening! Sometimes he agreed with her, and sometimes he didn't, but she didn't mind a little argument. In fact, she loved a good one.

And they hadn't left the dance floor since she'd turned around and found him standing there. He moved well, this stranger who refused to give her his name, with power and a simple grace. She felt oddly safe in his arms.

"I imagine that you, sir, are simply agreeing in order to please me."

"And why would I do that?"

"Let's be honest for a moment. Men are predictably single-minded where women are concerned. You're quite charming, and I'm sure you're very aware of that fact and have used it to your advantage many times in the past. You've no doubt been successful with ladies who are not educated as to their rights."

He didn't seem at all shocked or offended. Amazing. Of course, how was she to be sure with that mask covering so much of his face?

"And what rights are those, exactly?"

Charmaine smiled, and he grinned back. "The right to make one's own decisions. To plan one's life and follow that plan with the same diligence any man would."

"I think you've made the mistaken assumption that men always get what they want and women never do."

"So, it's a *mistaken* assumption, is it?"

"Most definitely."

"Then explain why men are free to work where and however they choose. Any profession, any place on earth. They control the money, they own the property, they make *all* the decisions, and the poor lowly female is expected to comply with the wishes of her husband or her father as if she had no will of her own. Why, women are no better than slaves in most households."

In most instances she would bring up the subject of marital continence here, but the very idea of having that discussion with this man made her blush. She could feel the heat rising to her cheeks, just thinking about it.

"And here I've been living all my life under the *mistaken* assumption that women want to be taken care of."

"Ha!" she countered, glad to send her thoughts in another direction. "Not all women are looking for a man to take care of them. What a preposterous notion."

"You don't need anyone to take care of you, do you, Charmaine Haley?" he asked softly.

"I most certainly do not."

"Then let's just dance."

The next dance was particularly fast. The music was lively, the dancers who crowded the floor livelier. Charmaine and her stranger reeled and twisted, turned and hopped until she was breathless. Literally.

She stopped moving, and her partner stilled with her. The music played on.

"Are you all right?" he asked, leaning down to place his face close to hers. "You're flushed."

"I need to sit down," she said. What she really needed was a deep breath of fresh air, and that wasn't going to happen until she got out of this darn corset. "And something cool to drink would be nice."

He was leading her toward the dining room. Charmaine looked up to find Verna Coleman and her two boys blocking the pathway to the punch and the chairs that lined the dining room walls. They weren't smiling.

Before she could bemoan the necessity of facing that particular family, the stranger spun her about and slipped through the dancers to the open patio doors.

The fresh cool air was heaven, after being in that crowded room all night. Charmaine closed her eyes and took a deep breath—well, as deep a breath as she could manage. It was wonderful—and then she heard Verna Coleman's bitter voice.

"I think they went out this door."

"This way," she whispered, grabbing the stranger's hand and pulling him into the darkness away from the patio. They passed through the garden, around a sharp bend in the well-tended path so that they would be out of sight. The music faded, the voices became distant and then died, and finally Charmaine slowed her step. She didn't release the stranger's hand until she stepped onto the gazebo at the edge of the garden.

She sank onto the bench and closed her eyes. Blessed quiet. Cool air. If only she could shed the tormenting corset, all would be right with the world.

The stranger sat beside her. Close, so close his arm brushed hers. "Are you all right?"

"Yes." She nodded, not knowing if he could see her in the darkness. The moon shone on half his face, on that leather mask and dark hair. "I just couldn't breathe," she whispered. The lowered voice was appropriate here in the darkness.

He raised his hand to touch her cheek, there below the mask. "You're warm."

"Yes."

She didn't protest when his hands slipped to the back of her head to untie the silk ribbons that held the mask in place. The cool air against her face felt heavenly, his fingers against the skin there even more so.

"You're very beautiful," he whispered.

Her heart skipped a beat. His words were romantic nonsense, as this entire evening had been, a practiced flirtation. Still, just for tonight—"I am not, and you shouldn't say such things—"

"You are," he interrupted. "And tonight I say whatever I want."

His fingers traced her face, danced down her cheeks and across her jaw, brushed over her lips and back again. "Will you let me kiss you, Charmaine Haley?"

"Yes," she breathed, without hesitation, without thinking at all.

His lips on hers were soft and reluctant, as if he was afraid she'd change her mind. They brushed lightly over hers, and then they settled in nicely, moving gently over her mouth. The sensation was intoxicating.

He tasted and smelled very pleasant, warm and amazingly different from anything she'd ever known, until this was *all* she knew. His taste and his smell, the feel of his mouth on hers, the beat of her heart and his.

Charmaine raised her hands to the back of his head, intent on removing the mask and revealing his face. He stopped her, his large hands gripping her wrists and pulling them away from the leather thongs that held his mask in place. He kissed her wrists, the palms of her hands, and he didn't release her.

"I want to see your face," she pleaded.

"No," he whispered, bringing his mouth to hers again.

"But why?" The question was a mere breath against his lips.

He sighed, softly, uncertainly. "I had planned to show you my face before the night was over, but now I can't. It would ruin everything."

"Why? How could it possibly—"

He silenced her with a kiss. "Tomorrow I'll be gone," he said. "Tonight is all we have, is all we'll ever have, and I don't want to spoil it."

There was a terrible finality in his words, and Charmaine's heart pounded with excitement and an unexplained terror. She'd never see him again. Something akin to panic rushed through her, a real dread at the certainty that she'd never feel this way again. She allowed her lips to fall against his, seeking without shame the overwhelming sensation she felt when his mouth touched hers.

His hands released hers and danced up her arms, over her shoulders to her neck. Long fingers delved into her hair, and with his tongue he parted her lips and teased her with more. This was more than wonderful, it was magical. Her body was singing, her blood was dancing, this was . . . this was everything Howard had warned her against.

She drew her head back sharply, drawing away from the lips that taunted her. The stranger was unprepared, and as he had his fingers twined in the pearl necklace she wore, it snapped, and pearls went everywhere. They bounced on the gazebo floor, fell into her bodice, rebounded off his black frock coat.

"What's wrong?"

"What's wrong?" she repeated as she came to her feet. "I can't . . . *this* is wrong! This is exactly why waltzing is sinful and should be outlawed."

In the moonlight she could see his smile, and there was something about that smile that was hauntingly familiar. Of course, he had smiled several times throughout the evening. "This has nothing to do with waltzing, Charmaine Haley," he whispered.

The intriguing stranger stood, slowly unfolding his long body from the bench, and Charmaine wanted nothing but for him to kiss her again. He took a step forward, toward her, but instead of taking her in his arms, he winced and stopped his progress.

"What is it?" Charmaine whispered.

He sat down on the bench and slowly removed one boot. When the black boot was in his hand he shook it, and then he turned it upside down. A single pearl rolled into the palm of his hand.

"I see," she said, stepping forward to get a better look at the pearl resting in the palm of hand. It looked so much tinier in his wide, dark palm that it had as one of many around her throat. She was almost upon him when she stepped on another one of the pesky pearls. She knew it was a pearl, because the bottom of her shoe slid over it so smoothly—and so quickly.

If she hadn't been wearing a darn corset, she would have been able to right herself in time, but as it was she fell stiffly forward and into the stranger's ill-prepared arms. The boot he'd been holding in one hand went flying, and as he caught her around the waist they went tumbling over the side of the gazebo. Strong arms tightened around her, and when they fell, his body cushioned the blow for her.

He landed flat on his back, and she landed atop him with a knee on either side of his waist and her skirts bunched around her thighs. After a breathless moment she actually began to laugh softly. It was fortunate that they'd had no audience. What a ridiculous sight they must have made, tumbling over backwards that way!

Her heart was pounding, her hair was falling in disarray about her face, and her expensive gown was falling off of one shoulder.

A hand came to her face, and her laughter died. Long fingers touched her cheek briefly and then moved to the back of her head, and after a pause where taking a breath was impossible, the stranger pulled her face to his and kissed her again. Hard this time, insistent, his tongue invading her mouth as she sat atop him. She had never been so close to any man before, never had her body pressed to his and her mouth joined in this impossible way. The rush of longing that coursed through her body was unexpected and unwanted and much too powerful for her to ignore.

"I'll kill you."

It took Charmaine a moment to realize that the husky voice had not come from the man beneath her. Evidently he realized it at the same time, because they popped up together, straightening hair and skirts and a slightly askew bodice as they came to their feet. It didn't help matters any that the hem of her skirt was tangled in the stranger's diamond stickpin, and it took them several seconds of shared fumbling to undo the entanglement.

"Daddy, I can explain," she said quickly as she turned to face him.

"No explanation is necessary," her father

said. "I can see quite well." He drew a gun from beneath his coat and pointed it in their direction. "Step away, Charmaine."

"No." She stepped in front of the stranger, knowing her father would never risk harming her. "Not until you put that gun away."

He shook his head.

"Mr. Haley," the stranger began.

"You shut up!" He waved the gun wildly. "Nobody touches my daughter, do you understand? *Nobody!*"

"Run," Charmaine whispered. The stranger didn't move. Instead of running away he rested a large hand comfortingly at the small of her back, silently joining her in her defiance of her father. She looked over her shoulder, for one last glimpse of what she could see of his face. The mask and the moonlight thwarted her. "Run."

"I'll never forget this night," he whispered, and her heart stopped.

Before she could respond, before she could even think of a response, he was gone. He had finally taken her advice and run.

Her father swung his gun around quickly, firing a wild shot into the darkness, and the town clock chimed.

Midnight.

Chapter Eight

The clock was pealing the last reverberating strain of midnight, as Ash limped on one booted foot and one in only a sock to the alley where he'd left Pumpkin.

Well, everything that could possibly go wrong had. His plan to embarrass Charmaine had gone out the window the first time she'd smiled at him. He didn't want to hurt her. He wanted this one night to be perfect—for her *and* for him. For Charmaine to be horrified that the man she'd danced with all night was just Ash Coleman—that was not part of any perfect evening.

He unhitched Pumpkin from the post,

jumped into the saddle, and leaned forward with a few soft words for the horse. And then he heard the voices, Stuart Haley's loudest and most furious bluster dominating them all as they headed this way.

If he didn't get out of this alley, he'd be dead.

With another whispered plea and a nudge of his heel to Pumpkin, they were off, flying from the alley and onto the street to surprised shouts. And then the gunfire started. After a moment of panic he realized the resounding shots came from only one gun. Stuart Haley's, no doubt.

The bullets whizzed past, too close for comfort, and Ash leaned over Pumpkin's neck to make a smaller target of himself. Getting himself shot wasn't exactly part of a perfect evening, either. He'd counted four gunshots, each and every one of them zinging by, much too close for comfort. Surely he was almost out of range. Haley had fired once there at the gazebo, so there was just one bullet left in that gun. Just one.

It was the final bullet that got him, grazing him low on his right and bootless leg and burning like hell. He faltered in the saddle, just a little, but Pumpkin didn't fail him. They flew away from Salley Creek and Stuart Haley and his posse.

Ash was well away from town before he was sure no one was following. Only then did he slow Pumpkin and look down at his leg. There to the side, just beneath his knee, was a furrow in the pants Nathan had taken from his trunk of costumes. His wounded leg continued to burn like the dickens but there wasn't much blood, so he figured it couldn't be too bad. All in all, it was a small price to pay.

The moon lit his way, as he meandered slowly toward home. It was a night to remember, this was. He'd danced with Charmaine half the evening, and it had been wonderful and somehow fitting, as if no one else in that room had the right to twirl her across the floor. She'd fit in his arms just right, moved with him without fault. Perfectly.

She still had sand, he realized with a smile in the dark. Charmaine said just what was on her mind no matter how outrageous. Decadent waltzing, ruinous novels, excessive excitement. Most of it was bluster, he'd realized from the start. She was repeating something she'd heard and thought she should agree with, but it wasn't genuine. All that talk about women's rights sure did get her fired up, though, and she was a picture when she was fired up.

And after all that he'd kissed her, and by God she'd kissed him back. A kiss that had fired up his blood and set it racing, that had awakened desires he'd purposely buried deep. In that instant, with that first kiss, Charmaine Haley had staked claim to his heart and his body, and she didn't even know it.

His warm memories turned cold with the sudden comprehension that none of it was real. He'd been someone else tonight, hiding behind that mask and pretending he could have whatever he wanted. Even Charmaine.

Mooning over what he couldn't have served no purpose. He didn't have time for courting, and even if he did it would be a waste of time in his present situation. Besides, she would never have kissed him if she'd known who he was.

Ash reached into his pocket and withdrew the white mask Charmaine had worn most of the night. He'd slipped it there after removing it from her face so he could kiss her, not consciously intending to steal it, but glad now that he had. Moonlight shone on pearls, made the white satin so bright it glowed with an unearthly radiance in the night.

He'd told her that he'd never forget this night, and it was the truth. Maybe she wasn't for him, but by God it had been perfect, for a while. Just for tonight, he reasoned. Just for tonight.

"I don't *know* who he is!" Charmaine shouted at her father again. "He was just a stranger passing through town. You'll never find him!"

He tossed a single boot onto the floor at her feet. "I don't believe it for a minute, young lady!"

They were standing in the middle of what had been the dance floor all night. It was cleared now, but for Charmaine, her father, and her very silent mother. After a wonderful evening her father had cleared the house of guests like a mad, raging bull. Even those who were supposed to spend the night were seeking refuge at the boarding house.

"It's the truth!"

"Then I'm glad I shot the sonofabitch!"

Charmaine felt like the rug had been pulled out from under her. Her knees wobbled, the room tilted and swam. "You did what?" she whispered.

"Now Stuart," her mother began calmly. "You don't know that you hit anything."

"Six shots and I damn well didn't miss every time," he seethed. "Sonofabitch flinched on that last shot. I got him all right."

Charmaine made a silent vow that she wouldn't cry. She wouldn't give her father the satisfaction. "There was no reason . . ." her voice trembled, so she closed her mouth and refused to say anything more.

"What have they done to you in Boston that you'd give yourself to some . . . some strange man who wanders in off the streets?"

"Give myself?" Charmaine whispered. "I didn't . . ."

Her father apparently didn't hear her. "What decent man from hereabouts will have you now? Maybe back East they'll stand for such behavior, but not in Kansas!"

It came to her suddenly, an epiphany that stilled her heart and her trembling knees. *What decent man from hereabouts will have you now?*

"I've tried to tell you I'm a modern woman," she said softly. "And you refuse to believe me. I do as I please. If I choose to dally with a strange man in the gazebo, I'll do so."

Her father turned an alarming shade of red.

"I'm sorry you stumbled upon my liaison, Daddy. I never meant to hurt you." He wasn't hurt, he was furious. She'd never seen him so angry. "I suppose there's nothing I can do about it now, but return to Boston as soon as possible and relieve you of the embarrassment of having me under your roof."

It was the perfect solution, and it had fallen into her lap. How fortuitous.

"Oh, no," he said much too calmly, and the color in his face returned almost to normal. "You're not going back to Boston."

"But you said it yourself, Daddy," she said, trying to match his calm. "No decent man from Salley Creek will have me after this unfortunate scandal. You yelled so loudly half of Kansas surely knows what happened here tonight. I am forever . . . sullied."

He smiled. He actually *smiled*. With a long step he came toward her, and Charmaine braced herself for whatever was to come. Her father had never hit her before, had never so much as spanked any one of his girls . . . but he'd never been in a rage like this before, either.

Before he reached her, he bent down and retrieved the boot her stranger had left behind. "He'll marry you," he said, studying the boot carefully. He turned it over, as if searching for some clue. "Damn big feet, this one's got. Shouldn't be too hard to find."

"He was just passing through town—"

Her father cut her off with an obscenity.

"Stuart!"

Charmaine watched her father's face soften as he turned to acknowledge his wife's admonishment. "Sorry, Maureen, but a man can only take so much. My daughter will not . . ." he struggled visibly for a word he could use in present company, "*dally* with a man and then act as if it means nothing!"

Returning his attention to Charmaine, he shouted again. "What's his name?"

"I don't know!" Her shout matched his, decibel for decibel. "He wouldn't tell me!"

Her father seemed to give in, to very slowly fall apart before her eyes. His anger faded, the flash in his eyes dulled, and he appeared suddenly smaller. "By God, I believe you. I wish I didn't. I wish I didn't have to listen to my own daughter talk about marriage as if it were a disease, and then turn around and . . . and . . ."

"Dally," Maureen said softly.

"Dally with a man whose name she doesn't

know." He shook his head slowly. "What's this world coming to?"

Charmaine wished she did know the stranger's name. Not that she would give it to her father, if she did. She wanted it for herself, for her memories. *Stranger* seemed awfully cold for a remembrance.

"If you don't find him," she said with a cold calm, "and you won't find him, I assure you, I'll return to Boston next week."

"Like hell you will."

"You can't stop me."

She hadn't meant it as a challenge, but it was clear her father had taken it as one. He crossed his arms over his chest, planted his feet far apart, and then he smiled. "We'll see, young lady," he said softly. "We'll see."

Nathan was waiting up, sitting by the fire with one of Oswald's books in his lap. He was not asleep, but his eyes drooped and he yawned as he turned to the opening door. After a moment's perusal, his eyes widened and he shot from the chair.

"What on earth happened to you?"

Ash limped into the house and slammed the door behind him. There was an odd satisfaction in that simple act.

What could he say? This was the most memorable night of his life. He'd danced, he'd kissed, he'd lost his heart—"I was shot."

Nathan assisted Ash to the chair by the fire, even though Ash insisted he didn't need any help. It was just a scratch, after all. Hurt like hell, but he'd live.

His godfather had to see for himself, of course, and wouldn't rest until the furrow in Ash's calf was cleaned and bandaged. He swore and mumbled as he did the job. When that was done Nathan retook his seat, and Ash leaned back and stared into the fire.

"I'm guessing it didn't go well," Nathan finally said, and there was such disappointment in his voice. You'd think he was the one who'd been shot.

"It went as well as could be expected," Ash said, sparing a glance for his godfather.

"She found you out, didn't she?" Nathan snapped. "I never would have thought it possible, you're so transformed, so completely different."

"She didn't find me out," Ash assured him. He began to smile. No, she'd had no idea he was the one. He could look into the fire and see her lips awaiting his expectantly, her smile, her laughing face as she sat atop him in the grass. He'd wanted her then, more than he'd ever wanted anything or anyone.

"I see the night wasn't a *complete* failure," Nathan said with a smile of his own.

"Not a complete failure," Ash conceded.

It was late, and Ash knew he should climb the

stairs and get to bed. Maybe he'd sleep for a few hours tonight, for a change.

"So you'll see her again?" Nathan pressed. "You'll call on her properly, and—"

"No," Ash said quickly and finally. "Tonight was fun, but this is where it ends." Ah, but what a night to remember.

The fire crackled, and for a while that was the only sound in the room. This house was a peaceful place, without Verna and her boys in it.

"I've had the most fabulous idea," Nathan said blandly. His even tone warned Ash that something was up. "Leave this place and come on the road with me. A bath, a shave, and a haircut, and you're altered beyond belief. You've Lila's blood in your veins, so there must be acting talent in you somewhere. Your good looks, Lila's genes, my training, and I'm back in business."

"I'm no actor."

"You fooled Miss Haley," Nathan cooed.

Yes, he'd fooled Charmaine all right, but there hadn't been any acting involved. He'd let down his guard for a few hours, but nothing had changed. "I'm a farmer, Nathan. I was born in this house and I'll most likely die here. I'm sure that sounds dull to a man who's traveled across the country time and again, but it's who I am. It's what I want."

He was a part of this place, it was a part of

him. Otherwise, he would have left after his father's death, leaving Verna and Elmo and Oswald to make their own way. He was and would forever be a farmer.

And Charmaine Haley would make a terrible farmer's wife.

Ruth was humming as she straightened the gown and turned back the bed. How could she? How could she be so curiously happy? Ruth, who rarely smiled and never laughed, was grinning like a silly goose and humming a tune that had been played earlier during the evening.

How could she be so inappropriately happy when Charmaine's world was falling apart?

"I'm glad to see *someone* had a good time tonight," Charmaine snapped.

"Oh yes, miss." Ruth was apparently oblivious to the sarcasm. "Everything was just beautiful, and the food was delicious, and the guests seemed to have a good time." Ruth cut a sly glance in Charmaine's direction. "And I met a very nice man."

"You did?" Charmaine forgot her own predicament, for a moment.

Ruth nodded, her head moving up and down in quick short snaps. "Yes ma'am, in the kitchen. He was looking for more of my apple pie, and he needed a seltzer for his stomach. I fetched a fresh pie from the oven and saw to his stomach, and we talked for quite some time."

"What did you talk about?" Charmaine asked, remembering her own conversation with the stranger.

"Oh, recipes and headache powders and cures for stomach ailments, that sort of thing."

It sounded dreadfully dull to Charmaine, but Ruth seemed satisfied.

When Ruth left her to make her own way to bed, Charmaine went to the window. Finally, she could breathe. She was going to burn that darn corset, and it would take an army to get her into one again.

She was weary, but how could she sleep? How could she ever sleep again? A dance, a kiss, a whispered *I'll never forget* . . . and her world was turned upside down.

Howard had warned her that one day she would meet a man who appealed to her baser emotions, to her lower self. He'd tried to prepare her . . . but mere words couldn't describe the way she'd felt when the stranger had kissed her. How did one fight something like that? How did one guard against a feeling that overpowered everything else, every thought, every conviction. . . .

And her father had shot him! She tried not to think of it, tried to convince herself that he'd missed all six times and the stranger had made a clean getaway.

But when she closed her eyes she saw him, wounded and bleeding, wasting away without her, calling her name. . . . She was distressed by the certain conviction that her stranger *needed* her.

Such excitement was surely not good for her constitution, but she found she wasn't anxious to put the stranger from her mind. The dancing and the conversation, that thrilling smile, the kissing in the gazebo. It was all so decadent . . . but it didn't *feel* decadent. It felt good, and pure, and right, and she wanted nothing more than to look out the window and see him standing there beneath the maple tree, staring up, waiting for her to lift the pane and invite him in.

Her eyes flew open and she sighed in dismay. Goodness, what was happening to her? She tried to reason out her unusual behavior. She'd been in emotional turmoil since arriving in Salley Creek. Her father was his usual demanding self, her mother was not herself at all, and everything had changed. And after an evening that was much too exciting, her father had taken a *gun* after the only man who'd ever made her question her beliefs.

It was late, she was tired, and everything she believed in had been tested tonight.

Her father would never find the stranger. The man who had robbed her of her senses as if she were a brainless child had to be, as he'd claimed, passing through Salley Creek never to return. And no one else would ever make her fall to such depths. No one. From now on, she'd be on her guard against tall, handsome strangers who were experts at dancing and kissing.

It was just as well that her father was doomed to failure.

And still she stepped to the window, lifted it slowly and quietly, and leaned forward to search the shadows of the maple tree that grew up to and beyond her window. She strained, listening intently for a sound that shouldn't be there, a rustling of leaves or a seductive whisper. Nothing.

She slammed the window shut.

Chapter Nine

He'd faced every man in town on this deceptively beautiful morning after the masked ball, with the boot that scoundrel had left behind in his hand and a silent and unnaturally pale Charmaine at his side. It was a frustrating quest. The men he confronted were either too short, or too fat, or they had incredibly small feet. With every failure, his anger grew. Stuart Haley would not be made a fool of! His daughter would not *dally* with a man unless she was by-God prepared to marry him!

It didn't take long at all to eliminate the men in town. Not that he'd expected to find the man he searched for sitting on his doorstep wearing only one boot. It wouldn't be easy, but this wasn't over, not by a long shot.

They were approaching the Coleman farm. From there, he would set his sights just beyond Salley Creek, to the ranches in the next county. The owner of this boot was probably some good-for-nothing cowboy enjoying a night on the town . . . with *his* daughter!

Of course, when all was said and done it would be right nice to have a cowman as a son-in-law.

"Daddy, you're wasting your time," Charmaine said with a forlorn sigh as they pulled up in front of the Coleman house. "I swear to you it wasn't Oswald or Elmo March, and Ash wasn't even there."

He snorted as he left the buggy and lifted his arms to assist Charmaine to the ground. He wanted to believe her, he truly did, but she'd changed so much . . . too much. His little girl would never lie to him, but this woman, well, he just wasn't sure.

"Then this won't take long, will it?" he snapped as he mounted the steps.

Truth was, he thought he remembered seeing those March boys while Charmaine was dancing with the low-life stranger who would marry her come hell or high water, but through his anger he couldn't be certain. Besides, maybe they knew who the sonofabitch was. *Somebody* had to know!

Verna Coleman opened the door before he reached it, a false smile on her face.

"Why, Mr. Haley, what a pleasant surprise," she said as she held the door opened wide. "And Charmaine," she said brightly. "Do come in."

He didn't like Verna Coleman, any more than he'd liked John in his day. She was friendly and always had been, and she ran with an acceptable bunch of churchgoing ladies in town . . . but her cheerful greetings made his skin crawl. No need to waste any time.

"I'm looking for the man who belongs to this boot."

He'd been up and out of the house before Verna and the boys had returned from town, and Nathan had still been asleep. It had been a quiet morning, the best kind, and after a productive morning in the fields Ash was headed in for a quick noon meal.

He groaned aloud when he saw the strange wagon in front of the house. Verna's friends, a house full of them no doubt, here to gossip about the ball.

Ash hesitated on the front steps. What if one of them recognized him with his short hair and a mere one day's beard growth? He didn't think it was likely, but it was a chance he couldn't take. Verna and her cohorts would have a field day with that bit of news, and word was sure to get back to Charmaine, sooner or later.

He took one step back. Hell, he was hungry, but his stomach would wait.

Too late. "Here's Ash now," Verna's shrill voice called as she threw open the door.

With a sigh, he pulled his hat down over his eyes, slumped his shoulders, and prayed for the best.

The last thing he expected to see as he entered the house was Oswald sitting by the cold fireplace, his foot held aloft while Stuart Haley compared it to a boot.

His boot.

Fortunately for Oswald, he had tiny feet for a tall man.

"I told you."

Ash spun around at the sound of Charmaine's soft voice, and saw her practically hiding in the corner. Primly dressed today in a pale green gown, she was as beautiful as ever, but there was none of the laughter and brightness he'd enjoyed last night. Not even a smile. In fact, Charmaine looked as if she'd passed a sleepless night, just as he had.

She wasn't looking at him, but was staring at her father, the angry man with a boot clutched in his hand.

Haley's eyes passed over Ash quickly and then settled on his daughter. "Let's go."

Charmaine looked at him then, smiled weakly, and muttered a low, "Hello, Ash." As she passed him, without even glancing up, she spoke again. "You should have been there last night. It was very interesting."

I was there. He wanted to say it, wanted to force her to look at him, but as always he kept his mouth shut.

She was apparently moving too slowly to suit Stuart Haley, so he took her arm and propelled her toward the door. The boot swung in one hand, and Charmaine was pulled roughly with the other, and Ash saw red. Daughter or not, Haley had no call to treat her that way.

It all happened at once. Ash reached out and knocked Stuart's hand away from Charmaine. As Haley spun around, Nathan appeared at the top of the stairs, dressed and groomed but yawning as if he'd just left his bed.

"What are you doing with Ash's boot?"

One could have heard a pin drop. No one moved, no one said a word. Charmaine stepped forward slowly, her head cocked to peer beneath the hat that was shading most of Ash's face. The jig was up. He took the hat off, looked her square in the eye, and she stopped in her tracks.

"You!" she whispered harshly, and the horror on her face was all too clear.

"This . . . this *sodbuster?*" Haley shouted.

Ash didn't even look at the man. His eyes remained on Charmaine's face, on the surprise and revulsion he saw there. Those emotions were quickly replaced with anger.

"You tricked me," she hissed. "You *lied* to me."

"You let this sodbuster *touch* you?" Haley shouted.

"Ash, what's going on here?" Verna demanded.

"Did I say something wrong?" Nathan asked innocently as he descended the stairs. "I merely wanted to know why this gentleman was leaving the house with one of Ash's good boots."

Everyone was talking at once, everyone but Ash and Charmaine. Noise, that's all it was, senseless, irritating noise that washed over and past. Charmaine hadn't taken her eyes off of him, and he could see the calculating way she studied his chin and his jaw, his mouth and his hands, and finally his eyes. Oh yes, she recognized him, all right.

The rush of noise stopped when Haley pulled his gun, nudged Charmaine aside, and poked the barrel of that gun smack into Ash's chest.

Ash looked calmly at the spot where steel met cotton. "Be hard to miss, this time," he said calmly.

"You sonofabitch," Haley muttered, and he cocked the trigger back with his thumb.

"Oh Daddy, stop it." Charmaine reached out and placed her small, pale hand beneath her father's forearm, forcing the arm and the weapon gently upward and to the side. The barrel passed perilously close to Ash's face before swinging away. "You're not going to shoot anyone."

He wanted to, Ash could see it in the older man's eyes. He wanted nothing more than to see Ash dead. For kissing his daughter?

"You're right, sweetheart," Haley said coldly. "I won't be shooting anyone today. At least, not until *after* the wedding."

"Who's getting married?"

Ash's simple question angered Haley even more, and the man waved his pistol wildly. "You are, you sonofabitch!"

"Not to *her?*" Ash shouted.

"Of course to her, you dimwit!"

Ash shook his head slowly. This made no sense, no sense at all.

"Daddy," Charmaine said softly. "You don't understand." She cut her eyes from Haley to Ash and back again.

Ash tried to help. "Look, Haley, it was just a prank. A stupid joke. It didn't mean anything." He looked to Charmaine for confirmation, but she just flinched, wincing and closing her eyes. When Ash turned back to Haley all he saw was the fist flying at his face.

It wasn't fair. Surely someone would jump up before this went any further and state the obvious, that this *wasn't fair!*

The ceremony was taking place in the parlor of the Haley house, since her father had rightly guessed that the preacher would object to the pistol and the threat of bloodshed in his church.

She and Ash stood side by side before Reverend Howell, a good two feet of space between them. Her father stood at Ash's other side, and held that six-shooter pointed at his ribs. Her mother sat calmly by, there on her favorite sofa, not saying a word.

Ash's family had followed them to town. Verna was absolutely giddy, Oswald was smug, and Elmo was passing his time whispering and laughing with Ruth. That odd Nathan Sweet, Ash's godfather, watched the entire proceeding with detached interest.

The minister directed his questions to Ash first. When he hesitated, just before his final *I do*, her father nudged him with the pistol.

When the preacher turned to Charmaine with her vows, she was ready to refuse, to shout out a loud *I don't!* and stalk away. Her father moved to stand behind and between her and her groom. Ha! He wouldn't dare shoot her, probably wouldn't even dare to point that nasty weapon in her direction. There was nothing he could do.

Reverend Howell waited for her *I do*, as did everyone else in the room. Her father smiled at her, waited almost patiently, and cocked the hammer of the pistol that was pointed at Ash's back.

"You wouldn't!" she hissed.

"With pleasure," he whispered.

Ash didn't turn to her, didn't beg her to say *I do* or *I don't*. He stared straight ahead, in the preacher's direction but not exactly at the preacher. In fact, he hadn't really looked at her since they'd left his farm.

"I can't go on." Reverend Howell slammed his Bible shut. "This makes a mockery of the sacred institution of marriage, and no amount of money directed to the good work of the church can make me participate . . ."

"So you'd rather I shoot him, too?"

Reverend Howell did have the good manners to look horrified at the suggestion. "Of course not."

"He compromised my daughter. He marries her and makes an honest woman of her, or I kill him here and now. It's as simple as that."

"Ash." The reverend turned his most serious face to the reluctant groom. "Is this true?"

"No." The single syllable was short, low, and decisive.

Charmaine backed away as her father leaned insistently between her and Ash to face the preacher. "He's a no-good lying sack o'—"

"Stuart," Maureen Haley's soft voice intruded.

"She admitted it to me herself," he continued. "Said that they . . . they . . ." he sputtered.

"Dallied."

Charmaine shot her mother a quick and

harsh glance. She was *not* helping matters!

Ash leaned forward slightly to see past the insistent father of the bride and lock his accusing eyes on her.

Should she admit that it was all a lie? Goodness, what would her father do to her then? How utterly embarrassing! But what choice did she have?

"I might have exaggerated just a tad," she whispered.

"Don't embarrass yourself by lying to me now," her father snapped.

He lifted the cocked and loaded weapon so that the barrel touched the base of Ash's skull. His finger was on the trigger.

The sight of that weapon touching Ash's hair and flesh made her heart pound. "Get that away from him right this minute," she ordered, but it did no good. "Nothing happened, this is all a huge misunderstanding."

Her father was deadly calm, and the muscles in his hand tightened and twitched. He didn't believe her, and he was apparently more than willing to carry out his threat to Ash. "You know what you have to do."

"I do! I do, I do, I do!" She stomped her foot.

The gun swung down and away, and with an easy movement he released the hammer.

The reverend pronounced them man and wife. Papers were signed. Verna Coleman beamed. Nathan Sweet looked oddly satisfied.

Her mother was serene and her father was mollified.

Charmaine was having a difficult time accepting this as real. This didn't happen, not in this day and age! Yet none of the guests seemed to realize that any part of the ceremony was out of the ordinary. She was the only one. Well, Ash, certainly, but she didn't dare look at him to see for herself.

While everyone else was occupied congratulating themselves on a job well done, she made her way to the hallway and to the staircase. All she wanted to do was close herself in her room and cry for hours. Everything was ruined, now. Her father would make her stay here, he'd put Ash to work on the ranch and, after tempers cooled, he'd mold Ash into the son he'd always wanted.

And where would that leave her? Exactly where she did *not* want to be. Married, enslaved, stuck here in Salley Creek for the rest of her life!

"Where do you think you're going?" She was just a few steps up the staircase, weary to the bone and in no mood to face Ash Coleman.

"I'm going to my room," she said primly. "It's been a difficult day."

"Your room?" he repeated. "Honey, your room isn't up there."

"Of course it is," she snipped. "I don't know where Mother will put you, but I'm sure—"

"You don't get it, Charmaine." It was the touch of humor in that angry, husky voice that alarmed her. "We're not living *here*."

"Of course we're living here." She took a few steps down to face the dolt.

A crowd was gathering behind him, her parents and the rest of the guests at their so-called wedding standing in the doorway to the parlor where they'd been married. So many smiles! How on earth could they be so obviously happy over this debacle?

"You're free to return to your farm of course," she said with a sharp glance to her treacherous father. "With your name on a piece of paper my reputation is restored and I am bound in some archaic way to this barbaric town. My father should be satisfied with that. You don't have to stay here at all."

Ash didn't say a word, but as she reached him he lifted his long arms, grabbed her, and launched her up and over his shoulder.

"Put me down! What do you think you're doing!"

"Taking you home," he said calmly.

"Wait right there." Her father, thank goodness. He'd put a stop to this nonsense.

She couldn't see what was going on. All she could see was Ash's back against her nose.

"Mr. Haley," Ash said calmly. "You're going to have to quit pulling that gun on me every time we disagree."

"I intended for you to stay here."

"I intend to go home," Ash said just as adamantly. "Now, I'm damn tired of looking down the barrel of that gun. Shoot me, or get out of the way."

Evidently her father decided to get out of the way, because Ash moved forward and there was no resulting explosion.

She grabbed a handful of Ash's cotton shirt and lifted her head. "Daddy!"

Her father was shaking his head, holstering his gun with more than a hint of resignation. He'd gotten his way! What was he moping about? Verna stepped away from the knot of onlookers to follow Ash, and she motioned for Elmo and Oswald to join her. Nathan Sweet joined the parade as well.

"You're not going to allow him to . . . to . . . to do this to me, are you?" Her words shook unsteadily with each jarring step that carried her toward the front door.

"You made your choice last night, Charmaine," her father said solemnly. "I've done all I can."

"My *choice?*" she screeched. With each step Ash took she was jostled, shaken until her vision blurred and a long strand of hair came loose and fell over her face. "You call this a *choice?*"

With his newly freed hand, her father waved good-bye.

Chapter Ten

"Is she coming down to supper, Ash?" Verna asked as she placed the plates and silverware neatly on the table. Supper was late, but Verna was actually cooking something that smelled and appeared edible. Stew and biscuits, and a small lopsided cake for desert.

Verna was so impressed, so thrilled to be connected—however tenuously—to the Haley family, that she was practically giddy. It was a side of her Ash would have been content never to have seen, but here she was—giggling and fussing over the details of the evening meal.

Of course, she would have preferred that Charmaine had married Elmo or Oswald, but a relation was a relation, and Verna's social standing in Salley Creek had just risen considerably.

"I don't know," he said, glancing toward the stairs. How was he supposed to know what Charmaine intended to do? He hadn't seen or heard a word from her for hours, since they'd arrived home and she'd closed herself in her room. Their room.

Married. He'd known that one day he would take a wife, but he'd never expected it to come about this way. He'd been prepared to court, when the time came, and he had very specific ideas about the kind of woman he'd eventually marry. An even-tempered woman who was accustomed to hard work. Someone who could cook and sew and help with the animals. Someone practical.

Charmaine wasn't practical or even-tempered, and she knew nothing about farm life. She was pretty and bright, and for a short time he'd believed he could fall in love with her. It was the kiss, he supposed—the dance, perhaps. A fantasy no more real than Nathan's theater.

Now he was married. To a woman who likely didn't know the first thing about living and working on a farm. To a woman who'd married him at gunpoint. To a woman who hated the very sight of him.

She'd barely looked at him at all on the way

home, staring away from him to the familiar landscape along the road from Salley Creek to the Coleman farm. She hadn't said a single word. Even Verna and the boys had the good sense to keep quiet, but he couldn't say the same for Nathan. He'd prattled on endlessly about the pleasant weather and the fine Haley home.

Nathan. The man seemed to think this was amusing. He hadn't laughed, not out loud, but Ash had caught his godfather smiling contentedly on more than one occasion since the wedding. Of course, if not for Nathan and his big mouth they wouldn't be in this mess. *What are you doing with Ash's boot?* Without that offhand comment none of this would have happened. Charmaine and her father would have walked past him with that damning boot in hand.

Had Nathan done it on purpose? Had he known what would happen?

"Well, go ask her!" Verna snapped, jerking Ash out of his reverie. "Tell her supper will be on the table in ten minutes."

He mounted the steps with dread in his bones. He should have left her there on the staircase of her father's house, as she had wanted. He should've walked away without a word. But he'd been so angry, so blindingly furious. With Charmaine, with her father . . . with himself.

And to be perfectly honest, something unexpected had welled up inside him. Something altogether extraordinary. When he'd watched her walk away from the preacher and the papers that made her his wife, some possessive demon deep in his heart had cried out *mine*.

Well, what's done was done, but this wasn't going to be easy.

"Charmaine," he called as he knocked on the door to his room—their room. "Supper's almost ready."

"I'm not hungry," she insisted. Her voice was muffled and thick, and a loud sniffle followed her statement. Crying? Of course she was crying. What else should he expect?

"Fine," he muttered. His hand rested on the doorknob. There was no lock on the door, wasn't a lock in the entire house, though he imagined Charmaine was wishing for one now. She didn't want to face him—didn't want to see him ever again.

His hand fell away from the door. There would be plenty of time for confrontations later.

Somehow, she'd fallen asleep. A few hours ago she'd been certain she'd never sleep again, but the nearly sleepless night after the ball and the long day that had followed, had exhausted her. She wasn't sure what had woken her, but she came awake all of a sudden. The house was quiet, the room was dark.

Charmaine rolled onto her side only to see

Ash standing at the window, his back to her, his newly shortened hair and bare, broad shoulders shining in the moonlight. The sight of him standing there startled her so that her heart leapt sharply in her chest, but she recovered quickly.

She'd never seen a man's bare back before, and she found it oddly fascinating. Ash's back wasn't smooth at all, but was knotted with muscles that moved when he shifted on his bare feet and crossed his arms over his chest. Ash had worked hard all his life, and it showed in his long lean body. There was surely nothing wrong with admiring something so . . . so admirable.

Thank goodness he was wearing trousers.

He couldn't know that she was awake. She didn't want to talk. And even more, much more, she didn't want him to think that just because they were married he had the right to crawl into this bed with her. If she was very still and very quiet . . .

"Did I wake you?" he asked softly.

"No," she whispered. Then, "I don't know."

He turned to look at her, and her heart skipped a beat. This was not the beautiful boy she remembered, and not the hairy farmer she'd seen covered in mud. This was the man from the masked ball, the man who had waltzed with tantalizing elegance and listened to her as if what she said meant something to him, the man

161

who had kissed her and turned her insides and her world upside down.

"What are you doing here?"

"This is my room—our room." He might have smiled, but perhaps it was just a twitch of those lips. "That'll take some getting used to."

"Isn't there another room? It's a big house—"

"I suppose I could ask Elmo and Oswald to share a room so you can have one of your own," he interrupted, "but it might be hard to explain your newfound modesty since we've already *dallied* in the gazebo."

She was glad of the darkness, glad Ash couldn't see the blush she felt rising hotly in her cheeks. It was her own fault . . . no, it was just as much Ash's fault! He'd deceived her on purpose, played with her emotions, pretended to be someone else so he could seduce her. . . .

"I lied," she snapped. "There, I said it. I thought you were long gone, since you were just 'passing through town,' and well . . . I thought if my reputation was sullied beyond repair, Daddy would send me back to Boston."

"Surprised you, didn't he?" Ash asked softly.

She had the urge to scream at him, but she didn't want to wake the entire household. "I'm still going back to Boston," she hissed the truth at him. "I don't know how I'll get there, or when, but I assure you I have no intention of staying here."

"It never occurred to me that you would." His voice was so low she could barely hear it.

He turned back to the window. Her eyes had adjusted to the darkness, and she saw, with a rush of relief, the pillow and blanket there on the floor near his feet. At least he hadn't been foolish enough to think he could share a bed with her.

She didn't intend to calmly accept what her father and Ash had done to her, but neither was she certain as to how best to proceed. Out-and-out defiance would mean war, with Ash and with her father. Perhaps if she pretended to accept the marriage until her father calmed down, she could arrange a visit to Boston to visit Felicity and Howard and finish up some fabricated old business. She just wouldn't come back. Once there, she could see to an annulment.

Planning for an annulment meant, of course, that her so-called marriage to Ash had to remain unconsummated. Since he seemed to have no inclination otherwise, and she certainly didn't intend to invite him into her bed, that shouldn't be a problem.

She really shouldn't take her anger out on him. Poor Ash, this really wasn't his fault.

"I'm sorry you were dragged into this," she said to his motionless back, her anger fading now that she had a plan. "I know you didn't want this any more than I did."

He didn't say anything, didn't argue or agree. He just stared out the window as if there was something fascinating out there.

"I had no idea my father—"

"What's done is done," he said sharply. "Let it rest." He didn't display any intention of lowering himself to the bedroll on the floor.

She couldn't leave it alone, couldn't let anything rest.

"Why did you do it, Ash?"

"Do what?"

"Pretend to be a stranger. Dance with me and . . . and everything." It probably was best not to actually mention the kissing or the softly whispered, *I'll never forget this night.*

"It was just a game, a prank," he said softly. "I had every intention of telling you who I was before the night was over."

A game. A prank. "So, you lied, too?"

"Yes."

Of course he'd lied, what a stupid question that was. He'd told her she was beautiful, that he would never forget their night. Childish antics.

"I hope this hasn't ruined any plans you might have had," she said sensibly, ignoring her rising disappointment. "Goodness, I don't know what's going on in your life. We've barely talked since I came back. Do you have a lady friend, Ash?"

He did turn to her then, not a simple twist of

his head but a complete turnabout to face her. Bare chest, black eye, and all. "No lady friend, Charmaine, and the only plans I ever had were for a quiet, simple life. I can't imagine being married to you will be quiet *or* simple." It was an insult, and he didn't even try to hide the fact.

"Well pardon me," she said haughtily. "You can be assured that being married to a . . . a sodbuster was not in *my* plans for the future."

"Is that a fact?"

"Of course it's a fact!" Her voice rose a bit too high and loud, and they both waited for the sounds of an awakened household.

But all was quiet.

"I remember differently," he whispered after a long and very quiet moment. "I remember a little girl who wiped her runny nose on the sleeve of my best shirt and announced that when she was old enough she would leave her mean old sisters and do me the great favor of being my wife."

His smile was much too wide.

"I did not have a runny nose," she said with as much dignity as she could muster. How mortifying! She remembered a few childish tears . . . but a *runny nose?*

"I definitely recall a *very* runny nose."

"And besides," Charmaine said quickly, "that was years ago. My feelings had been terribly hurt, and I was . . . I was . . ." she searched for a proper explanation while Ash's smile faded away. She couldn't tell him about her childish infatuation, not now.

"So you do remember?"

"Vaguely," she whispered.

"Well here I am, your wish come true," he said dryly. "I wonder if you'll find life as a sod-buster's wife as charming as you once thought it would be?"

"I should've let Daddy shoot you," Charmaine hissed lowly. "I should've said 'I don't!' and watched him blow your head off."

Ash turned again to the window and the chill midnight. "Maybe you should have."

"Stuart, quit pacing and come to bed," Maureen sat up and sighed. "It's well past midnight, and you've got a busy day tomorrow."

She didn't point out to him that the reason he had such a busy day ahead was because he'd neglected his daily chores to track Ash Coleman down and arrange the necessary wedding.

He sat on the edge of the bed and stared away from her. "Did I do the right thing?"

It was an uncommon occurrence for Stuart Haley to question his decisions.

"I don't know," she said honestly. "I hope so."

"It's just . . . Ash Coleman! Of all the men in this county, of all the men in Kansas . . ."

"Ash is not so bad as all that," she said soothingly. "You've just never forgiven his father for putting up that barbed wire. He's a perfectly nice young man, handsome and hardworking and . . ."

"That's enough," Stuart snapped. "I don't need to hear a list of Ash Coleman's attributes right now. Dammit, I expected them to stay here, to live here instead of on that, that *farm*."

Maureen smiled and placed the flat of her hand against her husband's back. "You got what you wanted, Stuart. Charmaine is married, she'll be staying close to home, and we'll get to see her children, our grandchildren, grow up." She raked her fingers across that familiar bare back. "Why, just a few days ago you were worried about her attitude toward men and marriage in general, and as I predicted, the right man came along and proved her silly theories wrong."

"And Ash Coleman is the *right* man?" he asked with a hint of disbelief.

"I believe so," she said with a certainty she didn't quite feel.

Stuart fell back against his pillows and threw an arm over his eyes. "My grandchildren will be sodbusters," he mumbled.

"Perhaps," she said soothingly.

"But what else could I do?"

"Stuart, darling." She peeled back his arm so she could look into his moonlit eyes. "You did the right thing," she said, telling him what he wanted and needed to hear.

"I hope so."

"No matter what she says about being a modern woman, Charmaine is not the kind of young lady to allow liberties unless she cares deeply for a man. Her behavior was inappropriate," she said sternly, "but things will be all right now. She'll settle in at the Coleman farm, and perhaps in time Ash will take an interest in this ranch."

"Do you think so?"

"Well," she traced a shadow on his shoulder with her finger. "He's right about one thing. You will have to stop pulling a gun on him every time you disagree."

Stuart grunted, as close to an agreement as Maureen expected she'd ever get.

He wrapped his arms around her and pulled her to him for a kiss. He was restless tonight, and it didn't look as if she'd get much sleep, either.

"Really, Stuart," she said as he rolled over her and tossed the heavy quilt aside. "Don't you think a man of your age should quit sleeping in the buff?"

He laughed, a low rumble in her ear. "No, I don't."

Charmaine was asleep again. How did she do it? How could she be angry and argumentative one minute, turn her back on him in disgust, and be asleep five minutes later?

When he was certain she was deeply asleep

he crossed the room silently to stand over her. In anger she'd said she wouldn't stay, and he believed her. It was for the best that she leave as soon as possible, that she slip away and be done with him and this sham of a marriage before she worked her way any deeper under his skin. Maybe he should help her, take her to town and with a false smile on his face put her on the train and wave good-bye.

And then again maybe he could make her stay. He could climb into bed with her right now, kiss her until she softened like she had in the gazebo, and take what was rightfully his as her husband. His body was telling him to do just that. He was hard and aching, and she was here in his bed. It was what he wanted, more than anything, more than she would ever know. Tonight and every night, he would take what was his. With a child growing inside her she'd have no choice but to stay.

It wasn't an option he considered for long. *No choice.* That would make for a miserable marriage all around, now wouldn't it?

She made a funny little noise, more a squeak than a snore, and stirred beneath the quilt. If she was mortified at the memory of a childish runny nose, what would she say if he told her she made odd noises in her sleep?

He ached for her, physically and somewhere deep inside, and still he smiled. Charmaine wouldn't be here long, but while she was here life would not be dull.

Chapter Eleven

To everyone's surprise, it was Elmo who offered
cheerfully to go to town to collect Charmaine's
belongings. Clothes, shoes, personal items—
she'd left it all behind when Ash had tossed her
over his shoulder and carried her out of the
house.

Charmaine considered riding to town with
Elmo, but she didn't want to face her father just
yet, and the idea of enduring the long ride to
town with Elmo was more than she could bear
at the moment. She'd no doubt be entertained
by more stories about his various aches and
pains, and the very idea was more than she
could stand right now. Nathan asked to ride

along, as he had a telegram to send, and the two of them set out shortly after breakfast.

Ash Coleman, that insensitive lout, had been gone from the house when she'd finally awakened. His bedding had been rolled up and stored behind a wide chest of drawers, there where no one was likely to spot it through the open bedroom door. The blanket and flat pillow were neatly folded, crisp and taut as if they'd not been touched. Charmaine wondered, once or twice as the morning passed, if Ash had gotten any sleep at all.

She didn't want another confrontation, but there were a few things they needed to get settled, and the sooner the better. Tempting as it was, she couldn't simply ignore the situation and the fact that Ash was her husband, and running away was not an option.

All morning she silently rehearsed what she would say when she saw him. Pacing in the room where she'd slept, she mouthed the words and used her hands for emphasis. Sitting in the rocking chair before the fire while Verna chattered away, she went over the words in her mind once again. She practiced her most austere posture and expression, and to complete the picture she pulled her hair into a tight bun at the back of her neck.

She expected Ash to come to the house for the noon meal, but he didn't. Oswald and Verna ate a hearty dinner, but Charmaine picked at the food on her plate, eating slowly, delaying, waiting. Even after Verna cleared the table, there was no sign of him.

"Doesn't Ash come to the house for dinner?" she asked as Verna retired to her rocking chair with a half-finished embroidery sampler. Oswald was already deeply involved in his newest novel.

Verna smiled coyly. "Missing your groom already? How very precious."

Missing her groom? *Precious!* Was the woman crazy? Didn't she remember the wedding at all? Charmaine shook her head gently, but Verna didn't seem to notice. "Surely he's hungry."

Verna squinted at her sampler, which was, Charmaine noted, a mess of knots and ill-formed letters. And why was she working on a piece of embroidery when there were dishes and laundry to be done? The layer of dirt by the front door could use a broom, too.

"Ash usually takes a couple of biscuits with him when he's going to be away from the house all day," Verna said without a hint of concern.

"A couple of biscuits? That hardly seems sufficient for a man who works so hard. . . ."

Verna placed her embroidery in her lap and looked Charmaine square in the eye. "You know, Ash does work much too hard. Now that you're married, you should convince him to move to town and take up with your father and that prosperous ranch of his."

"Could you and the boys handle everything here without him?" Charmaine asked, certain that they couldn't.

"Good heavens, no. We'd have to come to town with you." She smiled. "We're family, you know."

"I know," Charmaine said softly.

"When you marry one Coleman, you get the lot of us."

Charmaine had a stray and unkind thought that perhaps she really *should* have allowed her father to shoot Ash.

"Where is Ash working today, do you know?"

Verna gave Charmaine another sickening coy smile. "I really don't know. . . ."

"He's fixing that fence on the east edge of the property," Oswald interrupted without looking up from his book. "I believe he said he expected to be out there most of the day."

A couple of biscuits were certainly not sufficient for a man of Ash's size who did physical labor all day. "Perhaps I should take him something to eat."

Verna waved her hand lazily. "I'm sure he'll be fine. He always is."

Charmaine would not be put off. She left Verna and Oswald, and rummaged through the kitchen for a sufficient meal. She packed leftover fried chicken and an apple and a large

173

piece of pie, arranging it all in a basket she found in the pantry.

"I was saving that for Elmo."

Charmaine turned around to find Verna sulking in the kitchen doorway. "I'm sure he and Nathan will eat while they're in town. Mother will insist."

"But that's his favorite, custard pie."

What could only be called indignation almost overcame Charmaine. How dare this woman deny Ash sufficient food? He worked hard, he put the food on their table, and Verna was whining about a piece of pie? She refrained, with great effort, from telling Verna that Elmo looked as if he could do with a little less pie. "Make another," she said with a bright smile.

Verna parted her lips as if she had something to say, but she evidently thought twice. She closed her mouth without saying a word.

He would almost swear that someone had purposely destroyed this section of fence. Haley? Not his style. Oswald or Elmo? No, this required too much physical effort for either of his stepbrothers to accomplish. Verna? He could almost smile at the thought of her tearing into the fence and knocking down the post.

Ash had stopped just long enough to wipe his sweaty face on a sleeve when he saw Charmaine picking her way through the tall grass, the skirt of her plain green wedding dress in one hand, a small basket in the other.

He'd half-expected her to make a quiet escape while he was away from the house, to make her way to Salley Creek, beg borrow or steal a ticket to Boston, and be gone by the time he got home for supper.

Unreasonably, he was glad she was still here.

She dropped her skirt and lifted a hand to shade her eyes. "Hello," she said as she resumed her trek. "I brought you something to eat."

"I already ate."

"I know," she said shortly. "Biscuits. What kind of meal is that for a working man?"

Charmaine Haley—Charmaine *Coleman*—always managed to bewilder him. Last night she'd told him, in so many words, to go to hell. Today she was bringing him food and chastising him for not eating enough. Why did she care what and how much he ate?

"Besides," she said as she reached him. "We need to talk, and I thought it might be best to get this out of the way . . . privately."

Here it comes, he thought as he took the basket from her. She wasn't going to stay, but at least she was going to be honest with him about it. She picked a grassy spot that was high and dry, and sat down with her feet tucked under her skirt.

Ash sat down a couple of feet away and started removing food from the basket. She'd thought of everything, down to a plate and utensils, a neatly folded linen napkin, and a jar of cool tea.

"Go ahead," he said calmly, studying the food instead of Charmaine.

"You can eat first," she said almost shyly. "You must be hungry."

Ah, she was putting it off, delaying the inevitable, and that was unlike her. "I don't have all day. I'll eat, you talk."

"It's about this . . . marriage." She said the word *marriage* as if it truly pained her, as if it tasted bitter in her mouth.

"What about it?" He picked at the chicken.

Charmaine sighed, and Ash lifted his head to look at her instead of the food. Why did she have to be so beautiful? If she were ugly or even plain, maybe he could rouse some indifference. If she didn't look so damned delicate, maybe he wouldn't feel the need to protect her. If she didn't look so fragile, maybe he wouldn't be so certain she didn't belong on this farm.

"We really haven't had time to discuss any . . . details of our relationship."

"Details?"

Charmaine sighed deeply, frustrated and slightly indignant. What did she expect of him? That he could read her mind? Hell, he almost could. She hated it here, she hated him, she was looking for a way out.

"Last night you said you had no intention of staying, so why are you still here?"

She fidgeted and bit her bottom lip before answering. "I don't know. What am I supposed to do?"

"You're asking me?"

He ate while Charmaine hemmed and hawed and said a lot of nothing, mostly about how they hadn't had time to get to know one another properly, and managing the entire time not to look him directly in the eye. When he'd finished the meal she brought him, which only took a few minutes, he repacked the basket, wiped his face and hands, and moved to sit beside his wife.

"Charmaine." He took her chin in his hand and made her look at him. "Say it. Spit it out. Nothing you say will surprise me, I promise you."

"Marital continence," she blurted, and then she turned an alarming shade of red.

"What?"

She took a deep breath before speaking, lifted her chin in a pose that was almost defiant. "There's a higher union to be known in a truly modern marriage than that of . . . of the physical relationship. A husband and wife can and should be spiritual partners rather than . . . rather than . . ."

"I lied," Ash said as he dropped his hand from her chin. "You can surprise me."

"I should have Howard send along a selection of manuals explaining the benefits of a pure marriage."

"No, thank you."

"He explains things much more clearly than I can."

"Wonderful."

"It's for your own good."

Hell, he could tell she believed it. Her eyes were wide and clear and true, and as blue as the spring sky on a cloudless day. "My own good," he repeated.

"It's a well-known fact that seminal fluid comes from the brain," she said primly. "It's best not to waste such a precious commodity, but rather to conserve it so it can be expended more constructively, in thought."

"I should be a genius," he muttered.

"What?" she leaned forward and just an inch or so closer to him.

"Nothing," he said more clearly. "What you're saying is that you don't want me to touch you."

"Well . . . yes." She squirmed on the hard ground. "I didn't think you would object."

"You didn't?"

"Last night you didn't . . . I mean, you slept on the floor and you didn't . . . You don't even seem to *like* me very much."

"It's not exactly been my lifelong dream to spend my wedding night with an unwilling bride who cried herself to sleep," he interrupted harshly. "And it's not that I don't like you, Charmaine, it's just that you're not exactly the kind of woman I'd planned to marry."

She intended to stay? He should be angry, but he found there was a touch of relief somewhere deep inside that he couldn't deny. So she wasn't practical or hardworking . . . so she was as flighty as his mother had ever been. . . .

"I'm sure there have been other women in your life." She spoke with a no nonsense tone, but a becoming blush rose to her cheeks. "I know how difficult it is for men to contain their animal impulses. But it's for your own good, I promise you. You'll thank me, one day."

Maybe, but not for *this*.

"Eventually I'll want children," he said.

She paled, so quickly and so completely that he was afraid she would faint.

"Where do babies fit into your *pure* marriage?"

"When the time comes, and I think it will be several years before we're ready for children, we will do what we must—but no more than once a month. We'll wait after each encounter to see if we've been successful."

"Sounds like fun," he muttered, and this time she heard him.

"It's not supposed to be fun," she said sternly.

"Odd, I always heard different."

She shot to her feet. "I can't have a civilized

conversation with you. Why did I expect differently?"

He jumped up to cut off her escape. "Who filled your head with these ridiculous ideas?" She tried to step past him, but he was wider and faster and she had no chance. "You talk about the marriage bed as if it was medicine to be endured, just another unpleasant chore to undertake at the prescribed time. What about pleasure? Passion? Tell me Charmaine, have you already forgotten what it felt like to be kissed?"

"It was the dancing, and I think there must've been champagne in the punch," she protested as she tried again to sidestep him.

He grabbed her, a hand on her arm and another around her waist. "I didn't have any punch, and neither did you. At least, not after I arrived," he whispered, and suddenly she was very still.

"I was weak—"

He silenced her with a kiss she didn't want, found her lips with his and put a stop to her nonsense. She was stiff in his arms, unresponsive, but only for a moment. Her eyelids fluttered and closed, her lips softened, and then she melted. Her body against his, her mouth against his.

There was a maddening little noise deep in her throat that almost pushed him over the edge. She was his wife, and if she wasn't willing now she would be in a few minutes. He could feel her falling toward surrender, and by God he wanted her.

"I'm so scared," she whispered as she pulled her lips away from his. "This wasn't supposed to happen. This can't happen." She protested, but there was pure acceptance in her eyes. "And I must say, I think it's really unfair of you to use your experience against me," she said breathlessly.

He smiled down at her, and then he kissed her again. Now wasn't the time, he supposed, to tell her that he was as much a virgin as she was.

No waltz, no champagne punch, and still a simple kiss made her reel. Why now? Why Ash Coleman?

It was a test of her strength, of her convictions. Still, she'd thought herself stronger than this. He parted her lips with his tongue and then flicked it inside her mouth, and she thought her knees would buckle. She held on tight so she wouldn't collapse and fall to the ground, and her mouth moved against his as if she'd kissed him a thousand times and knew every sensitive curve of the lips that danced over hers.

The sensations went far beyond her lips. She felt this kiss throughout her entire body, from the top of her head to her toes. He was in her blood, somehow. He made her forget everything, in some way.

181

Instinctively, her body fell against his. She couldn't get close enough, couldn't touch or feel or kiss enough.

Weak, she was wonderfully weak. . . . "Stop," she whispered, and he did.

She couldn't do this, couldn't give up everything she wanted and believed in for a physical sensation, for the passion and pleasure Ash mentioned so enticingly. In any case, according to Felicity the kissing was nice but the rest was dreadful. To have a part of a man's body actually inside hers, to suffer the invasion Felicity had spoken of with such disdain . . . it didn't sound nice at all.

"I meant everything I said." She couldn't make herself sound stern, as she knew she should. "I'm not ready for this. I don't want . . . I can't . . ." Drawing away slightly, she had a very good and close view of the black eye her father had given Ash. She stroked the skin around it, softly and carefully. "I'm sorry he hit you, and I'm so sorry I got you into this mess with my stupid lies."

"If you have to be sorry for anything," he said, kissing her once again and then stepping away, "be sorry you meant everything you said."

She needed a little persuasion, that was all. A gentle push in the right direction.

Ash saw her, sweeping the porch with a vengeance, as he approached the house. She must feel something for him, or she wouldn't still be here. Charmaine Haley wasn't one to mindlessly obey her father or anyone else, no matter what kind of ceremony had taken place.

If she swept any harder she was going to take a layer of wood right off the porch.

"What's wrong?" he asked as he stepped onto the porch, and her head snapped up. She hadn't heard him coming, evidently.

"I'm married to you," she whispered hoarsely.

This was not going to be easy. "True enough," he said casually.

She stopped sweeping and leaned on the broom handle. "And that stepmother of yours is still angry because I brought you the last piece of pie and she was saving it for Elmo, who needs more pie in his stomach about as much as you need more dirt on that shirt." She studied the offensive shirt and sighed deeply. "Elmo snivels more than any man I've ever met, filling the house with a constant wail, and when Verna chimes in it's more than I can bear. And if Oswald suggests one more time that we all pack up and move in with my parents, I'm going to shoot him."

"The Haley solution."

Charmaine didn't appreciate his comment, but her only response was a cutting glance.

"Nathan's hiding in the barn," she continued. "Rubbing down the grays, I think."

"And you're hiding out here."

She was openly distressed, angry, and . . . confused. As confused as he was? Impossible.

Ash stepped onto the porch, but before he had taken two steps toward Charmaine she stiffened and took a step back. "You stay away from me," she said sternly. "I won't have any more of this afternoon's nonsense."

"Nonsense?"

She narrowed her eyes. "You know what I'm talking about, so don't pretend to be innocent. I will not allow you to seduce me, Ash Coleman. I've made up my mind about what I want, and you can't sway me."

"I can't?"

"No, you can't," she said, and her voice trembled, just a little.

He leaned against the porch rail and smiled at her. She was still shaken. Good. He wanted to shake up every one of her crazy notions. "And what is it again that you want?"

Ash expected another speech on marital continence and pure marriage and the conservation of seminal fluid. He expected another earful of hogwash.

He didn't expect what he got—a wide-eyed stare with a touch of fear in it, an uncertain waver of the hand that wasn't grasping the broom handle.

"Time," she whispered. "I need time."

Chapter Twelve

She had to do something and this, at least, was away from the house.

A barn had never been Charmaine's favorite place to pass an afternoon, yet it was quiet here but for the coo and shuffle of the animals. She was rubbing Pumpkin's legs with a burlap sack, a treat the mare seemed to enjoy immensely.

Every day she tried to find a chore that would allow her to escape the crowded house for a time. Nathan had shown her how to feed the chickens and milk the cows, a chore that had turned out to be every bit as disgusting as she'd suspected it would be. But no chore was as disgusting as spending time in Verna's company.

Ash was giving her what she'd asked for days ago. Time. Time to think, to plan, to calm her agitated soul. Time to build a wall he couldn't break through with a simple kiss. Simple? In her much too vivid memory there was nothing simple about it.

It had been sprinkling off and on all morning, and all of a sudden the rain came down hard. Heavy raindrops lashed against the barn's roof and sides, but the structure was sturdy. The sound of fat, insistent raindrops against the barn was soothing. Here she was safe, warm, and isolated.

Kneeling at Pumpkin's side, she rubbed gently with the burlap sack. The barn had an aroma all its own, but she was becoming accustomed to the smell. With a little luck she could spend an entire afternoon here, undisturbed. Verna and her sons wouldn't miss her, and she certainly wouldn't miss them.

They were an odd bunch. Just this morning she'd caught Verna with her ear to the wall of the kitchen as she tapped lightly against the raw wood. What was she listening for? And what did they do all day while Ash was away? Not cleaning, certainly, and Verna never spent any more time preparing the evening meal than was absolutely necessary.

She didn't hear Ash coming. He just burst into the barn, shaking off the rain as he came through the open double doors. He hung his dripping wet hat on a peg by that door, and then he began to unbutton his soaked shirt.

Her view of him, as she peered over a bale of hay, was clear, but he obviously had no idea she was here, as his fingers worked the buttons.

She should stand and make her presence known, before he went any further. It would be simple enough at this point, to stand and greet him civilly and warn him before he went any further.

But she didn't.

He peeled off the soaked shirt and hung it on yet another peg.

Charmaine's mouth went dry. Goodness. Ash was gorgeous in the moonlight, as she well remembered, but by the brighter light of even a cloudy day he was magnificent. In spite of everything she knew and wanted and believed, her fingers itched to trace the shadows on his skin, the muscles and the furrows, the nooks and crannies.

Ash lifted one arm above his head, working out a tight muscle, and she could see his ribs outlined clearly. She wanted to run her fingers over each and every one of those bones, she wanted to lay her mouth . . . she closed her eyes tight. This could not be happening.

One eye opened slowly. Ash stood outlined in the open door, watching the rain, his back to her as it had been that first night. Their disastrous wedding night. If she was very still and quiet he would never know she was here. She sank lower behind the hay.

"We needed this rain," he said casually, "but I was hoping to get a little more work done before it got this heavy."

Charmaine closed her eyes. How could he possibly know she was here? She hadn't made a sound, hadn't uttered a single word. Ash didn't know anything. He was . . . he was guessing.

"Well?" he said. "How long are you going to hide back there?"

She didn't budge.

"Fine," he said softly. "We'll play this however you want."

Charmaine very cautiously came up on her knees and peered over the bale of hay. Ash hadn't moved from his station in the open doorway. He watched the rain, the way a farmer might, with contentment and more regard than an ordinary man.

Her heart caught in her chest, her blood roared, and she reminded herself of everything that Howard and his manuals had taught her. Magnetic currents, that's all this was. A scientifically explained phenomena. Ash's magnetism was just stronger than any she'd encountered to this point, that's all.

It was a perfectly reasonable explanation, and still her heart raced.

"I don't blame you for hiding out here," he said as if they were carrying on a normal conversation. "Verna and the boys are a lot to take. I guess it doesn't make things any easier for you."

Charmaine rose up slowly, brushing straw from her pale blue skirt. "Nor for you," she said, smoothly ignoring the fact that she'd been hiding from him.

With his back to her, Ash smiled. He'd known it from the moment he'd stepped into the barn, that she was here somewhere. Heaven help him, he could sense her, he could feel her presence.

And now he could hear her, stepping closer, halting her progress while still several feet away.

He turned to watch her.

It hadn't been easy, but he'd done as she'd asked. He was giving her time.

Right now staying away from her was impossible. She was enchantingly fair, in a plain white blouse that would have been unnotable on any other woman, and a skirt that was the color of her eyes and streaked here and there with hay. Her cheeks turned a pretty pink, as she blushed and then tried to ignore it.

He took a step toward Charmaine, expecting her to back away. She didn't. She stood her ground and waited. The welcomed rain became harder, pounding the barn and soaking the fields outside this warm haven.

Charmaine lifted a hand as he reached her.

With fingers splayed, she held that hand between them. There was no move to back up or push him away, just a frown as she fluttered that hand gently.

"What are you doing?"

"Checking something," she whispered.

"Checking what?" He lifted his hand so that it was palm to palm with hers, almost but not quite touching.

Charmaine's eyes snapped upward to meet his. "Magnetism," she whispered. "This is purely scientific, I assure you."

He joined the palms of their hands and twined his fingers through hers. "Purely scientific."

"Yes."

With his free hand he outlined her face and one shoulder, down one arm to her hip, and in this perusal he never quite touched her. His hand skimmed a mere inch or less from her skin and her clothing. Magnetism, she said. The hand in his trembled.

"Oh, my," she breathed.

She lifted her free hand and did the same to him, tracing his jaw without actually touching it, skimming her palm just above his chest. Could she feel his heartbeat, with her hand not an inch from his flesh? It beat hard enough, that was certain.

Not touching her was the hardest thing he'd ever done. A finger slipped and brushed against her arm. The delicate hand that wavered at his side grazed briefly over his skin. He settled his hand firmly over her hip and she didn't move away.

Charmaine was his here and now, his for the taking. He knew it, as he lowered his mouth to hers.

She closed her eyes and welcomed his mouth with a sigh, as the hand that had floated above his chest settled over his heart, and in response his shaft grew hard and heavy. A simple touch, a kiss, and he was hers as surely as she was his.

Charmaine kissed him without reserve, parting her lips for him, taking and giving, and he wanted her so badly he could think of nothing else. She brushed her tongue against his bottom lip, moaned softly from deep in her throat. . . .

And then she stopped. All at once she dropped her hand and pulled her lips from his and yanked her fingers away. Two steps back and she ran into the bale of hay. With no other choice, she sat down quickly.

Her face was flushed, her eyes bright, her mouth swollen and red and well kissed.

"Interesting," she said breathlessly.

"Interesting?"

She nodded her head, and a few newly mussed strands of golden hair went astray. "I've read about magnetism, of course, but I've never actually experienced it so . . . so personally."

She took a deep breath and refused to look directly at him.

"What am I?" he snapped, frustrated and angry and confused once again. "A goddamn scientific experiment?"

"There's no need to be snippy," she chastised in a breathy voice. She leaned back just a little, and her legs fell apart of their own accord, opening slightly beneath that sky-blue skirt. Did she have any idea what she was doing?

She refused to meet him eye to eye, but her gaze was roaming freely and curiously. Those bright blue eyes focused on his bare chest, beyond his shoulder, on his battered boots. Eventually they found the evidence of his arousal, the hardened length snug beneath his damp Levis.

"Oh, my," she said as she sat up, snapped her knees together, and pulled her eyes away. A moment later she stood with a jerk. "You know, I really should get back to the house and see if I can help Verna with supper."

"It's pouring . . ."

She hurried past him, brushed his arm and kept on going. Out into the rain and in a blur to the house.

It was a nightmare. The days passed, one into another, and every morning when Charmaine woke she was surprised to find herself sleeping in Ash Coleman's bed. He, of course, continued to sleep on the floor. At least, she assumed he slept.

He was either downstairs before the fire or staring out the bedroom window when she went to sleep, and no matter how early in the morning she woke, he was always gone.

She and Ash had been married for a full two weeks, and during most of that time they'd barely spoken. That rainy afternoon in the barn just four days ago had been the exception, an exception she didn't dare repeat. Inappropriate desires had come to the surface much too strongly and much too quickly. Now all she had to do was close her eyes or glimpse Ash when he didn't know she was looking, and those feelings came back, as strong and undeniable as the moments they'd touched.

Impossible. She had to get out of here!

It was Saturday, and that meant Verna and her boys would be going to town. Last week Charmaine had stayed at home, keeping to the quiet house while Ash was busy in the barn, but today—today she would ride along. She had a couple of telegrams to send.

She'd prefer to handle this another way, but Ash was making that impossible. This was her last resort.

She dressed in a warm burgundy day dress, since the days and nights were turning cooler, and placed a matching hat upon her head. Perhaps she'd see her father while she was in town.

She hadn't seen him since the wedding, though her mother had dropped by twice to see how Charmaine was faring.

She wasn't faring well at all. Verna Coleman was spiteful and lazy, and those boys of hers had taken after her in both respects. It was Ash who kept this farm running, who did practically all the work while listening to the constant complaints. Nathan helped him out, here and there, and Oswald and Elmo would occasionally do a small chore, but Ash worked all the time.

Of course, he was probably keeping away from the house so he wouldn't have to see his bride any more than was necessary.

"Come along!" Verna snapped. "The wagon's hitched and ready to go."

Verna was not as friendly these days as she had been on the day of the wedding. You'd think she was still holding a grudge over that little piece of pie.

"I'm coming." Charmaine stepped onto the front porch of the Coleman house. It really was quite chilly. Elmo and Oswald were waiting, Elmo sitting in the driver's seat and Oswald waiting to assist his mother. He assisted Charmaine, too, into the back of the wagon since there was only room for three on the bench.

As she climbed into the wagon, she searched the barnyard for Ash. He was nowhere to be seen, but Nathan stepped from the house to watch them leave. For once, he wasn't smiling, and he didn't have anything to say—not even a pleasant farewell. He stood there on the porch with a frown on his face, and Charmaine could only watch from her bouncing seat as they took off down the road.

It was a nightmare. Instead of having foisted Oswald and the rest of the clan off on the Haleys, he had a new addition to his family. A reluctant wife.

The house was filled to bursting. Verna was as strident ever, and nothing would change the boys. Nathan had stayed much longer than Ash had expected he would, pitching in around the place and entertaining in the evening with stories of his life on the road. The only time Charmaine smiled was as Nathan told his tall tales around the evening fire.

For a few minutes he'd thought this marriage might work out after all, but the episode in the barn was like everything else with Charmaine. False and fleeting.

He came around the corner, and saw that the wagon he'd hitched up earlier was gone. For that, he could give thanks. A day without Verna and Elmo and Oswald was always a good day. He turned his eyes to the house. Charmaine would be there, puttering in the kitchen or trying to mend something. She wasn't very good at either. Maybe he should go in there and try to strike up a conversation. Maybe he should go in there and kiss her again and make damn sure she understood just what marriage was about. She wouldn't draw away from him again.

"She went with them." Nathan's soft voice disturbed the daydream, and Ash near jumped out of his skin.

"Charmaine?" Ash turned to the little man who stood in the open wide doorway of the barn.

Nathan nodded.

He'd known she would leave sooner or later. She didn't belong here, she was as miserable as he was . . . so why did his heart drop to his knees? "She won't be back," he said, as much to himself as to Nathan.

"You don't know that."

But he did. Every day when he came in he expected to find his wife gone. Her father would relent and rescue her from marriage to a sodbuster, or her mother would arrive in her fine carriage to whisk her away, or Charmaine would saddle Pumpkin and ride away on her own. Somehow, some way, she would find her way out of this marriage she didn't want. A marriage he didn't want any more than she did.

"I truly believed," Nathan said softly, "that once she was here . . . I mean, two people who are as obviously attracted as you two are can't share a bed and not find some sort of—"

Ash silenced his meddling godfather with a glare.

"Don't tell me you're not—" Nathan began.

"We don't want to have this discussion," Ash said coldly.

"You can't mean—"

"Mind your own business."

"Oh dear." Nathan brought a small and slightly dirty hand to his breast. "Oh *dear*."

Ash had no desire at the moment to discuss marital continence and the purity of marriage. Charmaine was gone, back to her nice big house, her solitary room, her overprotective father. He should be thanking his lucky stars.

But he wasn't.

"I don't understand women," he confessed. "I was just fourteen when Mom died, and the only other woman who ever lived here was Verna."

"Not exactly a shining example of womanhood," Nathan said dryly.

"Why can't a woman be straightforward like a man? One minute Charmaine says exactly what she thinks, and the next minute she says something that makes no sense at all. Hell, half the time it's like I'm supposed to be able to read her mind."

"A handy trick where females are involved," Nathan agreed.

Ash climbed onto the fence that surrounded the pigsty and sat down to face his godfather. "Sometimes I look at Charmaine and think . . . my God, this woman is my *wife*. What more could a man ask for? But of course she doesn't want to be here, and she doesn't want to be my wife, and I'm a fool for even dreaming that this will ever work."

"You love her," Nathan said with a smug smile.

Ash lifted a stifling hand. "I wouldn't go quite that far. It's useless anyway. She's not going to stay here."

Nathan sauntered toward the pigsty. "Go ahead, ask me," he said with a superior air.

"Ask you what?"

"About women. What they like, what they expect, what drives them wild."

"Nathan Sweet," Ash said with a wide smile. "An expert on women."

"Not an expert, by any means, but I have garnered a few rather astute observations over the years." He slicked back his hair with one indolent hand. "Observations I would be happy to share."

It was a long shot, but maybe the old man could help him understand what was going on with Charmaine. Maybe this turmoil wasn't all that unusual after all. "Tell me what you know, but . . ." He shook a finger in his godfather's direction. "If you try to give me a manual I'll strangle you with my bare hands, and that's a promise."

Once the telegrams had been sent, Charmaine made her way to the house to see her mother. If her father was there she'd have a civil greeting for him, and nothing more. How could she ever forgive him for doing this to her? It was embarrassing, degrading . . . and everyone who smiled and waved as she passed knew exactly what had happened.

To her surprise, a smiling Ruth answered the door. To her even greater surprise, Ruth rushed off to the kitchen after admitting Charmaine. Apparently, she was entertaining Elmo there.

Her mother was sitting in the parlor and absently stitching on a sampler that had been in progress for a number of months. She'd brought it to Boston on the last visit, and had given it as much attention then as she did now. Very little. She seemed relieved to have an excuse to set it aside.

"Charmaine, is everything all right?"

It occurred to Charmaine to tell her mother all her troubles, to rail against her and take out all the anger and confusion that was bottled up inside. To search for answers to the puzzling questions and contradictions in her heart. But the normally robust Maureen Haley was pale, and her eyes were not as bright as usual. In fact, she looked a bit dazed.

"I just dropped by to say hello and visit for a while," Charmaine said as she took a seat near her mother. "Everything's . . . fine."

Fine. What an audacious lie.

But the warm smile she received at that answer made the lie worthwhile.

Ruth very quickly served tea and cookies, and then bustled from the room to return to Elmo and the kitchen.

The initial conversation that followed Ruth's exit was stilted and formal. They talked about the weather, and Charmaine only shivered once, when her mother mentioned that heavy rainstorm they'd had this week. She couldn't help but notice that often her mother seemed to be elsewhere—thinking of something entirely different from their harmless conversation.

"Are you all right?" Charmaine leaned forward, a half-empty teacup in her hands.

She expected a *fine* as false as her own, but her mother turned teary eyes her way. "I'm being so silly," she whispered. "It happens to every woman of an age, and I knew it would happen to me, but I guess I wasn't really prepared."

"Prepared for what?" Charmaine placed her teacup on the table and moved to sit beside her mother on the sofa. She placed her arm around a stiff shoulder, feeling very odd to be comforting her mother the way her mother had always comforted her.

"The change." It was a low whisper. "The change of life that comes to every woman when she gets . . ." she sobbed. *"Old."*

"You're not old," Charmaine said staunchly as

she held her mother close. "You're . . . mature."

It was, evidently, the wrong thing to say. Charmaine watched in horror as her staid, calm, sensible mother burst into tears.

"There now," she said with a few soft pats to her mother's shaking back. "It's not as bad as all that. The change of life is perfectly normal. There are a number of excellent manuals available. I'm sure Howard would be happy to send you one."

"Oh, don't mention Howard to me. Him and his darned manuals and seminars, he almost ruined you." The tears stopped as the near-hysterical woman turned her full attention to Charmaine. "Why, if not for Ash . . ." she sniffled loudly. "If he hadn't come along and shown you the foolishness of your ideas . . . where would you be right now?"

In Boston, happily unwed. "We're not talking about me, we're talking about you."

"It's so silly." Maureen straightened herself and wiped her face daintily, swiping away the tears. "I'm just afraid that your father won't look at me the same way he always has. I'm afraid he won't . . ." There was that far-off expression again. "Won't find me attractive anymore."

"That *is* silly," Charmaine agreed with a smile. "He's always adored you the way a husband should, in a wonderfully pure and spiritual way."

"What? Oh yes, of course. Pure and spiritual." And then she started to cry again.

Chapter Thirteen

Charmaine was so jostled she was certain she would be feeling the lurch of the wagon as she tried to sleep tonight. There was an advantage, however, to being relegated to the bed of the wagon. Verna and her sons seemed to have forgotten about her, and they hadn't tried for miles to draw her into the conversation.

She wouldn't be here for much longer, so she could take anything. Abuse, neglect, harsh words, utter boredom. As soon as Jeanette and Felicity received those telegrams they'd be on the next train to rescue her from this unbearable situation.

Poor Ash, she shouldn't blame him for any of

this. It wasn't his fault they were married, and it certainly wasn't his fault that he was possessed of more magnetism than was normal. When he was clearheaded, he didn't want to be married any more than she did.

Maybe she could just appeal to his common sense, explain the situation, and see what his response was. He'd probably be happy to help her end this farce of a marriage. He had, after all, agreed to her insistence on a pure union. Of course he didn't like it much, and if she hadn't come to her senses in the barn this would be a pure union no longer.

Ash could help her, but asking him was a risk she couldn't take. What if he went to her father? It would be the perfect revenge, suitable punishment for the indignities he'd endured. Surely Ash knew that if Stuart Haley had any inkling his daughter was planning to return to Boston, he'd promptly put her under lock and key.

The wagon lurched as it came to a halt, but she was cushioned on all sides by the supplies Verna and Oswald had bought at the mercantile. She sat very still for a moment, as Verna and her boys left the wagon. Goodness, she felt like she was still moving.

With a hand on the sacks on either side, Charmaine rose slowly. Her knees wobbled, but just a little, and it didn't seem that the ground was spinning *too* terribly fast. Ash was just rising from the rocking chair on the front porch, the look on his face one of surprise and wonder.

Why did he have to look at her like that? Why did he have to be so handsome? Why did her heart lurch when he caught her eye that way? Magnetism, childish infatuation, a mysterious working of her heart. She had to ignore it all.

Elmo and Oswald were climbing the steps—empty handed of course—when Ash stopped them. He literally placed himself between them and the front door.

"My wife doesn't ride in the back of the wagon," he said in a low voice.

My wife.

"There's only room for three on the seat," Oswald argued. "She's the newcomer here. If she wants to ride along to town that's fine, but—"

Ash reached out calmly, grabbed the front of Oswald's shirt, and lifted the man so that only the tips of his toes touched the porch. "My wife doesn't ride in the back of the wagon," he repeated.

"Okay, okay," Oswald agreed quickly and shrilly. "Elmo can ride in the back next time."

Ash dropped his stepbrother, and Elmo and Oswald quickly slipped into the house.

My wife, he'd said. Twice. The sound of that calm, cool, assured voice sent shivers up her spine. She knew the fluttering in her heart was an inappropriate and silly response, but there was no denying it. *My wife.* It was more than those simple words and the way Ash said them.

The way he was looking at her right now made her want to melt away.

He came to the wagon and helped her to the ground, hands on her waist, his body close to hers. "Are you all right?"

"I'm a little dizzy," she admitted, and she slid an arm around his waist. Just for support until the ground stopped spinning.

Ash kept both arms around her, holding her close and steady. It really had been rather sweet of him to come to her defense, so she couldn't very well push him away. She lifted her face to look into his. Goodness, had his eyes always been such a captivating green? He'd taken to shaving almost every day, and he looked so much more handsome without all that hair on his face.

"I'm quite all right, now," she whispered.

"Good." He didn't move away, and neither did she.

A cold wind rushed over and between them, chilling her face and ruffling a strand of hair across Ash's cheek. Her heart caught in her throat, and she wanted, at that moment, to place her lips against his, to steal a bit of his warmth and comfort. Like a thief, she came up on her toes to bring her mouth closer to his.

He dipped his head to catch her lips, and the chill went away.

"How dare you!"

Verna came storming down the front steps as

Ash and Charmaine fell slowly apart.

"How dare you," she said again, "threaten my son! You ruffian! I will not allow you to speak in such a manner to either of my children!"

Ash seemed not to mind her outburst at all. In fact, he smiled. Goodness, he should smile more often. "My wife doesn't ride in the back of the wagon."

Charmaine spun around to grab a parcel from the back of the wagon, and found herself staring into Nathan Sweet's face. He stood just inside the barn and leaned against the door that was propped open, and was wearing such a smug grin that she was sure he'd seen the kiss. Well, she thought as she stared him down, there was nothing wrong with a little kiss. She and Ash were married, after all.

Oh, dear.

She'd never noticed before what a truly gentle man Ash Coleman was. He smiled at Nathan's stories, which were becoming repetitive for her and so *must* be for Ash, and he never raised his voice to Verna, no matter how mean and spiteful she was. Any other man would have kicked those lazy stepbrothers out long ago, but not Ash.

And he'd been good to her, given the circumstances.

Something in her heart softened as she watched him. The firelight on his face, the cant of his wide shoulders. And he kissed so wonderfully. Was she a fool to ignore what they both obviously wanted? She was, after all, a fully grown woman and Ash was all man. Dangerous thoughts to be having.

"What about you, Charmaine?" Nathan asked, and she realized she'd missed most of this particular conversation.

"I'm sorry," she said softly. "I must confess I was about to fall asleep in my chair. It was a busy day."

"Your favorite play," Nathan urged.

She started to tell him that the theater was frivolous entertainment, but she knew Nathan Sweet well enough to know that the theater was his life. It would hurt his feelings terribly. Besides, she did remember one pleasant outing, before she'd joined Howard in his crusades.

"The Count of Monte Cristo," she said, apologetic that it was not Shakespeare. "I saw it performed in Philadelphia a few years ago, when I was visiting Jeanette. It was quite a thrilling performance." And truthfully, it had been.

"You haven't seen my *Macbeth*," Nathan said with a challenge in his voice. "Now, *that's* thrilling."

Oswald jumped in with his own opinion, and Charmaine returned her attention to Ash. He stared into the fire, unaware of her perusal, and that was just as well.

"Ash," Verna said sharply. "I didn't have a

chance to wash up the supper dishes. You will finish that chore for me, won't you?"

Without a word of protest Ash started to rise. He was much too tired at the end of the day to be taking on Verna's responsibilities!

Charmaine started to give Verna a piece of her mind, but of course that would accomplish nothing but to make things unpleasant for everyone. "I'll do it," she said instead, waving Ash back to his seat.

She headed for the kitchen without so much as looking in Verna's direction.

She was unbuttoning the cuffs of her shirt-waist and preparing to roll the sleeves up and deal with the stack of dishes by the sink when Ash came into the kitchen.

"I don't mind," he said, heading for the dirty dishes. "Most nights I welcome any opportunity to slip away from Verna's gossip and Elmo's whining." He wore a half-smile as he rolled up his own cuffs.

She couldn't very well allow him to think that she was doing something nice for him. "That's precisely why I volunteered. And I adore Nathan, but he's beginning to repeat himself. I've heard the story about Lily Langtry three times."

"I'll wash, you dry," he said with a smile.

"I'll wash, *you* dry," she countered. "I still don't know where everything goes, and I swear if there's so much as a cup out of place, Verna pitches a fit."

"Does she give you a hard time when I'm not here?" Ash's smile faded.

"Not really," she said quickly. "She's just her normal self, which isn't very pleasant. Goodness, Ash," she said as he set a pan of water on the stove to warm. "You shouldn't let her talk to you the way she does." Charmaine lowered her voice. "She's an ungrateful, tyrannical, and thoroughly unpleasant woman."

"Yes, she is," he agreed as he turned to face her.

"Why on earth did your father marry her? He was such a fine man, funny and always smiling and with a kind word for everyone, why would he marry a woman like that?"

Ash didn't answer right away. He shifted his weight from one foot to another and gave her question serious thought. "He was lonely. Mom had been gone nine years. . . ."

"He had you."

That got another small smile out of him. "Anyway, he met Verna and she evidently did everything right. She was sweet as honey when they met, timid and agreeable. He told me that much. He didn't meet the boys until *after* he'd brought her home."

They washed and dried the dishes, taking their time, standing side by side and talking about Ash's father and the people they'd gone to school with who had moved on. Ash knew the whereabouts of several of those old friends who were now far from Salley Creek.

She told him a little about Boston, very carefully avoiding any mention of Howard and his seminars and manuals.

It was in the midst of a description of her trip to the seaside that he reached out and touched her neck, there beneath her ear. It was a soft brush of his fingers, but was enough to send her reeling backwards.

"Sorry," he said, returning his attention to the dishes that were piling up. "You had a little smudge of dirt there. I thought I could just . . ."

"I do?" She raised a hand to her neck and covered the spot Ash had touched.

"I think I got it." He turned his back on her to take a stack of plates to the cupboard.

"Oh." She returned to the pan of dishes, and noted with a touch of disappointment that there wasn't much left to do. Talking to Ash over dirty dishes was much more pleasant than an evening with the family. "Sorry I jumped so. You just surprised me a little."

"I should've warned you."

She still tingled where he had touched her. A simple brush of another human being's hand, and her heart was beating as rapidly as it had as she'd danced at that wonderful, disastrous masked ball. It was ridiculous! She understood what was happening here. Simple human attraction, the physical response of one human to another. She could touch Ash innocently without being assaulted by these improper sensations . . . couldn't she?

When he was back beside her, drying a tin cup, she reached past him. Her arm brushed his. "It looks like I missed a spot on this one," she said, wiping at a nonexistent spot on the cup. That one instant had answered her question. Apparently she *couldn't* touch Ash without awakening something inside her. Something she was certain was best kept unexplored.

When he'd seen the wagon coming and been presented with the familiar picture of Verna and Elmo and Oswald side by side and chattering away, something in him died a little. He'd known Charmaine wouldn't come back, so why did it hurt?

And then she'd risen from the back of the wagon like something out of a dream, a little unsteady and the most wonderful sight he'd ever seen.

He'd been drawn to her then, and had ended up standing before her trying to decide if she would run if he tried to kiss her. She came to him on her own, lifting up and slowly bringing her lips to his.

And then in the kitchen, when he'd brushed that speck of dirt from her neck, she'd jumped back like she'd been burned. He hadn't understood why, until she'd leaned across and against him for a cup that wasn't quite clean.

It was a cold, clear night. Winter wasn't here yet, but it was coming. Tonight's cold snap was just a promise of what was yet to come.

Moonlight shone through the window and touched a sleeping Charmaine. She was under two quilts, and still she shivered on occasion. Ash scooped his blanket from the floor and gently added it to the bedding. He wasn't going to get any sleep tonight anyway.

He was quiet and cautious, but her eyes fluttered open. "Ash, what are you doing up?" she asked dreamily.

"Can't sleep."

She murmured sleepily, rolled on one shoulder, and then fixed her eyes on him. "What time is it?"

He looked at the clock that was sitting on the dresser. The moonlight lit the face. "Almost midnight."

She was slowly waking up, her eyes becoming brighter, her voice clearer. "Aren't you cold?"

"Yes." Freezing, and that was just as well.

She looked down at the blanket he'd added to her bed. "It's bad enough that I've taken your bed, you can't part with your only blanket as well." She took the edge of the blanket, wrapped her pale, slender finger around the edge, and then she was still.

If she had any idea how much he wanted to crawl beneath that blanket with her, she'd no doubt give him another lecture on marital continence.

"Well," she said primly. "This is ridiculous." She scooted to the opposite side of the bed and held back the covers as if inviting him into the bed.

"Excuse me?"

"It's cold, we're reasonable adults, and we are married after all." Her voice was soft and very calm. "There's no reason why we can't share a bed on a cold night like tonight."

He should argue with her and tell her exactly why they couldn't share a bed. Didn't she understand? Didn't she know? Maybe she did. Maybe this was Charmaine's way of telling him she'd changed her mind about their pure marriage.

And then again, maybe she was just being considerate.

He climbed beneath the layers of covers. The warmth was heavenly, as he welcomed the heat from Charmaine's body that had been absorbed into the bedding. She had scooted all the way to the other edge of the bed, and lay perfectly still.

"Now, isn't that better?" she whispered.

"Yes."

"Maybe you can sleep now."

Not likely. "Maybe."

They were both silent for a few minutes. He could hear the ticking of the clock, Charmaine's breathing, and his own. There was nothing else.

"I saw my mother this afternoon," Charmaine blurted. "She was behaving so oddly."

"She's married to Stuart Haley," Ash grumbled. "I'm surprised she's not a raving lunatic."

He expected Charmaine to be insulted, but she laughed lightly. "That's true enough."

A simple conversation to take their minds off the fact that they shared a bed, that's what they needed.

"Who else did you see?"

"Delia and Eula. We had tea in the office of the mercantile while Winston ran the store for a few minutes." There was a hint of frustration in her voice. "We tried to have a civilized visit, but Sarah Elizabeth has recently added curse words to her vocabulary and she was quite disruptive."

He laughed. "A few months back she decided to decorate my boots with licorice that had come right out of her mouth. Hell, I didn't even know she was there until I moved away and damn near stepped on her."

"That's terrible," Charmaine said, but she laughed lightly.

She squirmed, just a little, and her foot brushed his. "Goodness, you are cold," she said as she drew her foot away.

"You think that's cold . . ." Ash reached out and touched her neck with his cold fingers, and she squealed softly, drawing away and pulling the blanket to her throat.

"Your hands are like ice," she said, and she reached out to take one hand between her own. Two warm small hands covered the hand he'd teased her with, and he drank in her heat the way a starving man would take in food.

She moved her palms slowly over his hand, until it was no longer cold, and then she reached for the other hand, lifting up slightly and leaning over his body. Did she have any idea what she was doing to him?

As Charmaine warmed his hand, he reached out to touch her cheek with newly warmed fingers.

"See?" she said. "That's much better. A minute ago those fingers were like ice."

Those warm fingers slipped from her cheek to her hair, where they disappeared into the golden strands, and she was suddenly still.

"There's no reason, I suppose," she whispered, "that we can't kiss for a little while. That will warm you up, I'm sure."

She brought her face to his for a sweet kiss, a brushing of her mouth against his and nothing more. It was torture. It was wonderful. She kissed him again, harder this time, and she pressed her chest to his. All that came between them was the thin night rail she wore, a gauzy bit of linen that did nothing to disguise the softness or the heat of her breasts.

He slipped his tongue inside her mouth, and she gasped. That little sound was almost more than he could bear, and he deepened the kiss. Charmaine tasted of passion and surrender, and she was his—at least for now.

He was hard and aching to be inside her, but for now they kissed, and kissed, and kissed some more. A few minutes ago he'd been freezing, and now he was hot. His blood, his flesh, his soul.

With one hand at the back of Ash's head, Charmaine tried to pull him closer, tried to pull his mouth ever tighter against her own. Her heart pounded, her blood roared, and she couldn't get enough of this. Of *him*.

She lifted her leg and hooked it over his hip and felt the startling evidence of his own desire, the hardened manhood, press against her leg. She hesitated, stilling her lips. What was she doing? How had she come so far so fast?

"Ash?" she whispered his name against his mouth, unable and unwilling to pull away.

His lips danced gently over hers. "Yes?"

It was on her lips to tell him to stop, that this was wrong, that this was not what she'd had in mind when she'd offered to share the warm bed. They'd come close before, danced to the edge of something tempting and unknown, and she'd always been able to pull away before they went too far. But tonight her body ached, and sang, and hungered.

My wife. He'd said the words just that afternoon with such possession and fire. She was his
wife, for better or for worse. Perhaps it was true
that neither of them had wanted this marriage,
and maybe the wedding had been unusual, and
she had been so angry . . . but right now her
body was telling her that there was more.

He waited. Maybe he expected her to tell him
to stop. Maybe he was prepared to spend another long cold night looking out the window.

"I don't know what to do next," she whispered, and his lips began to move again. He
kissed her until she lost all reason, touched her
breasts gently through the nightdress until she
wanted to cry, it was so wonderful.

Ash moved to tower above her, and while he
removed his trousers and hiked up her nightdress, his lips never left hers. He was cradled
between her spread legs, his long, hard body
stretched out and tense, and she waited. She'd
never thought to crave something this way, to
want his body inside hers—but she did. More
than that, she needed it.

He touched her, his hot, hard manhood teasing the entrance to her body. It was marvelous,
but she wanted more. A gentle push, and she
began to open for him. She felt it, the welcoming of her body to his, the response that would
allow him access. Another push, and she could
feel him inside her, stretching her surely to the
limit. He began to withdraw, and then plunged

deep, breaking past the barrier of her maiden-head and burying himself deep inside.

It was a shocking invasion, painful and brutal and oddly beautiful. Ash began to move above her, his body rocking in a primal rhythm she could feel to her bones. He moved within her, he moved over her, he kissed her again. Her hips rose and fell of their own volition, search-ing for perfection, searching for . . . something.

Ash began to move faster, his breathing came heavy, and he was hot—so very hot. She opened her eyes to see the gleam of sweat on his face and his broad chest. His eyes were locked on hers, his firm jaw was tensed, and in the moon-light he was beautiful.

He plunged deep and stayed there, whispered her name softly and quaked and emptied his seed into her. And then he melted around her, covering her body with his and laying his lips on her neck and her cheek and her lips.

"That was incredible," he whispered breath-lessly.

"It was?"

He lifted his head to look down at her, and he smiled. "We need a little practice, maybe," he admitted.

"Practice?"

"Well, we're both . . ." he shook his head. "Never mind."

"We're both what?"

He rolled over and brought her with him. "Today when I came back to the house and found that you'd gone to town with Verna, I didn't think you'd come back. I thought you'd be well on your way to Boston by now."

It was her plan, still. Wasn't it? She wasn't a farmer's wife, she was a modern woman. Suddenly she remembered the look on Ash's face when he'd seen her that afternoon. "So I gave you quite a start when I popped up out of the back of that wagon."

"Yes."

"Disappointed?"

He held her close and seemed to give the question serious thought. "No," he finally whispered.

Goodness, what was she going to do now?

"We're both *what?*" she asked to change the subject.

"Beginners," he admitted softly.

"Do you mean to tell me," she said softly, "that you've never done this before either?"

He shook his head slowly.

She was oddly elated at that bit of news. She'd always heard that men were incapable of controlling their urges, and so often turned to prostitutes and loose women for, well, relief. But not Ash Coleman. He'd waited for her just as she'd waited for him.

"I think we did very well for our first time," she whispered with a smile.

Ash kissed her one last time, pulled her down so that she rested her head against his shoulder, and almost immediately he fell into a deep sleep.

Chapter Fourteen

Was that sunlight? Ash opened his eyes slowly. The room was flooded with warming rays that followed the cold night. Coming awake to a bright light was startling. How long had it been since he'd slept past sunrise? So long ago he couldn't remember.

Charmaine was snuggled against him, and the memory of the night that had passed made him smile to himself. This changed everything. No more marital continence, no more sleeping on the floor, no more wondering when Charmaine was going to disappear.

They had a real marriage, now. So, maybe she wasn't your typical farm wife. Maybe she

221

couldn't cook or sew, and maybe she was afraid of the pigs . . . but she was still his wife.

She stirred as he did, and lifted her head slowly. She was wonderfully mussed, hair in shambles, nightdress askew, cheeks pink with sleep. This was a sight he could get used to seeing every day.

"Good morning," he said, and he reached out to touch one pink cheek and push away a strand of wayward golden hair.

Charmaine pinned her brilliant blue eyes on him, shook her head slowly, and backed away. "What have you done?"

"What have *I* done?"

"You seduced me," she whispered.

"*I* seduced *you?*"

Charmaine sat up and brought the blanket to her chin, suddenly shy. At least she had the good sense to look contrite. "Yes. You certainly knew what was going on here. You should have removed yourself from the room before things got out of hand. You took advantage of my . . . of my inexperience, and . . . and *seduced* me."

Ash sat up, his good mood gone. "Yeah, you figured me out. I seduced you by giving you my blanket, and then accepting *your* invitation to share the bed."

"You looked cold, what was I supposed to do?" she snapped, as if somehow this was all his fault.

"Kissing to warm me up was your idea, not mine."

"But you should have known better," she insisted weakly.

Ash grabbed his clothes and dressed with his back to her. He'd married a crazy woman. Last night she'd been the one to come to him, dammit, and now here she was acting like he'd forced himself upon her.

When he turned around Charmaine was furiously stripping off the sheets. "I have to wash these before anyone sees them. I bl-bl-bled a little."

He felt a stabbing of guilt, and the need to take Charmaine in his arms and make the pain go away. "Are you all right?" he asked, making an effort not to reveal either of his urges.

She nodded quickly. "This changes everything," she sniffled. *"Everything.* I wasn't supposed to l-l-like you." She held the balled-up sheets in her hands and stared at him accusingly. "How could you do this to me?"

It all made sense, her insistence on a *pure* marriage, her sudden withdrawal in the barn that afternoon, the distance that was always there . . . he'd been right all along. And, dammit, she'd told him as much on their wedding night. She had no intention of sticking around.

"When are you leaving?" he asked calmly. Her teary eyes widened, and she took in a deep breath.

"I don't know, but I can't stay here," she whispered. "I'm not cut out for this, Ash. Not for working on a farm or taking care of you or having . . . children." He could barely hear her by the time she finished her sentence. "I don't belong here."

He couldn't live like this. Waiting for her to leave, getting his hopes up that she'd stay and then having those hopes dashed. "Then get out."

"What?" It was a choked whisper.

"You heard me." He actually looked her in the eye. "You don't want to be here, so get out."

She clutched the sheets. "It's too soon. Daddy would be furious, and he'd chase after me no matter where I went and drag me back and dump me on your doorstep. After he's calmed down and turned his attention to another matter, then I should be able to slip away quietly. We'll just tell everyone we gave it our best but it didn't work out."

She'd thought this out thoroughly, had probably thought of nothing else since she'd said *I do! I do, I do, I do!*

"It really would be best if I stayed here until matters can be . . . arranged. It won't be long."

He wanted to tell her no, he wanted her gone today. Now. He couldn't stand to look at her anymore. "Sure. Stay as long as you want, Mrs. Coleman."

Ash scooped the blanket from the floor by the bed. "But I can't take this anymore. I'm damned tired of being jerked around like a dog on a leash." Soft and loving one minute, harsh and accusing the next, Charmaine would be the death of him. "I'll be sleeping in the barn until you leave."

"But . . . what will Verna and the boys think?"

Ash stopped with his hand on the doorknob. He didn't care what anyone thought, he only knew that he couldn't share a room with Charmaine and pretend she was truly his wife until she decided it was safe to leave. He couldn't live with the faint hope that she'd change her mind and stay.

Charmaine held on to the sheets as if they offered some kind of support, as she waited for Ash to answer. He just stood there, his back to her, the blanket hanging from one arm. Her eyes stung with the tears she held back. She couldn't allow this to happen. She absolutely positively could *not* fall in love with Ash Coleman.

Without turning to look at her, he finally answered. "I don't care what anyone thinks. Tell 'em we had a fight, if anyone asks. Tell 'em I'm a lousy husband."

"But you're not," she whispered.

He glanced over his shoulder, a look of mingled puzzlement and anger on his face. "Why get choosy now about the lies you tell, Mrs. Coleman?"

Why did he keep calling her Mrs. Coleman?

To remind her that she was his wife in every way, perhaps. Maybe to make her feel guilty. And she did feel incredibly guilty.

He slammed the door on his way out, and Charmaine lowered herself slowly to the side of the bed. What had she done? A moment of weakness, and all her plans were ruined. A single touch, and she had put aside everything she believed in for physical pleasure.

Felicity had been so completely negative about the marital embrace. Horrid, she'd said. Degrading.

But last night hadn't been horrid *or* degrading. Not at all. It had been overpowering and a little painful at first, but all in all it was quite . . . agreeable. Maybe Howard was doing something wrong.

Charmaine Haley was not one to cry over spilt milk. What's done was done, and there was nothing she could do but move forward. She should look at this as an experience, an investigation of sorts. If she was going to return to Boston and join Howard on the lecture circuit, it would be helpful to understand exactly how the physical elements of a relationship threatened to overcome the more pure spiritual attachment. Goodness knew her baser instincts had overcome her good sense last night.

And all it had taken was a touch. . . .

"Charmaine!" Verna's biting voice was accompanied by a pounding on the door. "Are you ready?"

"Ready for what?" Charmaine asked weakly.

"Church! You didn't go last week, or the week before. People will talk." Poor Verna, she was so concerned about what people thought.

"I'm not feeling well."

Verna's sigh was audible through the closed door. "Very well. I'll make your excuses."

"Thank you," Charmaine mumbled.

"But we have a standing in this community, and next week I'll expect you to join me."

If she was still here next week. "Of course."

It was Sunday, and that meant no field work for the day. But the animals still had to be fed, and there was enough work to keep Ash busy in the barn.

Anything to keep his mind off Charmaine.

"The first time's always the hardest."

Ash nearly dropped the shovel he was cleaning out the stall with, as Nathan's articulate voice interrupted his thoughts.

"What?" It *showed?*

"Of course it is," Nathan said calmly. "You think you're never going to disagree, and then some little thing crops up and there you go—your first fight."

First *fight*.

"You and Charmaine are both so transparent," Nathan continued. "She's furiously doing laundry and you're attacking these stalls like you're going to find treasure under there somewhere." He wrinkled his pert nose. "Can I help?"

"No." Ash returned to his chore. "You've helped quite enough."

"No need to be impertinent."

Ash waited for Nathan to leave, but he didn't. He leaned against the doorjamb and seemed to wait himself.

"I don't understand women," Ash admitted.

"Ah," Nathan breathed, and it was a wise, knowing *ah*. "This conversation again. To be honest, I don't think any man is expected to understand women. You might just as well accept that you'll never understand Charmaine, and get on with your life."

Ash propped the shovel against the stall and went to the door for a breath of fresh air. "I don't know what she wants," he confessed. "One minute I think I know exactly what she wants and the next minute, out of the blue, she changes her mind. I don't know if I can take it."

"Of course you can take it," Nathan said, with a hearty slap to Ash's back. "Man has been 'taking it' since time began. I know it seems impossible, but eventually you and Charmaine will come to an understanding."

If only it were that simple. "She's leaving."

Finally, Nathan was shocked. "Leaving? Good heavens, what kind of a fight was this?"

Ash stared up and toward the window to his

room. "It wasn't a fight, Nathan, it was . . . the truth. This is a forced marriage that started with a lie. Neither of us wanted it, and it's not going to last. It's just as well. She can't cook, she can't sew, she's scared of all the animals but Pumpkin. . . ."

"Your mother was the same way when she came here. You should have seen her, chasing chickens and milking cows from the wrong side, and ruining half your father's shirts trying to wash and mend them. She learned, just as Charmaine will learn."

Ash tore his eyes away from the vacant second-floor window. "There was one very big difference, Nathan, and you know damn well what it is. When my mother came here she came of her own free will. She loved her husband, and *this* is where she wanted to be."

He didn't have to finish, didn't have to say aloud that Charmaine would rather be anywhere than here. And as for love? Never. Even if they were married for a hundred years, Charmaine wouldn't come to love him.

He could love her, though. He could feel it already, growing in his heart even as he tried to quell it. Loving Charmaine would ruin his life, but he wasn't sure he could stop.

"And still . . ." he said, memories he didn't want coming to the surface, "it was hard on her. As much as she loved my father, as much as she wanted to be here . . . she was never strong enough. I thought maybe Charmaine was, but it was a mistake."

"Lila was happy here," Nathan said defensively.

"Most of the time," Ash agreed. "You weren't here in '74 when the locusts descended on us. You didn't see her stand on the porch and scream. . . ."

"You were just a baby . . ."

"I was four years old," Ash interrupted. "And I can still close my eyes and see it. The darkness that came so fast, the grasshoppers everywhere. They ate everything green, and then they started on the bridles and saddles and shovel handles. My mother stood on the front porch and screamed until she couldn't make a sound."

He didn't tell Nathan that he'd had nightmares for years that the grasshoppers hadn't stopped there. In his nighttime terrors the locusts kept going, through the house, through the people in it.

"Dad was in town, and by the time he got home she was losing the baby she carried. I didn't know that then, of course, I only knew that she was bleeding and screaming and I knew that somehow those damn insects were responsible."

After that there had been no more children. Losing that baby had damaged her, physically, mentally.

"She never talked about that time," Nathan said softly.

Ash shook his head. "No. She tried to ignore it, to pretend that it never happened. But you see, she wasn't strong enough for this life, and it killed her."

"I can't believe that."

Of course Nathan couldn't believe it. If he'd thought his precious Lila was in danger he would have done everything in his power to save her. The little man would have done battle with demons, if necessary.

"It would be the same with Charmaine," Ash said gruffly. "What am I supposed to do, force her to live and die here?"

"You're depressing me," Nathan said with a sigh. "I think I'll saddle Pumpkin and go for a nice long ride in the countryside."

"Sure," Ash mumbled as he returned to his work.

"And I think you should give your wife a little more credit. She's stronger than you know, I imagine. While I'm gone, and you and Charmaine have the place to yourselves, why not try to talk some sense into her?" Nathan suggested in an offhanded way. "Women are volatile creatures, stormy one minute, calm the next. Who knows, maybe Charmaine's winds have changed."

Ash shook his head and returned to his chore as Nathan took the saddle from the wall.

*   *   *

Maureen closed her eyes and reclined on the sofa. Well, she was going to have to relent and go see the doctor, like it or not. Her head was spinning, and her stomach was twirling nauseatingly. Was this normal? What if it was something worse than the change of life? A terrible disease, perhaps. She'd been healthy all her life, and this speculation over her failing health was disturbing, to say the least.

She had tried to convince herself that this illness was a result of her age and the unnatural amount of excitement in the household as of late. Charmaine's return, the ball, the wedding . . . but as time passed and life returned to normal, her health had not improved.

Everyone else was out of the house, Stuart on the range and Jane at her sister's, so when someone knocked loudly on the door she groaned and rose to answer. Perhaps it would be Charmaine, come for another visit. That thought cheered her enough that her headache all but disappeared.

But it was that odd little man, Ash's friend, who stood at the door with his hat in his hand.

"Mrs. Haley," he said with a bright smile. "Just the woman I wanted to see."

Charmaine made the bed with clean sheets, while those she'd soiled last night hung on the line outside the kitchen door. She thought she'd feel better when the bed was crisply made, but that wasn't the case.

Ash Coleman would make some woman a wonderful husband, one day. When she was gone and the divorce was final and any lingering scandal had died down. He was hardworking and handsome and really very sweet, most of the time. And last night . . .

She tossed a pillow onto the bed. This couldn't be happening to her! She wasn't twelve any more, she was twenty-one, fully grown and mature and very certain about what she wanted from life.

She wanted her life to mean something. She wanted to do something *important*. Falling in love with Ash Coleman and considering, for even a moment, staying here, was out of the question.

But her life of seminars with Howard suddenly seemed lonely. Funny, for they'd always been exciting to her, before. Before she'd made the mistake of coming back to Salley Creek. Before the ball. Before she'd begun to wonder if she would always miss Ash the way she missed him now.

Goodness, he was in the barn! How could you miss a man who was no more than a few hundred feet away?

She should have better control of herself. She wasn't a misinformed child, she was an educated woman who understood very well what had taken place last night. Her physical impulses had overridden her common sense, it was as simple as that.

But it wasn't simple at all. She wasn't emotional like Jeanette and she never had been, yet her emotions were in turmoil. Of course, this wasn't love! Love was harmonious. Neat and tidy and warm, and a comfort to those who found it. *This*, whatever it was, was complicated and dreadful. It was turning her insides around and muddling her normally clear mind. Her heart *hurt*, and for the first time in her life she didn't know what she wanted.

Charmaine threw herself, face first, onto the bed. Her life was in shambles.

Chapter Fifteen

Damn, it was turning cold fast. Ash hurried from the barn to the house for a quick evening meal, and then it would be back into the cold for him.

He'd been sleeping in the barn for three days, and but for one snide comment from Verna everyone in the house ignored the new sleeping arrangements. He didn't sleep any better in the barn than he did in the house, but at least now he could blame the weather or the hard cot or Charmaine for his sleepless nights.

He heard the shouting before he so much as set foot onto the steps to the porch.

"I will not allow it!" Verna's voice was high-pitched and sharp.

And who was the recipient of that acid tongue tonight? Elmo? Oswald? His smile faded. It had better not be Charmaine.

His question was answered before he opened the door, by Elmo's unusually strong reply. "I'm going, and you can't stop me."

"But what about the treasure?" Verna hissed as Ash opened the door.

The three of them turned sharply to the door. Verna's face paled, and Elmo had the good manners to look ashamed. Oswald was cool as always.

"What treasure?" Ash asked as he closed the door behind him, shutting out the cold wind.

Verna's eyes narrowed. "You know very well what treasure. The Montgomery treasure your mother brought with her when she came to this house, the treasure your father talked about on his deathbed. 'Be sure Ash remembers where the treasure is. Lila wanted him to have it.'"

"Funny, Verna," Ash said emotionlessly as he stripped off his heavy coat. "You've never asked me about the Montgomery treasure."

She reached out and slapped Elmo on the arm. "See what you've done? We'll never get it now!"

Charmaine came to the top of the stairs, and she watched the scene with apparent interest. Nathan was not far behind her. He'd been dressing for dinner, as he did every evening—even when the meal was nothing more than tasteless stew or burnt chicken.

"Would everyone like to see the Montgomery treasure?" Ash asked softly. Nathan smiled widely, and Charmaine waited with curious expectation on her face. Verna's eyes became bright, and Oswald grinned wickedly.

Ash moved the rocking chair Verna sat in every night, threw back the tattered rug, and dropped to his haunches. It had been a long time, but he was sure he hadn't forgotten. He pressed against one floorboard, and it held fast. He moved to the next, and this time when he pushed hard the floorboard popped up to reveal Lila Montgomery's secret hiding place.

"You idiot," Verna hissed. Ash didn't turn to see which son she admonished. "I told you to search this room!"

"I did!" Oswald snapped. "Several times!"

Ash didn't listen to their continuing argument. He lifted another board and then he reached into the space beneath the floorboard and wrapped his fingers around the wooden box that held his mother's treasure.

It had been years since he'd gone through the contents, and he placed the box on the floor and lifted the lid carefully. There was a silent crowd around him, now. Verna and her boys, Nathan and Charmaine, all looking down at the valuables within.

"The Montgomery family Bible," he said, lifting the largest and heaviest item in the box. He gently turned back the cover to reveal the family history written carefully there. His name was the last entry in this book. "Her favorite book of poems." He took the slim volume from the box and leafed through the yellowed pages. How many evenings had she read to him from this book? There had always been something of the dreamer in her, something fragile and much too soft for the life she had chosen.

"Is that it?" Verna wailed.

"Oh, no," Ash said as he delved one more time into the box. "We can't forget the Montgomery family blessing."

"The *what?*"

Ash smiled grimly at Oswald's outburst. "The Montgomery family blessing has been handed down from generation to generation for more than a hundred years. Now *that's* a treasure."

Charmaine's curious eyes were fastened on the contents of the box—and then on him. "Lila Montgomery, my mother," he said, speaking only to Charmaine, "was a young woman when the War Between the States began. Her family was untouched, at first, and then everything went wrong. She saw her father die, and then her brothers, and then her mother." He never spoke of this, because he felt his mother's agony for these ancestors he had never met. But for his wife—temporary though she may be—he would tell it.

"When the Yankees came through and burned her home, she only had a few minutes to grab that which was most precious to her. She left her father's gold watch, her mother's ruby necklace, and the family silver, and she gathered these treasures and made her way West."

"What an idiot!" Verna snapped.

Ash ignored his stepmother. Charmaine's eyes filled with tears, and she placed a comforting hand on his shoulder. The compassionate touch was warm and wonderful and all too brief. With a flutter that hand lifted away, and Ash replaced the treasures carefully and returned the box to its proper place.

"I can't believe we wasted all this time searching for a couple of books and a piece of paper!" Oswald shouted.

"That . . . that's *it?*" Elmo asked softly.

Verna paced. "There has to be more. There *has* to be."

Ash almost laughed. It was rather ridiculous, the way Oswald stormed and Elmo stuttered and Verna ranted. His eyes met and held Charmaine's, blue eyes bright still with tears for his mother. But she smiled, surely recognizing as he did the absurdity of the current situation.

All this time they'd been searching for buried riches, gold and silver and gems, when there was nothing to be found. If they had discovered Lila Montgomery Coleman's treasure, in the course of their search, they wouldn't have recognized it as the treasure they sought. They didn't know what *riches* were.

Oswald sputtered at some new accusation from his mother, lifting his chin and talking incoherently. In response, Nathan suddenly laughed out loud. He got a venomous glare from Verna for his trouble.

"So, there's no problem if I leave first thing in the morning?"

All eyes turned to Elmo.

"You can't run off with that . . . that *servant.*"

"I like Ruth," Elmo said defensively. "And she likes me. Mrs. Haley said they didn't want Ruth to travel alone, and anyway she thought I might be interested in going to school there in Boston."

"School?" Verna said with a shake of her head.

"You're too old to go back to school," Oswald sneered.

"Who will take care of you?" Verna moaned.

Elmo straightened a spine Ash had thought impossibly weak. "I'll take care of myself."

That silenced everyone. "Maybe I'm not cut out for life on a farm, but that doesn't mean I can't do anything at all," he continued. "And after I get some schooling and find a job, I'm going to ask Ruth to marry me."

"She's not going to marry you," Oswald scoffed.

Elmo stared his brother down. "She already said that when the time comes, if I ask, she'll say yes. You're just jealous. . . ."

"Jealous because of that *mouse?* I don't think so!"

Ash backed up a step as Elmo closed in on his older brother. "Don't ever say anything bad about Ruth, or I'll knock out a couple of those pretty teeth."

"Now, now," Verna said calmly. "See what you've done, Elmo? You've allowed a woman to come between you and your only brother."

Elmo would not be swayed. Seems the boy had backbone after all.

"Ash," he said as he broke away from his mother and brother. "I hate to see you sleeping in the barn, with it so cold. He cut a cautious glance to Charmaine. "I think I'll pack up and head on to Salley Creek tonight, so you take my room."

Ash took the hand Elmo extended. "Good luck in Boston. I hear it's a great place. The kind of place a body goes and never wants to leave." He glanced over Elmo's shoulder to Charmaine, and watched her smile fade.

When they learned that Elmo was fully prepared to walk to Salley Creek, Nathan offered the use of Pumpkin. Elmo was to leave the horse at the Haleys', and someone would collect the mare in a day or two.

Verna shed a couple of crocodile tears, and Oswald told his little brother more than once that there was *no way* he'd survive in the big city, but Elmo would not be dissuaded. He rode off with a satchel of clothes, and a hopeful smile on his face.

He didn't even delay for dinner.

Charmaine watched the clock on the bedside table as the minutes and the hours ticked away. Goodness, it was almost one in the morning and she was still wide awake. Maybe she was sleepless because Ash was back in the house, instead of in the barn where he'd been for the past several nights.

She was miserable, but still she smiled in the dark. She never would have thought Elmo March had a romantic bone in his body, but evidently she was wrong. He was riding away from his family and his home for an unknown future with the woman he loved.

Charmaine scooted up on her elbows. She'd never get to sleep tonight!

It was a small noise, a bump in the night . . . but it caught her attention. Someone was up. Nathan or Ash, unable to sleep? Or Verna or Oswald, pilfering the Montgomery treasure.

She slipped out of bed and grabbed her wrapper against the chill. That parsimonious Verna had done quite enough to Ash, in her opinion. She was spiteful and lazy and didn't take care of him the way she should.

Charmaine opened the door silently. If she caught that woman *near* Ash's treasure . . .

The fire was dying, but flickers of light lit the main room as Charmaine made her way slowly down the stairs. Someone was sitting on the floor behind the rocking chair, a dark shape she couldn't make out. The chair had been moved, the rug pulled back, and the treasure box was opened on the floor.

By the time she was close enough to be sure it was Ash, it was too late to turn back.

"What are you doing up?" she whispered.

Ash didn't jump or turn around at the sound of her voice, so she was sure he'd heard her coming. "I haven't looked through here for a long time, and since I couldn't sleep I thought I'd dig it up again."

He held a sheet of paper in his hand, but it was too dark for Charmaine to read over his shoulder. "Is that the Montgomery family blessing?"

She took a step forward so she could see his face, one half of it, anyway. He smiled in the dark, and touched the paper in his lap with fingers she knew to be gentle in spite of their size and strength. "Yes."

"Read it to me?" She sat on the floor beside but not too near him, on another small rug.

Ash shook his head. "It's nonsense."

"Read it to me anyway."

He twisted his head to look at her, at last. "My mother believed in fairies and ghosts and ogres and unicorns. I think, after what she went through in the war, that belief helped her survive. Another world, where good always triumphs and evil is always vanquished, makes sense after what she went through."

"I guess so," Charmaine whispered.

"She told me this blessing came from the fairies, and it had been passed down for more than a hundred years, from Montgomery to Montgomery. It was a sacred gift, she said, a secret from those who had not been so honored by the fairies. When I was about ten years old I realized that this blessing is written in her hand."

"You didn't tell her, did you?"

Ash grinned. "Of course not. Even then I knew that she needed me to believe." He turned his eyes to the paper in his lap. "Maybe by that time she believed it herself."

"I'd still like to hear it."

He was silent for a few long moments, and she didn't know if he would comply or not. When he did begin to read, or to recite, it was in a voice so low she had to strain to hear it. "A Montgomery of pure soul and kind heart will survive the harshest tests in this life and have as his reward the most precious gift of all. One true love to cherish until the end of time."

Her heart skipped a beat. "That's beautiful."

"It's nonsense," he snapped as he returned all the treasures carefully to the box. "Pretty words to make my mother feel safe, that's all they are."

One true love. It was a ridiculous notion, as Howard would certainly remind her. Romantic nonsense, fanciful rubbish . . . but no less touching.

"Go to bed, Charmaine," Ash whispered as he rolled the carpet over his mother's secret hiding place that was no longer a secret.

"I'm not tired." She hugged her knees to her chest and studied the dying fire. "I don't know why, I should be exhausted but I lie in bed and I just can't make myself be still. I squirm and can't get comfortable, and I keep thinking about Elmo and Ruth, and . . ." and when she'd hear from Jeanette or Felicity. She really didn't want to mention that at the moment, "and . . . and just everything."

Ash took her hand and drew her to her feet with a jerk. She fell against his chest, into his arms, and he didn't let her go. "I said, go to bed," he whispered.

"*I* said I'm not . . ."

He silenced her with a kiss, not a soft and delicate meeting of their mouths, but a harsh kiss that stole her words and her breath. She tried to pull away, but Ash's stilling hand at the back of her head stopped her. His tongue plunged deep into her mouth, moving and exploring, and she came up on her toes, just slightly.

She couldn't take much more of this. She was dissolving, her body, her will, every promise she'd made to herself since becoming this man's wife. Surely his heart beat in rhythm with hers, surely he could feel what he was doing to her. It was an unerring impulse that made her lift one hand to Ash's arm, to rest it there on muscle so hard and warm she sometimes craved this simple touch.

It was pure instinct that made her lips part in invitation for an even deeper kiss.

Without warning Ash released her, and she stumbled back before catching her balance. Already he'd turned his back to her. "Go to bed, Charmaine," he whispered.

She started to take his advice, backing slowly toward the staircase. He was right, of course. They had no future, not even a real, true past. There was no happily ever after waiting for them. But she didn't *want* to sleep alone. She didn't *want* to spend another night alone in that cold bedroom.

She wanted Ash to love her.

The realization startled her, even as she admitted in her heart it was what she'd wanted all along.

This time she did surprise him, sneaking up behind him to lay her hands on his waist. He jumped slightly before he spun around.

"Dammit, don't do this to me," he whispered hoarsely.

She smiled and stood on her toes to kiss him, a gentler beginning this time. "I want you to share the bed with me again," she whispered, and Ash groaned into her mouth.

"Don't . . ." he began.

She silenced him as he had silenced her a few minutes earlier, with a kiss, a silent demand as her tongue tested softly.

"You're not going to stay," he whispered brusquely. "You don't belong here and I can't . . . you can't . . ."

"But we can have this, can't we?" she answered. "We both want it, we both need it. I can't say I truly understand why I feel this way, but I can't deny it either." She laid her mouth against his, softly, urgently.

With a sigh into her mouth, Ash lifted her from her feet and carried her up the stairs. His mouth never left hers, and his every step was unerringly steady as he carried her to their bedroom. He even had the presence of mind to close the bedroom door softly.

She'd never wanted anything so badly in her life, never needed anything this way. It was overwhelming and frighteningly undeniable.

By the side of the bed, Ash worked the knot of her wrapper and then slipped it off her shoulders. His fingers trembled slightly, as he slid them over her shoulders and down her arms, testing her flesh as surely as his mouth had tested hers.

The nightdress was in the way, binding her throat and her shoulders, chafing her as it never had before. "Maybe I should just take this off," she whispered, already working the ribbons at her throat. Ash helped, pulling the linen over her head when the ties were loosened.

She stood before him completely naked, only slightly chilled in spite of the cool air. She should be shy, embarrassed. No one had seen her this way before, *no one*. But she wasn't embarrassed *or* shy. Ash reached out to touch her bare shoulder, to touch with gentle fingers the rising flesh of her breasts. And he kissed her again, as those fingers brushed lightly over a nipple that hardened at his touch.

The need was aching and unexpectedly powerful. "And I think," she whispered breathlessly, "that you should take this off," she said, brushing her fingers over the waistband of Ash's trousers.

In a moment Ash had discarded his trousers as carelessly as he'd discarded her nightclothes, and they stood together, naked in the moonlight.

Goodness, he was beautiful. His face, his body, his very soul. Who wouldn't love a man like this?

"Can I touch you?" she whispered.

"Yes."

She closed her fingers over and around his swollen manhood. It was silk and steel, hot and hard. And larger than she'd expected. If she hadn't already taken it into her body she would have thought it impossible. She stroked the length with gentle fingertips.

"Enough," he said harshly, taking her wrist and moving her hand away. And then he touched her; big, gentle hands brushing over her breasts and her ribcage, her stomach and her hips, the rounded curves of her backside.

When one of those hands parted her thighs and touched the flesh that ached and throbbed for him, she thought she would drop to the floor with the intensity of the sensations that flooded her. As if he knew, as if he felt what she did, he lowered her gently to the bed.

And kissed her while he towered above her and continued to stroke the damp folds of the most private part of her body. Of their own accord, her legs spread to give him access, and her hips rocked against his hand. It was startling and unexpected, the sensations that shot like fiery sparks through her body. The stirrings grew and became almost insistent, and then he moved his hand away.

What was he doing? Why was he waiting? *Ash.* She tried to say his name, tried to whisper it against his mouth, but the sound that came out of her mouth was an unintelligible moan.

249

Then he was there, thrusting, filling her bit by bit until he was buried inside her.

She took his face in her hands and kissed him softly. There had to be something more to this than the physical. Something special, something . . . blessed.

Could she be Ash's one true love?

He moved again, rocking gently, stroking her body, and as before her body answered. She lifted her hips to take all of him, and her body pitched with and against his in an ancient rhythm.

She couldn't breathe, she couldn't think. Her body reached and danced and sang, until something unheard of happened to her.

She fractured. Shattered, actually. It started from the center of her being, grew until it was a force that could not be contained, and then it shattered. She held on to Ash to keep from falling apart, clutched him as her insides quaked and her breath returned to her in a rush.

One last time he plunged deep, and then he quaked quite a bit himself.

She'd never known anything could be so powerful and wonderful, so exhilarating and exhausting.

"Ash?" she breathed.

He closed his lips over hers, softly, as if he were as drained as she. "Yes," he murmured. At least, she thought it was a yes.

"Was that extraordinary?"

"Yes, Charmaine, that was definitely extraordinary."

"No wonder," she whispered knowingly, "it's so difficult to convince married couples of the integrity of a pure union."

He laughed, a low, warm rumble against her mouth. "Should be damn near impossible."

"I never knew," she whispered. "I never had any idea that it would be so . . . so perfectly wonderful. Magnetic forces so powerful, an energy that has to be electric, it's so strong . . ."

Ash silenced her with a finger over her lips. "Don't analyze it," he said softly. "Not tonight."

He looked into her eyes and brushed back a strand of hair that had fallen across her cheek. Would he ask her to stay? If he did, if he whispered the words right now, she would say yes without hesitation. For the moment—for the first time in weeks—her heart and her mind were perfectly clear, and she knew what she wanted.

But of course, he wouldn't ask. He wanted a wife who could cook and sew and help out around the place. How many times had he told her she didn't belong here, that she wasn't the kind of woman he'd intended to marry? He wanted a helpmate, not a bedmate. A partner, not a lover. They had this, a physical attraction that was more powerful than she'd imagined was possible, but it wasn't enough.

Ash was probably awaiting the proper time for her to leave as anxiously—more anxiously—than she was.

Chapter Sixteen

Ash woke slowly, after sleeping for several hours in Charmaine's bed. He'd dreamed, pleasant unformed dreams that stayed faintly with him as he woke, content and well rested. Who'd have thought that the cure for his insomnia was Charmaine Haley?

She was a lovely little thing, soft and fragile—well, perhaps not as fragile as she appeared to be. Right now she was nuzzled against him for comfort and warmth, her leg thrown over his and one small hand resting on his chest, her face a match for the contentment he felt.

His happiness was disturbed by one question he couldn't push away. Why did she make plans to leave one minute and invite him into her bed the next? It was a kind of torture, but he couldn't believe she was purposely tormenting him. Maybe in spite of all her lecturing and protests, the physical aspects of marriage appealed to her as strongly as they appealed to him. Maybe she wanted him the same way he wanted her. With every fiber of his being.

Her body was pressed to his, skin to skin from chest to thigh. He peeled the sheet back slowly.

She was beautiful, with her creamy unblemished skin, and those curves in all the right places. And she was his, for the moment, his wife, his lover. He could look at her and be amazed . . . and then know, in a terrifying moment, that she would never stay.

Their marriage had begun with a lie. Two lies, to be honest. If he had only told her who he was, the night of the ball, nothing ever would have happened. If she had just told her father the truth, instead of fabricating a wicked romp in the gazebo, there never would have been any shotgun wedding.

And so he couldn't be sorry.

He wanted her again. Needed to lose himself in this perfect body. Moving languidly he kissed her shoulder, the warm white skin that rested against his, and she stirred. He brushed his fingers over the swell of her breasts, finding and teasing rosy nipples tenderly until she opened her eyes and smiled at him.

The last time Charmaine had awakened in his arms she'd been angry and hurting and filled with regret. If she regretted what had happened last night, he'd know very soon. He held his breath.

"Good morning," she whispered, and there was no regret in her voice or her eyes.

He answered her with a smile as he rolled her onto her back. Already he was hard and eager, but he waited. He kissed her, soft and then hard, and she kissed him back ardently. He took his lips from hers and touched them to the tender flesh of her breasts, tasting and exploring, and finally flicking his tongue over a hardened nipple.

She arched up and into him, spreading her legs slightly wider in unmistakable invitation, and it was all he could do not to thrust inside her. He waited, tasting one nipple and then the other, touching the damp entrance to her body, sliding one finger inside of her.

Her eyes were closed, her lips barely parted. What a magnificent sight she was. Her hands roamed over his body in an exploration of her own, soft hands that danced over his chest and his side, the curve of his hip, until she touched his manhood with gentle fingers that threatened to send him over the edge.

When he filled her she whispered his name, and it was the most beautiful sound he'd ever heard. She wrapped around him so tight and so hot he was ready to explode, but he waited. He wanted to feel her come apart beneath him, as she had last night. He wanted her to lose control in his arms.

He wanted her to love him.

A few strokes and she was reaching for more. He buried himself deep, and it happened. She moaned as the spasms wracked her body, and then he let himself go. She drained him, body and soul, taking everything he had to offer and more. He emptied everything he was, everything he had into her welcoming body.

A moment later, Charmaine lay contented in his arms, drifting toward sleep again.

The worst had happened. He would never again be happy without her. And he knew just as well that she would never be happy here.

Of all the chores she'd taken on, this was her least favorite. She took the cow's teat between two fingers and pulled gently. Nothing.

At least she had the relative quiet and privacy the barn afforded. That was worth something, she supposed. She pulled a little bit harder. Nothing.

She was no longer afraid that the cow would trample her. At first, as Nathan had shown her the intricacies of this chore, she'd been certain there would be some sort of revolt to follow this personal attack . . . but the good-natured cows didn't seem to mind at all.

"You're going to have to put a little more into it than that."

Ash's voice startled her, and she glanced to the side to see his big battered boots and denim-encased legs nearby. "I'm just getting warmed up," she said as she returned to the task. She took hold and squeezed and pulled, and at last milk came spurting out. It missed the pail by a good three inches, taking off at an angle, but there *was* milk.

"Here, I'll do it," Ash said, and he took a single step forward before she stopped him with a sharp reply.

"You will not."

He didn't take another step toward her, but leaned against a stall and watched.

If she was to convince Ash that she belonged here, she had to make herself useful. She concentrated on the chore, a simple task usually relegated to children, and gave it every bit of determination she possessed. And it worked. Milk came forth, streaming into the pail as she found her rhythm.

"I didn't know you could milk a cow," Ash said softly.

"I've only done it a few times. Nathan taught me." She glanced up to look at Ash, and a stream of milk missed the pail and dampened the hem of her skirt. "Damnation," she muttered as she adjusted her grip.

Ash smiled, but he had the good sense not to

laugh. "You don't have to do this, you know."

"It was Elmo's job, and from what I saw you ended up doing it most of the time, anyway," she said sensibly. "I saw you head out here this morning, before you went to the field. I should have done it then but . . ."

"You were sleeping when I left the room."

"I woke up as soon as you closed the door," she admitted. It hadn't been the closing of the door that awakened her, rather it was the absence of Ash in the bed.

"I don't mind."

"Of course you don't mind, but this has to be done twice a day, and I just don't see how you have time to add this to your schedule," she insisted. "You can't do everything yourself, Ash, there simply are not enough hours in the day. While I'm here I might as well make myself useful."

She glanced up and saw Ash, who hadn't so much as moved a muscle, grinning at her, a wide wicked grin.

"You know what I mean, Ash Coleman," she said, trying to be stern and failing miserably.

"I didn't say a word."

"You didn't have to."

When she finished with the milking, Ash took the pail and placed it beside the open door. He turned to face her with that wicked grin in place, blocking the exit with his long legs and broad shoulders. Just looking at him made her weak in the knees.

"What *are* you thinking?" she asked, fairly sure she knew exactly what was on his mind.

Ash didn't answer, but stepped forward and took her in his arms. She fit there, easily, comfortably, perfectly. One kiss, and her body responded with astonishing quickness. Her heart quickened, her arms tightened around him, her body readied itself for his.

It was just a kiss, she reminded herself. Nothing more. After all, this was late afternoon, broad daylight. It was just a kiss.

Ash lifted her from her feet and carried her away from the door.

"Where are we going?" she asked as she lifted her mouth from his.

"There's a cot in the tack room," he whispered. "A cot where for three days I lay in the cold thinking about you, thinking about this . . ."

"We can't . . ." her body melted against his, in spite of her protests. "Sexual excess isn't good for men. It causes all kinds of disease, headaches, and nervousness and . . . and weakness of the brain."

He carried her into the tack room and slammed the door shut with his foot. "Hogwash."

"But . . . but there are manuals. . . ."

He silenced her with a kiss. "I don't believe it."

"But . . . last night, and the night before that, and the morning in between . . ."

Ash set her on her feet, keeping one long arm tightly around her. His mouth danced over her throat, a hand touched her sensitive breasts, one and then the other. "Do you want me?" he whispered, his voice all but lost against her throat.

"Yes, but . . ."

He rose to kiss her mouth, to still whatever protests she might have, no matter how reasonable they might be.

"It's commonly accepted that twelve times a year is all that's healthy," she said breathlessly.

Ash laughed huskily. "Twelve times a *year*?"

"That does seem . . . unnecessarily restrictive," she conceded.

Ash lowered her to the cot and slipped his hands beneath her skirt. "It doesn't matter what anyone else thinks or preaches, Charmaine. Do you want me?" He touched the nub at the entrance to her body, stroked and teased.

"Yes," she breathed, and Ash joined her on the cot, towered above her.

"I want you," he whispered.

It wasn't that simple, it couldn't be.

Ash kissed her deeply, swirling his tongue seductively in her mouth.

It was that simple, for now.

*   *   *

Charmaine knocked on the door as if this was no longer her home, and of course it wasn't. While she waited for someone to answer, she straightened the dark green felt hat that matched her riding outfit. She glanced over her shoulder at the boy who was leading Pumpkin to the stables, and gave him a weak smile. Why was she nervous? This was a simple visit, and her motives were sound and reasonable.

Actually, it was best not to examine those motives too closely.

Maureen Haley answered the door herself, and Charmaine was glad to see that her mother was looking well. Her color was good, her eyes bright. She'd begun to worry. Her mother was, after all, no longer a girl.

"Is everything all right?" Maureen asked as she took Charmaine's arm and led her into the house.

"Fine, actually." More fine than she'd ever expected, but there was no reason to elaborate. "We haven't really visited in so long, and Verna was on one of her rampages today, so I thought it best to get away for a while." She thought it best not to mention any of the telegrams she'd sent.

And besides, her given excuses were the truth. Verna had been in a foul mood in the days since Elmo left. That, combined with the fact that the Montgomery treasure was of no worth to her, had brought out an even more bitter side of her personality.

"I'll have Jane make us some tea. . . ."

Charmaine placed her hand on her mother's arm. "Not just yet. Is there somewhere we can talk privately?"

The concern on her mother's face stole some of the brightness and color. "I knew there was something wrong," she said as she led Charmaine to the parlor and closed the double doors behind them.

Charmaine sat on the sofa, and removed the hat she'd taken the time to straighten just moments earlier. How best to proceed without giving away too much?

Maureen sat beside her and took her hands, comforting her in a motherly fashion. "What is it?"

She wouldn't chicken out now, not because she was having second thoughts that manifested themselves as knots in her stomach. "I need your advice."

Maureen nodded solemnly. "Of course." She took a deep breath and very obviously steeled herself for the worst.

"I wasn't really prepared for marriage," Charmaine confessed. "In truth, I had decided never to marry."

"I know," Maureen said softly.

"My education was superb, and my studies have continued with reading and seminars . . .

but there's so much I don't know. . . ."

Maureen nodded her head and stroked the top of Charmaine's hand. "I felt the same way. So many changes so very quickly. The . . ." she took another deep breath, "intimate aspects of marriage . . ."

"No," Charmaine said quickly, horrified at the notion of having that conversation with her mother. "Not *that*."

"Then what?"

Charmaine hesitated. This was the biggest and most momentous step she'd taken in her entire life. More important than any seminar or manual, more life-altering than any decision she'd ever made. "I want you to teach me to cook."

"To cook?"

"Yes." She couldn't sit still, so she freed herself from her mother's grip and paced in front of the sofa. "I can't even make a decent cup of tea, much less cook an edible meal." Her education had been excellent in most respects. Domestic arts were not taught, however, not at her exclusive school. And Felicity always had servants to take care of such matters.

"Verna is a terrible cook, and she doesn't feed Ash nearly enough. Why, there are times I can swear I see his ribs." She could feel the heat of a blush rising on her cheeks. Her and her big mouth. Now her mother would know she'd seen Ash naked.

"I haven't done much cooking lately, but Jane and I together should be able to—"

"And sewing," Charmaine interrupted before her mother could even finish her sentence. "I was taught about samplers and such, but not practical matters such as mending and darning. I tried, but I'm not very good at it."

"That will be simple enough."

"And laundry," she added. "I think I ruined one of Ash's shirts yesterday, and I can't seem to get *anything* clean."

Charmaine stopped pacing and looked down at her mother. She was presented with a warm smile.

"I say we start in the kitchen. After all, the way to a man's heart is through his stomach."

As her mother led her toward the back of the house, Charmaine had a flash of self-doubt. What if she couldn't do this? What if she was a miserable failure?

Ash would never ask her to stay if he didn't think she'd make a decent farm wife.

Ash couldn't remember the last time he'd come home at the end of the day with a smile like this on his face. He was cold, he was tired, and every muscle in his body ached.

But Charmaine was waiting for him. A quiet, smiling face over the dinner table, a welcoming, warm body in his bed at night.

It wouldn't last. He had accepted that fact, as

well as he could. She wouldn't be happy here for long, and she had her damned ambitions . . . but for now, while it lasted . . .

There was a tantalizing aroma filling the house, and it almost knocked him down as he opened the door. He must really be hungry if Verna's cooking had his mouth watering this way.

Verna was sitting before the fire, the scowl she'd worn constantly in the week since Elmo had left firmly in place. She rocked, short, angry bursts of energy. Whatever he was smelling was probably gone—or poisoned.

She snapped her head around as he closed the door. "I've been running this house two years," she hissed. "I don't need some spoiled brat coming in here to . . . to take over!"

He didn't need to ask who the spoiled brat in question was. At that moment, Charmaine came to the open doorway between the main room and the kitchen, wiping her hands on a flour-dusted apron. Pale hair that was usually neatly styled fell in tendrils from a bun atop her head, brushing her face and neck, and there was a smudge of something on her cheek. She smiled, and blushed, and she was the most beautiful sight he'd ever laid eyes on.

"You cooked," he said softly.

She nodded her head. "I hope you like it."

"I've gotta clean up." He headed up the stairs for a basin of water, a towel, and a clean shirt.

As he reached the top of the stairs he practically ran Nathan down.

Nathan was dressed for dinner in one of his best suits, gray with red trim. His hair was slicked back and he smelled like a barber shop. "What's the grin for?" Nathan whispered.

He couldn't stop it, couldn't even tone it down. "She cooked," he whispered, giving the words the significance they deserved. "And yesterday I caught her milking the cow."

Nathan returned his smile. "I know. Never again doubt the works of the master, my boy. Never again."

In a matter of minutes he was cleaned and changed and headed back down the stairs with an unnatural spring in his step.

Charmaine seemed to be holding the rest of the household at bay until he arrived. Only then did she allow anyone into the kitchen.

There was a feast on the table. A huge roast, creamed potatoes, biscuits, peas, and corn. And on the stove he spied two pies. Apple, if his nose didn't lie.

"I didn't know you could cook," he said as he held Charmaine's chair for her.

"Neither did I," she admitted softly.

Verna was reserved, but Nathan and Oswald were as obviously delighted with the meal as he was. After Verna's cooking, this was a spread fit for a king.

Everything was perfect. The biscuits were

flaky and the vegetables weren't overcooked or undercooked. There were no lumps in the potatoes, and they didn't run all over his plate, either. And the roast, it was nicely seasoned and so tender it all but melted in his mouth.

There was a rousing round of compliments from the men at the table, and even Verna was not so spiteful as to ignore the food in front of her.

Nathan studied a forkful of roast. "I do believe this is the tastiest beef I've ever put in my mouth."

Charmaine blushed. "Mother gave it to me this morning, and then she told me how to prepare it and shared a few seasonings."

"This is Haley beef?" Ash asked.

Charmaine's smile faded, just a little. "Yes, isn't that all right?"

He placed a forkful in his mouth and savored as he chewed and swallowed. "Makes it taste all the better."

Charmaine smiled again, Nathan laughed, even Oswald grinned.

The dishes were done, the pie they hadn't eaten stored away for tomorrow, and Charmaine settled in a chair by the fire. Goodness, she'd had no idea cooking was so tiring. It was worth it though, to see Ash's face as he'd surveyed the table, to see him eat a decent meal.

Actually, she enjoyed cooking. It was rather a

surprise to find that she enjoyed such a domestic chore, but it was gratifying to watch everything come together neatly. The lessons, given with great enthusiasm by Charmaine's mother and the never-failing Jane, had gone well. Jane had even declared that Charmaine had a gift.

Oswald was reading, Verna was mending a skirt, and Nathan had closed his eyes but was surely not asleep in his chair. Ash was sitting on the floor by the fireplace, apparently lost in thought, and Charmaine left her chair to join him there.

"What are you thinking about?" she whispered.

He answered softly in her ear. "I don't think I'd better tell you right now, not with all these ears around."

"How rude," Verna snapped. "If you have something to say, kindly say it loud enough for the rest of us to hear."

"Just complimenting Charmaine on that pie again," Ash said with a smile. Verna snorted, and Oswald added his mumbled agreement.

How ironic that after spending so many hours railing against a life of servitude, she found such joy in something so simple as preparing a meal. How ironic that after railing against physical subservience, she found it wasn't subservience at all, but a shared pleasure that didn't seem to affect Ash's brain adversely at all.

She turned her head to find Nathan staring at her with a small smile on his face. He was always watching, it seemed, and he saw more than most, she was certain.

He was holding that stare, eye to eye, when he made his announcement. "I have enjoyed my stay here more than you'll ever know, but it's time for me to move on."

Verna sniffed. "I'd begun to think you'd moved in permanently."

Oswald didn't lift his nose from his book.

"Where will you go?" Ash asked softly.

"Kansas City, to start," Nathan said, and she was sure there were stars in his eyes. "There's an investor there who's expressed an interest in supporting the arts by assisting me in getting back on the road. We've been in communication for quite some time, and he'd like to have the show in tip-top shape for a Christmas gala in Kansas City. To start I'll put a troupe together, arrange a few performances, and in a matter of months I'll be on my feet again." He grinned widely at Charmaine. "Sure I can't interest you in a starring role, my Juliet?"

"No, thank you," she said sternly.

"What about you, Oswald?" Nathan asked, turning his attention to the man, who lowered his book slowly.

"What about me?" Oswald asked suspiciously.

She could almost see Nathan's mind at work.

"Ever thought about becoming an actor?"

Oswald scoffed, giving the suggestion his disdain, and returned his attention to the book.

"You're probably right," Nathan said with a touch of melancholy in his voice. "Not everyone can take the late nights, the senseless adoration, the constant excitement."

Oswald lowered the book and actually closed it. "I've never acted before."

Nathan grinned. "I've seen you reading Shakespeare."

"Of course."

"We'd start you off with a few small roles, of course, but with a little training, you'd make a magnificent Hamlet."

Oswald grinned brightly. "Do you really think so?"

"I'm sure of it," Nathan said stoutly.

"I will not watch another of my boys wander off to the big city and . . . and leave me *here* all alone." Verna insisted. "Oswald's not going anywhere!"

Oswald grimaced. "I don't think I can take another winter here, Mother. Last year, during that big snowstorm, we were stuck in this house for days. I'm not a farmer, I hate those blasted animals, and . . . and there's no treasure to look for anymore. At least that was *fun*. Even knocking down fence posts on occasion to keep Ash away from the house for a few hours was mildly entertaining, but there's no need to do that, now."

Ash stiffened, and Oswald looked his way. "Sorry, Ash."

Nathan jumped in. "That's right, my boy. You're not a farmer, you're an actor."

"You stop that," Verna insisted. "He's not going anywhere. I won't allow both my sons to desert me within the span of a week!"

Nathan leaned back in his chair. He looked as if he had the situation well in hand. "You know, I'll need a new wardrobe mistress," he said with a wave of his hand. "Someone to help the actresses dress quickly and make alterations and plan the overall color scheme that's presented on stage. It's an extremely important job." He looked squarely at Verna. "Would you be interested?"

She puffed a little, but didn't say no.

"It's an undertaking that requires extensive travel. We usually find ourselves in a different city every week," he said. "But . . . we stay in the finest hotels, we eat in the finest restaurants. Why, you'll likely never have to cook a meal again."

Ash's hand tightened at Charmaine's side. She could feel it, the tension as he waited for an answer.

"It's tempting," Verna admitted. "When will you be leaving?"

"In the morning."

"Tomorrow?" Verna shouted. "Why, I can't possibly . . ."

"We move on at a moment's notice," Nathan said in an enticing whisper. "No ties, no responsibilities but to the play and the audience. What lies beyond the horizon, Verna?" His voice remained soft. "Have you forgotten?"

"Tomorrow," she repeated, but in a hoarse whisper.

Nathan leaned forward, tense yet smiling, with just a hint of a mercenary twinkle in his eye. "What do you say?"

Chapter Seventeen

It was a grand morning, bright and cold, as Oswald and Verna loaded their belongings into Nathan's wagon. Of course, if they'd been in the midst of a tornado Ash would have thought this particular morning grand.

Once Verna had made up her mind she didn't seem to have a single second thought. With the truth of the Montgomery treasure revealed to her at last, she wanted off this farm as much as Ash wanted her gone. And evidently the idea of living in hotel to hotel from one town to the next appealed to her, as it obviously did to Oswald.

Verna and Oswald were seated up top, while Nathan loaded the last of his own belongings into the wagon. Ash stepped quietly to stand behind his godfather, until he was close enough to whisper and be heard.

"I owe you for this."

Nathan glanced over his shoulder with a wide smile. "That you do, my boy. That you do."

"This is above and beyond your duties as a godfather, Nathan, and I'll never forget it. Do you really think Oswald will make an actor?"

Nathan closed the squeaking wagon gate and turned to face Ash. The smile faded. "Yes, I do actually. *If* he's willing to learn. God knows he's got the ego of a star performer."

"And Verna?"

"Verna will no doubt have husband number three snagged before spring rolls around." Nathan reached up and placed his arm over Ash's shoulder. It was an awkward position for the shorter man, so Ash leaned forward slightly. "I'll work her hard enough until then."

"Good luck."

At long last, the house without Verna and her boys underfoot, without the nagging and the whining and the insults. It would be just him . . . and Charmaine, for as long as she stayed.

"Don't waste this opportunity, my boy," Nathan whispered, and at that moment Charmaine stepped onto the porch. "You've got her all to yourself, now. Make the best of it."

"Charmaine's not going to stay." Ash said this as much to himself as to Nathan. Believing otherwise was dangerous. "She never intended to and nothing's changed."

She was looking to the wagon with a rather forlorn look in her eyes. After her difficult weeks here, she couldn't possibly be distressed about the departure of Verna and Oswald. Maybe it was more than that. Maybe, in spite of the truce they'd come to, she was dreading the prospect of sharing the house with him alone.

"Ha!" Nathan scoffed softly. "Even I can see that *everything's* changed. She milks cows and feeds chicken, she learned to cook for you. . . ."

"She's just killing time until her father cools off and she can slip away without worrying about him coming after her."

"No . . ."

"She told me so herself."

"If you tell her that you love her . . ."

"Forget it," Ash said sharply.

"But it's true," Nathan hissed. "Don't lie to me, because I know you better than anyone else, and I can always tell when you're lying. It's in your eyes . . . Lila's eyes. I can see even when you're lying to yourself."

It was the truth, and Ash didn't waste any more breath denying what Nathan saw. "Sometimes I look at her and it hits me like a thunderbolt. This woman is my *wife*. And then it hits me again, the knowledge that she never wanted to be and she'll leave in a heartbeat when the opportunity rolls around."

"I don't believe it," Nathan said stubbornly.

Ash glanced at the woman in question, as she paced the front porch with her eyes on the wagon. She really did look distressed. Charmaine didn't belong here, she belonged in the city, with her seminars and her manuals and her . . .

"What do women do in Boston . . . for entertainment?"

"They have oyster parties and go to the theater, for the most part." Nathan said with a grin.

"What else?" Ash asked seriously.

Nathan hesitated. "Sleighing and ice skating in the winter and picnicking in the summer. Games played after dinner, a buggy ride in the park. Poetry reading and musical events great and small. What exactly are you up to?"

"Nothing," Ash said softly.

He gave Nathan a hearty hug and another soft thanks, and then Charmaine came down the porch steps to say her own good-byes. Verna and Oswald were as cool to her as they'd been to Ash when he'd said good bye, but Nathan insisted on a hug and a kiss from his Juliet.

As they watched the wagon pull away, there was a tear in Charmaine's eye.

"What's wrong?" Hell, he knew what was wrong. She didn't want to be alone with him any more than she wanted to be married to him.

But she surprised him with her answer. "I'll miss Pumpkin."

This couldn't be right. Doc Whitfield had made a mistake, a terrible, terrible mistake.

She almost ran over Sarah Lewis, as the woman exited the Markam mercantile.

"Why, good afternoon, Maureen."

"Ha!" she said without looking at the woman, without even slowing her step.

Behind her there was a muffled and indignant, "Why, I never . . ."

Doc Whitfield was wrong, he had to be. What he suggested was impossible, preposterous. But even as she denied what she'd heard, she knew it was the truth.

Forty-five year old women didn't have babies. Well, perhaps they did, but *she* didn't. It was ludicrous.

More than fifteen years ago, Doc Whitfield had told her she wouldn't have any more children. She remembered that horrid meeting as if it were yesterday, and she'd reminded him of it just a few minutes ago. He was certain his diagnosis had been that it was highly unlikely that she'd conceive again, not impossible . . . but as far as Maureen was concerned that was splitting hairs.

Stuart was just riding in as she approached the house, and she changed course to intercept him. He gave her a wide smile as he dismounted and tossed the reins to the waiting stable boy, but that smile faded as she came near.

"What's wrong?" He reached for her, but she snatched her arm away.

"How could you?" she whispered.

"How could I *what?*"

He was truly puzzled, looking so innocent and concerned. Ha! *He* wasn't the one who was pregnant. *He* wasn't the one who was tired all the time and nauseated most every morning and already getting fat.

"Men!" she said, and then she spun on her heel to walk away.

He followed closely, around the house and up the stairs, through the front door and finally into the parlor. She tried to shut him out there, but he squeezed in before she could close the door in his face.

"What is going on here?" he demanded, tossing his hat aside. "Have you been talking to Charmaine?"

Maureen sat on the sofa and tried to gather her composure. She was going to have to tell him, sooner or later.

"I saw the doctor this afternoon."

He paled, and she could actually see the fear in his eyes. "What's wrong?"

The tears welled in her eyes. This couldn't be happening. Not now. She was a *grandmother*, for goodness sake. "I'm going to have a baby," she wailed.

Impossibly, Stuart went even paler. "A baby?"

Maureen nodded quickly.

When he smiled she wanted to punch him in the mouth. "A baby," he whispered. "After all these years." He sat beside her and placed a long arm over her shoulder. "Why are you crying? This is wonderful news."

"Wonderful news!" She tried to edge away from him, but he held tight. "I'm too old to have a baby! My daughters should be having babies, not me!"

"Did the Doc say you were too old?" he whispered. "Does he expect problems?"

Maureen shook her head. "He said I'm disgustingly healthy for a woman of my age, and I should have no complications."

"Good," he sighed with relief.

"But what does he know?" she snapped. "He's the one who told me there would be no more children!"

Stuart laid a hand against her face, a hand that was surprisingly gentle. A tear fell, and he brushed it away with his thumb. "You know, we always wanted more babies. So maybe we're a little old. . . ."

"A *little* old!"

He grinned, a wide smile that deepened the wrinkles on his face and made her heart beat faster. "I couldn't be happier."

"Of course you're happy." She tried to sound stern but fell far short. "You don't have to carry this child and give birth in the spring. Oh, and what will people say?"

"Who gives a—"

"Stuart."

"Who cares?"

Maureen gave in and fell against him, burying her head against his chest. "I'm scared," she whispered, admitting it for the first time. "I'm not a young woman, and . . ."

He wouldn't allow her to say it. "I'll take such good care of you," he said, "you'll wish you were pregnant all the time."

She sniffled.

"We'll hire extra help, and I'll stay home more. Hell, what's the good of having all this money if I can't spend it?" His hands brushed her hair. "I love you too much to allow anything to happen to you."

"It's not that simple."

"And another thing," he said, ignoring her. "When the girls were little I missed so much. Getting the ranch started, chasing rustlers, cattle drives, I was away from home more than I was here. This time, I don't want to miss anything."

Maureen lifted her head to look at him. Maybe this was not such a disaster after all. Maybe everything would work out for the best. Stuart was certainly happy about it. Didn't he realize that a child in the house would turn their comfortable world upside down?

The constant demands, the sleepless nights. The inevitable dilemmas of growing up. The heartache and pain, when the child suffered heartache and pain.

A child's laughter and tears. The unconditional love that comes only from a child. Another child to love and raise. Maybe this would be another beautiful daughter, and then again maybe it would be the son Stuart had always wanted. She was afraid to mention that possibility aloud, afraid she'd jinx whatever chance they had.

"You need a nap before supper," he demanded, rising and taking her hand to pull her gently to her feet, surprising her by sweeping her up and into his arms.

"What are you doing?"

"There will be no unnecessary walking in the next six months or so."

"You can't carry me everywhere."

"I don't see why not."

She turned the doorknob and Stuart pushed the door open to carry her from the parlor. They were halfway up the stairs when the strain began to show on his face.

"Okay," he conceded breathlessly as they reached the second floor. "Maybe we're not as young as we used to be, but we're not exactly a couple of old geezers, either."

She laughed. Minutes ago she would have thought merriment impossible, but as Stuart carried her to their bed she placed her head on his shoulder and laughed out loud. As he very carefully placed her on the bed, he let out a sigh of relief.

"What would you think about fixing up one of the downstairs rooms as a bedchamber . . . just for a few months?"

She took his face in her hands and kissed him lightly. "I love you, Stuart. I'm so sorry I yelled at you earlier."

"It's all right," he whispered. "Scared me a little bit, I can tell you that. You've never yelled at me like that before, and I thought surely something terrible had happened."

She still wasn't convinced that this wasn't terrible, but she felt much better.

Stuart sat down on the bed beside her and fell back. "You know," he said, still slightly breathless. "Maybe I need a before supper nap myself."

A fragrant stew was simmering on the stove, and the biscuits were almost done. A cherry cobbler was cooling on the table, its perfectly browned lattice crust and the red filling making it almost too pretty to eat.

Why was she so nervous? It wasn't like she'd never been alone with Ash before.

But when he slammed the front door shut she nearly jumped out of her skin. Fortunately he couldn't see her, and she had time to compose herself before he stepped into the kitchen.

"That smells great." He smiled at her, and the result was most distressing. She loved him more today than she had as a silly child. She loved him more every day, and it was tearing her apart.

He didn't want her to stay. Goodness, he'd been the one with a gun to his head as they were married, he'd been the one to declare on more than one occasion that she'd make a terrible farmer's wife.

While he cleaned up she set the table and filled two bowls with stew. She placed the biscuits on the table, along with butter and jam. Ash would want coffee with lots of milk and sugar, and she'd have tea. By the time he came to the table everything was in place.

"I guess it was lonely around here today," he said with a smile.

"A little," she confessed. "But it was blessedly quiet and peaceful. I don't think I realized how much Verna talked until she was gone."

He nodded his head in agreement and dug in. It was surprisingly gratifying to watch Ash enjoy the meal she had prepared, oddly delightful.

"Do you skate?" he asked abruptly.

"Skate?"

"Ice-skate," he clarified. "I ran across a couple of old pairs of skates in the tack room this afternoon, and I just wondered . . ."

"I love to skate," she said quickly.

"The pond freezes over in the wintertime," he

said. "Sometimes in December, always in January . . . I mean, if you're still here then we might could . . ."

"That would be great . . . if I'm still here."

She looked into her half-eaten bowl of stew. What did she have to do to prove herself? What would it take to get Ash to ask her to stay?

What if he never asked? After all, she'd told him she didn't intend to stay . . . more than once. She'd made it very clear that she didn't want to be here any more than he wanted her here.

His father had said she had *sand*, and she'd certainly never been one to hold her tongue. Why was it so hard to find the right words now? Where was her courage? Her courage was disturbingly absent, her tongue distressingly uncooperative . . . just when she needed it most!

If she didn't speak up Ash would never ask her to stay.

"I would hate to leave you here all alone during the winter," she blurted. "Maybe, if you don't mind, I'll stay until spring."

He didn't lift his eyes from his near empty bowl. "Sure. Whatever you want."

"I mean, with Verna gone you need someone to cook for you, and to launder your clothes and keep the house," she said quickly. "And what if you went skating all alone and fell through the ice and there was no one there to help you?

Goodness, I would feel as if I were deserting you if I left you during the winter."

"Then stay until spring," he said softly, without looking up.

"Spring," she said dreamily. "I do love spring here. In Boston it's still cold and it rains an awful lot. It's actually a pretty dismal place in the spring. I guess spring's a busy time on a farm, planting . . . whatever and getting the garden started and . . ."

"Yes," Ash answered, and he lifted his head slowly. "It's a busy time."

Charmaine couldn't look him in the eye, not yet. She stirred her stew and watched the fascinating rotation of a perfectly square piece of beef through the thick gravy. "I would hate to leave while you're so busy," she said rationally. "Maybe summer would be better. Yes, definitely summer."

"The winter wheat is harvested in June, July," Ash said absently. "I usually hire a few hands to help out, but they have to be fed and the days are long and . . ."

"Autumn," Charmaine finally gathered the courage to look at him again. "Oh, but you plant the winter wheat in the autumn, don't you?"

"Yes."

"Well, that brings us full circle, doesn't it?"

Why didn't he *say* something? He just sat there and stared at her with those green eyes that looked right through her. She should have kept her mouth shut, just this once! He was probably trying to find some diplomatic way to send her on her way . . .

"What are you trying to say, Charmaine?" His voice was husky, not much more than a whisper.

"I'm not trying to say anything," she said sensibly, placing her spoon on the table and rising to clear her dishes away. "I'm just . . . rambling, that's all. Just rambling."

He caught her wrist and pulled her with a gentle jerk onto his lap. "You never ramble. As a matter of fact, you're the only woman I've ever known who doesn't ramble. Well, except for that day you tried to convince me that marital continence would be good for me."

Wasn't he listening to her? She'd done everything but ask outright if he would have her. "Maybe it would!" she snapped as she tried to rise. Ash pulled her easily back into his lap.

"I don't think so," he said softly, and then he forced her to look at him.

"You're impossible."

"Stay," he said simply.

It was the one word she wanted to hear more than anything. Her heart was melting, and when he kissed her she was lost.

"Not until spring," he said as he pulled his lips from her, "not until autumn . . . forever."

"Forever," she whispered.

He kissed her again, a deep and passionate

kiss she had learned to answer well. Her tongue swept over his lower lip and then flicked into his mouth, and with a soft moan he drew it deeper. His manhood swelled and hardened against her hip, and she could feel the answering response of her own body. Her nipples grew hard and tight, and at her innermost core she ached for him.

They fit together so well, mouth to mouth and body to body. Surely that meant something. There was never any awkwardness in the way they came together, just an easy and natural connection. It was as if this was meant to be.

"I need you." It was a huskily whispered plea as he lifted her and set her on the edge of the table.

"I know."

"Now."

"Yes."

She heard something hit the floor, but it was distant and unimportant. Ash was all she knew, all she wanted to know as he lifted her skirt and found the sensitive flesh that already throbbed for him. He stroked her gently, circled his thumb against the nub at the entrance to her body until she was arching off the table to meet his caress.

She heard him working the buttons of his denim trousers, though she could see nothing for the yards of fabric of her own skirt that flowed softly between them. His eyes never left her, and she could see, in that moment, what she wanted to see. Love, a love as impossibly deep as her own.

With a gentle hand at her hip he eased her closer to the edge of the table, lifted her legs and wrapped them around his waist, and then he entered her slowly, pushing inside to fill her completely. For a moment he was still, and then he began to withdraw just as slowly. When she thought he would leave her he thrust to fill her again, and she rocked forward to meet him.

Already she knew his body well, and he knew hers. They moved in an unconscious rhythm, a passionate and perfect dance, a meeting of body and soul. There was more, and she felt it as surely as the union of their bodies. It was a joining of their hearts.

Too soon the climax of her pleasure came, in an intense explosion that burst through her body with the power of a lightning bolt. Ash's culmination came on top of hers, with a raw and powerful thrust that surely took him deeper than ever before.

She'd never felt this close to another human being, hadn't known it was possible. It was so much more than physical pleasure, so much more than the fact that his body was a part of hers.

His very soul had mingled with hers, making her a different person, a better person. For the first time in her life she was complete.

He gathered her into his arms, holding her close and kissing softly her mouth, her jaw, the side of her neck. "Stay," he whispered.

"Forever." She should tell him now that she loved him, whisper the words that were, for some reason, very difficult to articulate. She should simply blurt it out. *I love you, Ash.*

"It was the skates, wasn't it?" he whispered, and she pulled away to see a bright smile blooming on his face.

And the perfect moment had passed. She returned his smile, certain that another perfect moment would come soon enough.

Chapter Eighteen

It was a soft, cold rain that had already soaked him to the bone, and Ash ran through the gentle drops and toward the house. In the past three days, since Charmaine had said she'd stay, his life had been perfect. He had a comfortable, peaceful home and, in his bed at night, a wife he loved more than anything. This was everything he'd ever dreamed of, but he'd never expected to actually see his dream come true.

He left his dripping wet hat and soaked boots on the front porch, and Charmaine met him at the door with a thick towel she all but attacked him with.

"Goodness, you're soaked to the skin," she

said as she rubbed the towel over his body. "You get out of these wet clothes right this minute, before you catch your death of cold."

"Yes, ma'am," he said obligingly, unbuttoning his shirt and following her to the kitchen. The long tin tub was sitting in the middle of the floor, and as he watched she added another steaming pot of water to the bath. "We're going to take a bath?"

"*You're* going to take a bath," she said, "a good hot one to take the chill off your bones."

"You can take the chill off my bones," he said as he stripped the wet shirt off.

"Not today, I can't," she mumbled.

"Why not?" he asked as he stripped off cold wet denim.

Charmaine's only answer was a despairing glance he read quite easily.

"Oh." He lowered himself into the warm water and closed his eyes. She was right. The warmth seeped into his bones and leeched away the cold.

The next thing he knew Charmaine was kneeling behind him, a washrag in her hand. She scrubbed his shoulders gently. "I shouldn't be disappointed, should I? I mean, it's a little early for children, and I did try to be careful about the days. Well, at least I did think about it those first few times. A woman's only fertile a few days a month, you know."

"No, I didn't know that."

Linda Jones

"Well, it's true. A woman can plan her family if she's very cautious. There's no need to have one baby right after another until one's health has been ruined." Her voice was a little too sharp, a little too clear.

"Are you disappointed?" he asked softly.

She was silent for a few minutes, and her hand dipped over his shoulder to his chest where it stilled. "Yes," she admitted with a reticent sigh. "It makes no sense, no sense at all. I never wanted children, I was always a little . . ." she paused, and Ash took her hand and drew her to his side so he could see her face.

"Always a little what?"

"Afraid," she confessed. "You should have heard Felicity scream when she gave birth to Hester. There was so much blood, and . . . and . . ." She paled with the memory. "And sweat and strain to the point where I was sure she was going to die. Felicity said it was the most excruciating pain she'd ever imagined, and she stayed in bed for two weeks afterward."

"It's not easy, I imagine."

"Not easy!" With a wide smile, Charmaine playfully splashed water onto his chest. "Spoken like a man who will never have to go through such an ordeal."

He took her hand in his wet one and held on tight. He imagined when the time came he'd feel every pain Charmaine did, but he couldn't

292

tell her that. Not yet. Just the thought of her in that kind of pain made him queasy.

"I don't want you to be afraid."

"I'm not, not really," she said with a sigh. "I mean, I was wrong about everything else, so maybe I'm wrong about this, too."

"Wrong about what?" he prodded.

"You know good and well . . ."

"Not really."

She made herself more comfortably there by the tub, but she left her hand in his. "I was wrong about marriage," she said with a sigh. "Marital continence and domestic chores and men in general."

With a wide grin on his face, Ash pulled Charmaine close for a sweet kiss.

"Of course," she said as she pulled away. "You're not like men in general. Why, do you know that most men would run and hide from a simple conversation such as this one? They're afraid to discuss personal matters, even with their own wives."

She was suddenly thoughtful, pursed lips and averted eyes hinting that she wasn't finished. "Can I ask you a very personal question?"

"Sure."

Charmaine looked him straight in the eye then, as if she was getting set to gauge his initial reaction to this question. "Why did you never . . . What I mean to ask is, why were there no women before me?"

"Maybe I couldn't find another woman who would have me," he joked.

Charmaine splashed water on his chest. "Horsefeathers. I don't buy that for a moment."

"Maybe I was waiting for you to grow up and come home," he offered, a little more seriously.

"You haven't thought of me for years, and I darn well know it. I was just a runny-nosed kid, remember?"

She wanted an answer, a real one, the truth. "What was I supposed to do?" he asked softly. "Visit the rooms over the saloon and take my pleasure with a woman who's made herself available to any man with a couple of bucks to spare?"

"Many men do," she said. "Maybe even most men."

He shook his head slowly. "I wouldn't know about that. I only know that option didn't appeal to me."

"You could have gotten married years ago," she said. Her voice was sensible, but she was no longer meeting his eyes. She swirled the water with her hand and watched the resulting ripples. "There are any number of single ladies in town looking to find a husband."

"I couldn't bring a decent woman here, not with Verna and her boys here to make her life hell. Besides, I had enough obligations without taking on another one."

A rush of color came to her face. "And then

my father takes a gun to you and . . ."

He placed a damp hand on her cheek and forced her to look at him. "Let's just say I was waiting for you to grow up and leave it at that."

"I shouldn't have asked."

"It's all right. I like being married to a woman who speaks her mind."

"Then you really are one of a kind."

An effortless smile spread across his face. "I like being married to a woman who has sand."

She returned his grin, giving him a wide and bright smile that somehow touched his heart. "That's why I love you." Her smile faded. "Well, I mean . . . I didn't intend to just . . ."

"Do you?"

She took her bottom lip between her teeth. Charmaine? Shy? Rather than answer, she leaned over and kissed him gently.

"Ash," she whispered against his mouth.

A furious pounding on the front door interrupted her, and Charmaine jumped back and up. Ash felt a rush of frustration. So close, so damn close.

Before she left the kitchen, he heard the front door swing open, and a woman's shrill voice called out sharply. "Charmaine!"

Charmaine's surprised voice answered. "Jeanette?"

Her sister stood in the open doorway, only slightly damp, and beyond the porch there waited a carriage. A moment later, Howard appeared behind her, stripping off his slicker and dropping it on the porch.

Something must have been terribly wrong for the two of them to come all this way, and to travel to the farm in this weather.

"Felicity," she whispered. "Oh no, something's happened?"

Jeanette and Howard exchanged a cryptic glance.

"Let's not discuss Felicity," Jeanette said sharply.

Jeanette had always been the beauty of the Haley girls. Tall and shapely without being round, she had the perfect silhouette. Her hair was a shade darker than Charmaine's, and was just a little bit curly. Her features were classic, the nose straight and strong, the eyes wide and bright blue. Her appearance was always flawless, from her hair to her face to her fashionable clothes. Charmaine had always felt frumpy next to her sister.

"We're here for you," Howard said, stepping past Jeanette to confront Charmaine. "You poor dear." He took her hands in his and shook his head slowly. "I only wish I could have gotten here sooner."

"But, why *are* you here?"

Howard laid a hand against her face. "You poor dear," he said again. "What has he done to you? You're not even thinking clearly. The telegram," he reminded her. "We came as soon as we could."

"But . . . didn't you get the second telegram I sent?" she asked breathlessly.

Howard shook his head, and Jeanette looked puzzled.

"I'm afraid you've wasted a trip. Everything's fine here."

Ash stepped into the room, still buttoning his dry shirt. His hair was wet and was dripping water onto his shoulders, and his feet were bare. "What's going on?"

Howard stiffened and lifted his chin defiantly. "I suppose this man is Ash Coleman."

"Yes. My . . . husband."

Howard reached into an inner pocket of his jacket and withdrew a crumpled telegram. "We're here because of this plea for assistance."

Charmaine tried to snatch the telegram from Howard's hand, but Ash was quicker, and Charmaine watched in horror as the slip of paper flew past her shoulder.

"Married to Ash Coleman," he read aloud. "Please save me." His voice faded away until she could barely hear it.

"I sent another telegram, just a few days later," she said quickly, disengaging her hands from Howard's and turning to face Ash. Goodness, he was furious, every bit as angry as he'd been on the day of the wedding. "I told them to ignore the first telegram."

He wouldn't look her in the eye. With great care, he folded the telegram and returned it to Howard. "Well, here she is. Save her."

He walked past without so much as looking at her, onto the porch where he stepped into his boots, and back out into the rain.

"I should have known it was too good to be true," Ash muttered. "Hell, deep down I *did* know, I just ignored it. I'm such an imbecile I have to see it in writing, right before my very eyes."

Betsy's mind was elsewhere, but Lady was paying attention. He stroked the mare's nose.

" 'Married to Ash Coleman. Please save me.' " He repeated the words he could still see. "I don't know why I was so surprised that it felt like a kick in the gut. She doesn't belong here and she never did. Everything that happened, everything good, was no more real than that damned masked ball."

What the hell was taking them so long? Charmaine had had time to pack her things and jump into the carriage with her sister and her brother-in-law, but the carriage sat deserted in front of the house. Maybe they were waiting for the rain to let up.

At least they knew there was no baby. All those nights in their bed, that fast and furious coming together on the kitchen table, the afternoon in the tack room, the evening in front of the fire. . . . It was good that he knew, otherwise he would have wondered, always. . . .

The front door slammed. He could hear it through the rain and the open barn door, but he didn't turn around. He had no desire to watch Charmaine load her belongings into that fine carriage and ride away.

But when the carriage began to move he went to the doorway. Slanted rain splattered his face and his once dry clothes, but he didn't move. Howard Stillwell, that jackass, had donned his slicker and was driving the carriage himself. And inside . . . inside a small white hand reached up and pulled the shade down so he could see nothing.

He told himself that it was for the best. All they had was Charmaine's scientific and reasonably explained magnetic attraction. Something that made him want her to the exclusion of all else, something that made a single touch ignite the passions of a lifetime. Science. Not love.

When the front door of the house opened, and Charmaine stood framed in the doorway, his heart stopped. Science, hell. Why was she still here?

She stepped onto the porch and waved him in with an uncertain flutter of her hand, and a moment later he was running through the rain.

"You didn't let me explain," she said as he stepped onto the porch and she backed into the house. She'd built a fire, and the warmth that emanated from the house was inviting. Still, he hesitated.

"What's to explain? I'd say the telegram was quite clear."

He stood in the doorway and stared at his wife. Charmaine Haley Coleman, contrite, embarrassed . . . pale as she'd been on their wedding day.

"Come in the house and close the door," she said softly. "You're letting out the heat."

He could close the door and return to the barn and force himself to be perfectly happy. He should do just that, back away. Run away. "Why are you still here? Jeanette and Howard came to your rescue, and yet you're still here. What happened?"

"I told them I didn't want to go," she admitted in a voice so low he had to strain to hear her.

He stepped into the house and closed the door behind him. "Took a while to convince them, didn't it?"

"Yes, it did."

Charmaine was afraid. He could see it in her wide eyes and hear it in her normally strong voice that now quavered. Yes, he was angry, but she had no reason to be afraid of him. She should know him well enough to be certain of that fact.

"And Howard had some news, I'm afraid," she whispered.

Ash stepped closer to the fire. He wasn't

soaked this time. A few minutes by the fire and he'd be dry and warm. "What kind of news?"

"It's Felicity." Her voice shook.

"Is she ill?"

Charmaine shook her head slowly. "She's . . . she's left Howard and run off with the *gardener*."

Staid little Felicity, who had been high-and-mighty by the age of eight? "No kidding."

Charmaine shook her head. "It's true. His name is Tavish. Goodness, I don't even know if that's his first name or his last. He's a Scot, a very tall redheaded man who's been with Howard for years. Evidently they've been carrying on for the past year, and now Felicity's expecting his child and they've run off together."

"Must have been quite a shock for Howard."

She nodded, and at last met his gaze straight on. "It's been devastating for him. He wants me to return to Boston with him and stand at his side, just for a while. Otherwise, he'll feel that everyone is laughing at him. If he has my support . . ."

"When are you leaving?"

She took a single step forward and placed a hand on his still-damp sleeve. "I told him I would think about it, but only for a visit. Once he's on his feet again and this scandal is behind him, he'll be fine. You must understand, Howard has been so very kind to me, and my sister has . . . has humiliated and disgraced him. I

301

must do my part to repair the damage."

"When are you leaving?" he asked again.

"Ash." She stood squarely in front of him and grasped the front of his shirt with both hands. "I did send a second telegram to Felicity and Jeanette, telling them that I was fine and there was no need . . ."

"To save you," he finished for her.

She lifted her head and looked him in the eye. God, he couldn't think with her this close, couldn't breathe. Her body touched his lightly, her breath warmed him. Her heart beat for him.

"I was angry when I sent that telegram. Angry and confused and . . ."

"You don't have to explain."

"Maybe you could come with me," she whispered. "It will just be for a few weeks . . ."

He laughed at her. "I can't leave, not even for a few days. This is a farm, *my* farm, and there's work to be done every day."

"Daddy could have his hands take care of things for a while," she suggested.

"Absolutely not," he said with a harsh and humorless laugh.

"I won't be gone long."

It was a lie. Once Charmaine was back in Boston she'd stay there, and he knew it even if she didn't. "When are you leaving?" he asked again, hoping she would answer this time. Not knowing was killing him by inches.

"Next week, on the Thursday train."

"With Jeanette and Howard?"

She nodded silently. "You do believe me, don't you, about the second telegram? You know I'll be back."

"Yes," he lied.

She believed him. Her sigh of relief was audible. "I don't blame you for being angry," she said softly. "You do forgive me . . . don't you?"

Didn't she know that he would forgive her anything? She could rip out his heart and stomp on it, and he wouldn't stop loving her. It was a terrible curse, or else a fatal failing. He wasn't sure which at the moment, and didn't care.

"Sure," he said without enthusiasm.

"Oh, and I know you won't be happy about this, but . . . there's going to be a family dinner Sunday after church. We're expected to be there."

Great. Sunday dinner with Stuart Haley, Howard Stillwell, and three-quarters of the Haley women. It was sure to be an interesting mix of heaven and hell.

"She seems happy enough," Jeanette said with more than a trace of disbelief in her soft voice. "But goodness gracious, Mother, there was a bathtub in the kitchen!"

Maureen smiled at her daughter. Jeanette perched on the edge of the chair nearest the sofa and twiddled her thumbs nervously. "You girls bathed in a tin tub in the kitchen until we moved into this house."

"Well, it just seems very . . . undignified."

It now seemed that sending her daughters East to be educated had been a terrible mistake. Charmaine had joined in Howard Stillwell's ridiculous crusades, Felicity had put aside her morals and her good sense to run from her husband with another man, and Jeanette had turned into a snob.

"What did you think of Ash?" she asked, to change the subject as well as to gather information.

Jeanette screwed up her nose. "I don't really know. He was only there for a moment before he became angry and stormed out of the house."

Maureen sighed. Of course he was angry. She'd been a bit heartbroken herself upon reading the telegram. It must have been devastating for Ash.

Everything had been going along so well. She'd executed Nathan Sweet's plan to get Elmo out of Salley Creek, and the little man had held up his end of the bargain by taking Oswald and Verna on the road with him. Alone, Ash and Charmaine had a chance. And now this.

"He was somewhat . . . well, more handsome than I remembered," Jeanette allowed. "In a rather crude way. Of course, he was just a child when I left Salley Creek." She narrowed her eyes and pursed her lips once again. "He's practically a complete stranger, and you made Charmaine marry him. How could you?"

If Jeanette had seen the two of them together at the ball, she wouldn't question the integrity of this marriage. It had come about in an unconventional way, yes, but it wasn't wrong. "Charmaine and Ash found themselves in a compromising position. I should say your *father* found them in a compromising position, one that indicated a wedding was called for."

Jeanette's face went blank with surprise. "Charmaine?"

"Yes, Charmaine. And I think . . . no, I *know* that she loves Ash Coleman very much."

"She always was sweet on him," Jeanette said thoughtfully, "but I thought it was a childish infatuation. Not love. Are you sure?"

Yes, she was very sure. She'd seen it in Charmaine's eyes as she'd given all her attention to Jane's instructions on cooking. She'd seen it when Charmaine got angry about the way Verna treated her husband. She'd seen it in a hundred little clues Charmaine surely didn't realize she gave.

And anyone who knew Charmaine knew she wouldn't still be on that farm if she didn't want to be.

"Yes," she assured Jeanette. "What did she say to you when you tried to convince her to leave that farm?"

Jeanette fidgeted uncomfortably. "First she said she was married, and so she couldn't possibly leave."

As if that would stop Charmaine from doing exactly what she wanted to do.

"Then she said Ash needed her there, that he couldn't cook and clean for himself because he works so many hours on the farm. Howard was livid about that, I can tell you. He told Charmaine that Ash could hire a housekeeper to handle the domestic duties."

"And what did Charmaine say to that?"

Maureen was pleased to see that Jeanette was at least giving some serious thought to what she'd seen and heard at the Coleman farm. "She sat down in a rocking chair and refused to budge. Crossed her arms over her chest, stuck out her chin the same way she did when she was six, and said she wasn't going anywhere."

"Would she have said that if she didn't love her husband?"

"Probably not. She did," Jeanette added with renewed energy, "agree to go to Boston with Howard for a couple of weeks. She was very distressed upon hearing the news about Felicity."

"As we all were." She still had trouble believing that her eldest and most sensible daughter would do something so outrageous as leave her husband and run off with another man. And if Howard was to be believed, she was carrying the man's child. Maureen shook off the pain of that news. Until she had heard from Felicity, she would not pass judgement.

For the moment she would concentrate on more immediate matters. It was definitely not a good idea for Charmaine to return to Boston with Howard Stillwell, not even for a short visit. Howard seemed to be more concerned about Charmaine's situation than his own, and that just didn't feel right. It was unnatural, and more than a little unnerving.

Chapter Nineteen

Ash ate his supper and seemed to enjoy it, but he hadn't so much as looked at her, not once since the meal had begun. He hadn't really looked at her since yesterday when she'd tried so ineptly to explain away that darn telegram.

It wasn't like her to be at a loss for words, but she couldn't think of a single thing to say that would make Ash feel better. She'd apologized several times, but those apologies didn't seem to touch Ash at all. He told her to forget it . . . but he hadn't.

Between Ash's hurt feelings and the knowledge that she was responsible, and the startling news about Felicity and the gardener, Charmaine was thoroughly miserable.

Felicity and Tavish. It was unthinkable, preposterous, and the most scandalous disgrace of Charmaine's life. She tried to remember Tavish clearly, to remember more than the fact that he was an incredibly tall man with red hair, but she'd never so much as carried on a conversation with the man.

Felicity had, though. Several mornings Charmaine had seen her sister walking in the garden with Tavish, pointing at this rosebush or that, gesturing gracefully at a bed of flowers. He had walked beside her, hands clasped behind his back, head bent to hear her words clearly.

She now doubted their conversation had anything to do with roses and flower beds.

Felicity was usually so practical, it made no sense, no sense at all. . . . Charmaine rested her gaze on the stoic profile of her husband. Unless Tavish had turned Felicity's world upside down, as Ash had hers. Unless she found such comfort and joy in his touch that nothing else mattered. Unless she loved him.

Charmaine knew now that what Felicity and Howard had found in their marriage was not love. There had been caring there, at one time perhaps, a mutual respect . . . but not love. She couldn't imagine sending Ash off to his own room at night, sleeping alone when she could be nestled in his arms. Purity and chastity were all well and good, but there was a spiritual core to her love for Ash that was as pure as anything she'd ever known.

If Felicity had found that with Tavish, how could Charmaine denounce it? How could she stand at Howard's side and condemn her own sister?

Yesterday's shock aside, she knew she couldn't do it. At the family dinner tomorrow she'd pull Howard aside and tell him that she couldn't go back to Boston, that her place was here with Ash.

And when Ash's anger faded, as it surely would, she would tell him how much she loved him. He didn't love her, of course, so it would be difficult to say the words. But with time, he would come to love her. Of that she was certain.

"How am I supposed to sleep with that man under my roof?" Stuart whispered huskily as he paced before the moonlit window. "He must have done something to Felicity to make her behave in such an irresponsible manner. She's always been an honest, reliable girl, and she would never do anything so . . . so dishonorable without a damn good reason."

Maureen was propped up on a number of fat pillows, her thick braid falling over one shoulder, her hands folded primly on her lap. She wasn't sure what distressed her husband more, the news that his married daughter had run off with another man, or the fact that Howard Stillwell slept just down the hall.

"Let's reserve judgement until we hear from Felicity," she said calmly. "And as for Howard, well, he'll be gone in a few days."

"Taking Charmaine with him," Stuart whispered. "He says it's temporary, but I don't believe it. She'll get to Boston and its seminars and social life, and she won't come back."

Maureen smiled. Her husband was loving and passionate and protective, but he was also occasionally blind. "I think Charmaine will have the good sense to change her mind before Thursday rolls around."

Stuart snorted softly.

"And if she doesn't, do you really think Ash will allow her to go?"

Stuart made his way to the edge of the bed. "Allow her? This is Charmaine we're talking about."

"A very *changed* Charmaine," she said as she took his hand. "You haven't been paying attention to the tempering of your youngest daughter."

He sat beside her with a heavy sigh. "I haven't seen her enough lately to know if she's changed or not. She's been avoiding me since the wedding. I guess she still hasn't forgiven me for making her marry Ash."

"Oh, I think she's forgiven you," Maureen whispered.

Stuart shook his head slowly.

"You'll see," she said, stroking the top of Stuart's hand. "Tomorrow."

"I don't think so."

"Come to bed." Maureen patted a waiting pillow. "I need my rest, you know, and I can't sleep without you beside me."

He obliged, crawling into the bed and taking her in his arms. "There now. I didn't mean to keep you awake so late. I'm sorry."

She nuzzled her head against his shoulder, finding that perfect fit. "I think we should tell the children tomorrow, while we have Jeanette and Charmaine together."

"Whatever you want," he whispered, and then he kissed the top of her head.

Ash looked wonderfully handsome in his gray suit, with his hair neatly trimmed and his face freshly shaven. If only he would smile.

They walked from church to the house, the lot of them. Jane was at the forefront, her steps quick as she hurried to the house and her kitchen. Charmaine's father and mother walked at a leisurely pace behind her, side by side and step for step. The distance between Jane and the Haleys steadily increased.

Howard and Jeanette were a few steps behind Stuart and Maureen Haley, their heads together in a conspiratorial fashion. Jeanette looked marvelous in her strawberry dress and matching hat, and Howard had donned a somber brown suit that he often wore for his lectures.

Charmaine purposely slowed her pace and slipped her arm through Ash's. For the next couple of hours, they'd be surrounded by her family and she wouldn't have so much as a private word with her husband. How could she have even considered going to Boston for two weeks!

"They're not so bad, you know," she whispered when Howard and Jeanette were well ahead of them and could not hear.

"Who's not so bad?" Ash's voice was low and lifeless.

"My family," she said with a forced smile. "Mother and Daddy, Jeanette and Howard. They just take some getting used to, that's all."

He didn't respond, and goodness, he always grabbed any opportunity to insult her father.

"You're still pouting, aren't you?" she accused softly.

"I am not pouting." At least he finally looked squarely at her as he defended himself.

"Call it what you will. . . ."

He came to an abrupt stop and faced her fully, glaring down at her. "I'm here, heading to Sunday dinner with four people who'd just as soon shoot me as feed me."

"That's not—"

313

"I'll probably have to eat in the barn, being a *sodbuster* and all."

"Ash, don't be—"

"I'm here, but don't expect me to be happy about it, all right?"

He took her arm and resumed the trek to the house. "Well," she said primly. "You're being so difficult I shouldn't even tell you that I decided not to go to Boston with Howard after all."

She expected him to be happy about the announcement, but if he was pleased at all he hid it well. "Don't stay on my account."

"I most certainly am *not* staying on your account, Ash Coleman." It was a lie, but she wouldn't grovel in front of any man, not even her husband. "I simply feel it would be inappropriate to so publicly support Howard. Felicity is my sister, after all, no matter what foolishness she's done."

"Whatever you want," he said in a low voice she had to strain to hear.

Everyone else had gone inside by the time Ash and Charmaine reached the front porch. They hesitated before the closed door, arm in arm still. He *could* lean down and kiss her. He *could* tell her he was happy she wasn't going to Boston. He *could* whisper *I love you*.

Instead of any of those pleasant options, he opened the door and led her inside.

* * *

314

"You can't mean it, Charmaine," Howard said in disbelief. "I need you. I can't hold my head up in Boston after what Felicity's done to me, not without your staunch support."

She'd managed to find a moment to pull Howard aside, asking him to join her in her father's study before dinner was served. Right off she'd told him she wasn't going to Boston, and she had expected a polite "I understand" in response. How mistaken she'd been.

"My place is here with Ash," she insisted. "Besides that, I can't publicly denounce my own sister, and that seems to be what you have in mind."

She'd never seen Howard so angry before. His fists balled at his sides, his eyes narrowed, and his face turned red. "She ran off with the *gardener!*"

"Are you angry because Felicity left you, or because she left with a servant? Goodness, Howard," she said quickly, reading the answer in his eyes, chastising him even though her initial response had been much the same.

"Yes," he said sharply, and with a stiff hand he slicked back his straight brown hair. She'd thought her sister's husband attractive enough in the past, if a bit small and sharp-featured. Right now he was downright ugly. "I'll admit it. Do you think I don't know my colleagues and friends are laughing behind my back? They're

315

having a grand time with this scandal, I can assure you."

"Some of them, perhaps," she admitted. "The more shallow of your acquaintances."

"*All* of them," he insisted. "Every last one."

He took a step toward her, and Charmaine nervously stepped back and toward the closed door.

"You must come back with me," he said softly. "They won't laugh at me, then. We won't let them." There was a glitter in his pale eyes she didn't like at all, a set to his mouth she didn't like at all. Howard was desperate, and he was determined not to leave her behind.

Charmaine was not one to easily admit defeat, but she recognized this as an argument she couldn't win. Not alone, in any case. Not now. With Ash beside her, Howard would have to accept her refusal. At the moment, her only objective was to get out of this room and away from Howard.

And she'd thought this would be easy.

"Let me think about it a bit more," she said, moving easily toward the door. "I didn't realize how very . . ." Desperate wasn't a word she could use. ". . . how very distraught you are over all this. Perhaps something can be arranged after all."

She didn't hear the door swing open, but when she turned around Ash was standing there, his hand on the doorknob, his eyes pinned on her. He didn't look at all surprised.

"Splendid!" Howard said grandly. "I knew we could work something out."

Charmaine kept her eyes on Ash. This was her chance to have this done with. In her heart she knew her husband wouldn't let her go. They could stand together and refuse Howard's unreasonable request here and now.

"Unless, of course, Ash objects. I hate to leave him on the farm all alone, he might need . . ."

"You do what you want," he said lowly. "Dinner's ready." And with that curt announcement, he spun around and walked away.

He'd rather be facedown in the pigsty again than sitting at Stuart Haley's dining room table with practically the entire clan. And to top it off they were all jabbering at once. Charmaine and Jeanette, sitting directly opposite Ash, had their fair heads together. Charmaine in her brilliant blue and Jeanette in her deep pink, they looked like two bright birds who would take off without warning and fly away. Their voices were soft, musical tones that drifted to him without clear meaning.

Neither of them had eaten much. How could they, unless they'd devised a way to eat and talk and be ladylike all at the same time? He imagined Felicity was a topic of conversation, as well as travel plans, but on occasion their eyes turned to him.

Maureen Haley, regal as always, was talking with Howard Stillwell, who sat at Ash's right. He did most of the talking, about the recent upheaval in his life. Ash could almost sympathize with the man, but he seemed more peeved than distressed, as if Felicity's departure were a great inconvenience.

Mrs. Haley did her best to comfort him, with soft words of consolation that struck Ash as slightly insincere.

Of course, Stuart Haley had to have his say, and his comments were directed first to Howard and then to his wife and on occasion to his daughters.

And then he looked Ash square in the eye. "Cattle," Haley said with a knowing nod of his head. "That's what your place needs."

He didn't want to have this conversation right now, but Haley was staring hard and waiting for a response. "I don't think so, sir."

Haley grinned. "Sure it is! I'll start you off with a few head. Let's call it a wedding present."

A wedding present? The man really was off his rocker. "No, thank you."

Haley's smile faded. "No reason to get snippy."

"Daddy, Ash wasn't snippy. You, however, are being your overbearing self once again."

Charmaine had apparently been paying attention to everything, not just her conversation with Jeanette. Dammit, he didn't want her fighting his battles for him.

"But it makes perfect sense," Haley said to Charmaine. "There's more money in beef than there is in wheat. I think about it and it just makes me sick, all that land, gone to waste."

"My land doesn't go to waste," Ash said through gritted teeth, and Haley turned his attention to this side of the table again.

"Sorry if you don't agree, son, but it makes no business sense at all for you to refuse a *gift* of several head of cattle. Independence is one thing. As a matter of fact I greatly admire independence. But bullheaded stubbornness is another thing altogether."

"Maybe you should hold a gun to my head until I agree to take those cattle home with me." The words were out of Ash's mouth before he thought, and they managed to silence the entire table. Charmaine's face went white, Maureen Haley pursed her lips, and Howard stared at the plate before him. Jeanette kicked him under the table.

"Why you . . ." Haley said, and with his hands on the table he started to rise.

Maureen put a stop to whatever Haley's intentions might have been. She stood quickly. "We have an announcement."

Stuart came to his feet, but he was staring at his wife, not at Ash. "Now?"

"Why not?" she sighed. "Everyone's here. We might as well get this over with."

"Is something wrong?" Charmaine asked. For the moment, everyone seemed to forget that Ash had just compared his wife to a side of beef.

Haley rounded the table quickly, and took his wife's hand. With a nod of her head, Maureen gave him permission to proceed.

Haley turned his eyes and his attention to his daughters. "Your mother and I are going to have another baby."

They waited for a reaction. Charmaine and Jeanette, side by side, wore almost identical stunned expressions.

Jeanette recovered first. "This is a joke, isn't it?" she said, and color flooded her face. "Well, it isn't very funny!"

Stuart shook his head, and a small smile crossed his face. "It's no joke, sweetheart. Come spring you're going to have a little brother or sister."

"Are you sure?" Charmaine asked, leaning slightly forward. "Absolutely without a doubt sure?"

It was Maureen who answered with a smile to match her husband's. "Absolutely without a doubt."

Howard was white as a sheet. "This is scandalous," he muttered.

"What?" Haley asked, his smile vanishing.

Howard lifted his head and smiled wanly. "I said, what a surprise this must be."

Haley relaxed. "Well, it was that. But it's a happy surprise."

Jeanette stood, a petulant frown on her face. "This is just not fair," she moaned. "You're a grandmother, for goodness sake." A single tear slipped down her cheek.

"It's certainly nothing for you to cry about," Maureen said rather sternly. "I'm the one having this child, not you."

"I don't mean to be selfish, really I don't," she sniffled. "But I so wanted you to come to Philadelphia in the spring to be with me when I have my first child, but you'll be *here* and I'll be a thousand miles away. It's just not fair."

"Jeanette," Maureen Haley said with a huge smile. She stepped away from her husband to give her daughter a hug. "Why didn't you tell me?"

"I was waiting for the perfect moment." Jeanette sniffled. "First there was Charmaine's situation, which I sorely misunderstood, and of course we're all terribly upset about Felicity, and I wanted the moment when I shared my news to be perfect."

"Any time you share such good news, it's perfect," Maureen assured her daughter.

Three of the four Haley women were expecting. Ash looked at an unusually quiet Charmaine, who'd shared her disappointment over not being pregnant just days ago. She was pale, but not unusually so. Her eyes found and held his, as if she knew what he was thinking. No matter what she said to appease him, he knew she was going to leave with Howard on Thursday and she wasn't coming back. Their chance had come and gone.

Ash was still angry, Felicity was God knew where with a *gardener*, and now this.

Charmaine paced in front of her seated mother and sister, here in the parlor that was Maureen Haley's domain. Jeanette occasionally wiped a single tear from her cheek, though she had reclaimed her composure and seemed to be suffering more from sentimentality than sorrow.

Their mother was calm as could be, smiling and happy, irrationally content. "Charmaine, would you sit down," she ordered softly. "You're making me dizzy."

Charmaine obliged, taking the nearest chair and sitting on the very edge. "I just don't understand how you could allow this to happen," she said sensibly. "There are ways to prevent conception, and for a woman of your age to even consider having a child is . . ."

"You overstep your bounds."

"But I don't understand. . . ."

"Perhaps you don't need to understand," her mother snapped.

Charmaine sunk back into her chair. Ash was furious with her, Howard thought that she'd decided to return with him to Boston, and now her mother was angry because she had dared to speak her mind.

She was not very diplomatic in her handling of delicate situations, she realized.

"Are you truly happy?" she asked, and her mother smiled.

"Yes. I wasn't at first, I must admit. This baby came as quite a surprise to your father and me, and I . . . I initially had the same reservations you do about carrying a child and giving birth at my age. But Doctor Whitfield assures me I'm healthy enough to see this baby through to the end, and it will be wonderful to have a child in this house again."

Jeanette dabbed at her eyes with a lace-trimmed handkerchief. "I didn't mean to cry. Lately it seems that I sob at the drop of a hat. Robert originally forbade me to come with Howard, but I cried so he finally relented. He would have come along, but one of the partners of his firm has him working a very important case."

"He must be thrilled," Charmaine said, an unwelcome envy rising within her. She, the woman who had declared so vehemently that she would never marry and have children, jealous because she was the only female in her family not carrying a child.

Ash would make a good father, when the time came. He was tenderhearted and protective and caring. The perfect father. The perfect husband. She could see it so clearly, the two of them surrounded by their children, filling that house with love and laughter. Ash could tell the children stories by the fire at night, and she would see that they were fed and clothed and well-read. She would teach her daughters to be strong and her sons to be tender.

What was it going to take to make Ash forgive her? He said he had, when she asked, but she didn't believe him. Ash Coleman was much too honest a man to be a successful liar. His eyes didn't catch and hold hers the way they once had, and he didn't smile at all anymore.

A stupid, impulsive telegram, and he just refused to ignore it! All she wanted was for him to smile at her again, was that so much to ask?

She was fooling herself. What she really wanted was for Ash to love her as deeply and completely as she loved him. She wanted everything. Love, family, happiness. She wanted to be Ash's one true love for all time.

Nothing else would do.

Chapter Twenty

Of all the people in the world to spend a Sunday afternoon with, Stuart Haley and Howard Stillwell were at the bottom of Ash's list.

Here in the very room where he'd heard Charmaine tell Stillwell that something could be arranged, Stuart Haley sat behind his desk and puffed on a fat cigar, and Stillwell sat in a comfortable chair with his hands in his lap and a pursed frown on his face. Ash stood near the door, poised for escape.

It was quite clear that neither Haley nor Stillwell was any happier with their present company than Ash was. Haley had muttered something insulting under his breath when both of his son-in-laws had declined his offer of an after-dinner cigar. When Howard had very primly refused the whiskey Haley poured, the old man had rolled his eyes in despair.

Ash had downed his whiskey in one swallow. And then he'd downed Howard's. He wasn't a drinking man, but by God it couldn't hurt.

The silence stretched uncomfortably, but when Howard opened his mouth Ash wished for a few more precious moments of quiet.

"I understand you had quite an interesting wedding," he said, his beady eyes fastened on Ash.

"You could call it that."

Howard shook his head slowly. "What kind of uncivilized place is this, where a woman can be forced to marry at gunpoint?"

"It's just a minor detail," Ash said sharply, "but the gun was pointed at *me.*"

Howard turned his attentions to the man behind the desk. "Charmaine doesn't belong here, and she certainly doesn't belong on a . . . on a *farm.*" He actually shuddered, as if revolted at the very idea. "It's unthinkable that a woman like Charmaine might spend her entire life hidden away in this dreary section of the country in that dreary little house. What an unconscionable waste. She's intelligent and forthright and in Boston, with my help, she can make a difference in this rapidly decaying world we live in."

"Hogwash," Stuart said without hesitation.

"Charmaine made her choice when she dallied in the gazebo while she should have been dancing and behaving like a proper young lady." If looks could kill, Ash knew he'd be dead now.

"Even a young woman who shows a rare lapse of good judgement should be allowed to choose her own husband, or even the right to live a full and happy life without one," Howard insisted. "Charmaine is curious, astute, charming. She has such potential in Boston. Did you know she was considering writing a manual of her own? Her role in my seminars has grown steadily, and in a few years she might even have given lectures of her own. A woman like that will never be happy on a farm."

The hell of it was, Howard Stillwell was right. Ash sauntered to Haley's desk and poured another whiskey. For courage. To kill the pain of the truth. "To be perfectly honest," he said as he studied the short glass that was filled to the rim, "there was no dallying going on that night." He tossed the whiskey back, emptying the glass and then forcefully returning it to the desk.

He grinned widely at the man before him. "That's right, Stuart, you shot me for nothing."

Haley's face turned an alarming shade of red. "Charmaine admitted to me herself . . ."

"Charmaine said what she thought she had to say to get back to Boston. You made a wrong assumption when you stumbled on us that night, and she went along with it so she could

327

go back where she belongs." He refilled his glass with whiskey. "Where she wants to be."

"Poor dear," Howard mumbled. "She must have been terrified."

"Yeah," Ash said, and his voice slurred just a little. Terrified of being stuck in this place for the rest of her life. Terrified of being married to a sodbuster. He downed this glass as quickly as he had the last one, tossing it back and relishing the burn. "So when you take her to Boston on Thursday . . . keep her there."

His insides flamed. It was the whiskey, but more than that it was the certainty that no matter how much it hurt, this was best for Charmaine.

Stuart shot to his feet. "You can't put my daughter aside like this."

Ash forced a smile, and with both hands he ripped his shirt open. Buttons dropped to the floor as he presented Stuart Haley his heart. "Shoot me," he said, his smile never fading. "Go ahead. I know you, Haley, you've got a six-shooter in one of those drawers, maybe a derringer up your sleeve. Put me out of my misery."

He might as well be dead. Charmaine deserved better. She deserved a choice, a bright and beautiful life, and what she wanted—what she'd always wanted—was Boston. He wouldn't sit around and mope, knowing in his head that she wasn't coming back, hoping in his heart that she would. It would be pure hell.

Ash's head pounded, and he could feel every heartbeat in his chest, the rush of heated blood through his veins. Haley stared at him like he was crazy, and maybe he was.

He had to get out of here. Haley would tell Charmaine that she was free at long last . . . he sure couldn't do it himself. He couldn't look at Charmaine and smile and wish her a nice life in Boston and pretend it wasn't killing him to send her away.

Ash turned his back on Haley and Stillwell and stalked from the room, slamming the door behind him. The hallway to the front door was incredibly long, and if he didn't get out of here soon he was going to suffocate.

A doorway near the front door opened slowly, and Charmaine stepped into the hall, placing herself between Ash and an easy escape. Jeanette and Mrs. Haley were close behind her, looking curiously his way. Why had he slammed the damned door! He should have left quietly, sneaking out like the coward he was.

Charmaine looked him up and down, and the response in her eyes and her expressive face was one of concern and . . . no, not love. "What's wrong?"

He wanted to tell her nothing was wrong. He wanted to assure her that everything was fine and take her home.

But nothing was fine. His life would never be *fine* again. Because the only way to make Charmaine truly happy was to let her go.

She'd proved it to him again and again.

That would show Daddy, wouldn't it, if I spent the entire evening dancing with a Coleman.

I do! I do, I do, I do!

I never had any intention of staying here. . . .

Married to Ash Coleman. Please save me.

"Ash?" she prompted.

His head swam, the hallway and the women in it tilted slightly to one side. Dammit, he didn't drink. Why had he downed Haley's whiskey like an old drunk?

Charmaine waited a moment for a response, and then she came toward him. Floating, like something out of a dream. Frowning, knowing just by looking at him that something was terribly, terribly wrong.

Before she reached him he stepped away, skirting around her and heading for the door. "I need to speak to you outside," he said softly.

They were rounding the house, headed for the stables, when Charmaine was finally able to snag Ash's arm and force him to turn around. An ominously cold gust of wind chilled her.

Ash stood before her with his gray jacket askew and his shirt hanging open and an icy gleam in his usually warm green eyes.

"I think you should stay here until Thursday." He brushed a strand of windblown hair from his eyes. "I'll bring your things by tomorrow."

"What?" His words were perfectly clear, but she didn't understand. "Why would I stay here? I told you I decided not to—"

"It's over," he interrupted her. "You go back to Boston and stay there, and I'll . . . I'll find myself another wife."

"Another wife? Ash!" She grabbed a flapping bit of his dancing shirt. "What is this? Did Daddy—"

He knocked her hand gently away, the way he might swat away a bothersome fly. "*Daddy* has nothing to do with this," he said gruffly. "A man should have a choice when it comes to the woman he's going to spend his life with. Neither of us had a choice, Runt, and I don't know about you, but I don't like having cattle *or* women forced on me."

She dropped her hand and took a step back. "But I thought we decided . . ."

"We had fun in bed," he said coldly. "And on the table, and on the floor in front of the fire, and that one time in the barn." He actually smirked, making all those wonderful memories somehow shameful. "But I don't think either of us should make important decisions based on . . . what did you call it? Lower impulses. Magnetic forces. Most people just call it lust. Whatever the hell it was, I imagine it will be the same with any other woman."

"Ash!"

"I'll find out soon enough."

331

It couldn't be true.

But she'd seen how miserable he'd been all day, on the ride to town and all through dinner. "You've been planning this all along, haven't you?"

He shrugged broad shoulders. "Just since your sister and Howard came to the farm to save you. It's the perfect solution. You've got your escort back to Boston, and with Verna and her boys out of the way I can have my pick of women from hereabouts."

"Your *pick!*"

Ash grinned at her, but it wasn't the warm smile she was accustomed to. It was positively wicked. "Any comely woman who can cook a decent meal and warm my bed will do."

She didn't believe him. Couldn't. What they had was special, and he couldn't just send her away without a care. She searched for an explanation, and quickly found one. "It's the telegram, isn't it?" she whispered. "You can't forgive me for that one impetuous mistake."

He took a moment to give her reasoning serious thought, and then he averted his eyes. "Yeah, that's it. 'Married to Ash Coleman. Please save me.'"

"That was before—"

"Besides, with Verna and the boys gone, I can have the place to myself for a while. It's what I always wanted, you know. Peace and quiet. A home that's a haven, not a battleground." He swayed a little, as if the wind was driving him back.

"You're drunk!"

He shook his head, and Charmaine leaned forward to smell the whiskey on his breath. "I am not," he said steadily. "I'm clearheaded, for once, and I know exactly what I want."

She didn't want to know. She had to ask. "And what's that?"

"I want you to go back to Boston." He swayed slightly as a gust buffeted them, but his eyes were clear and steady. "Hell, maybe you can even write a manual about us, and stand up in front of an interested crowd and analyze the most intimate aspects of this farce of a marriage."

"I would never—"

He continued as if he didn't hear. "I want to choose my own wife, next time, and I just . . . I just want this nightmare to be over."

Charmaine spun around before Ash could see the tears that sprung to her eyes. A nightmare! Their marriage was a *nightmare*? It hurt, more than she'd ever known words could. She wouldn't break down and cry in front of him! Not now, not ever.

Of course he wanted to choose his own wife. She couldn't blame him, could she? For not loving her, for being unforgiving, for wanting to have a say in his own future. Back straight, she walked away.

* * *

"What did you say to Ash?" Maureen demanded once again.

Stuart spread his arms, palms upward in supplication. "Nothing. I swear it. We were having a perfectly normal conversation, and then he went berserk." That was close enough to the truth, he decided. He didn't want to upset Maureen any more than she already was.

"Charmaine wants to go back to Boston. It's what she's wanted all along, and maybe we should take her wishes into consideration," he said reasonably.

Maureen came up off the sofa like a shot. "Ha! You don't care a whit for Charmaine's wishes or anyone else's. You're the most selfish man I've ever known! If I wasn't carrying another child, you'd be doing your damnedest to see that Charmaine stays here with Ash."

It wasn't good for her to get excited like this. He took her arm and sat on the sofa, forcing her to come with him. "It was foolish of me to think I could make Charmaine marry someone she doesn't love. I was foolish . . ."

"But she does love Ash, I just know it," Maureen said despairingly. "And now he's broken her heart and she's miserable. You did this, somehow, and you're going to have to fix it!"

When Charmaine had come back into the house, tears streamed down her face. She made not a sound, and it was the eeriest, most heartbreaking picture he'd ever seen. Charmaine with her back straight and her head held high and those tears that just wouldn't stop. She hadn't answered anyone's questions, she'd climbed the stairs without making a sound and closed herself in her room. That had been hours ago, and there hadn't been so much as a stirring from that room since.

And he should know. He'd pressed his ear to the locked door of her bedroom more than once, straining to hear something—anything. If he hadn't heard the bed squeak just once, he would have broken the door down to make sure Charmaine was all right.

Fix it?

"I don't think I can, Maureen."

Charmaine opened the window and welcomed the cold air that rushed over her body. Some time ago she'd gone through the ritual of preparing herself for bed, removing her dress and stockings, washing her face and braiding her hair. Her chemise would do for sleepwear tonight.

Cold air washed over her bare arms and her damp face. She should be dry by now, completely drained of tears, but when she least expected it they came back.

She knew, had known all along, that Ash didn't love her. How could he? She'd been forced upon him like those cattle Daddy had tried to give him. But things had changed, hadn't they? She and Ash had laughed and talked and begun to appreciate one another. He had to feel something for her besides lust.

But apparently any woman would do.

A fresh onslaught of tears took her by surprise. This was his way of getting revenge. Forced to marry her against his will, he'd made her love him, he'd made her think that they could have a life together. He'd used her body and her heart against her, asked her to stay forever, made her think he needed her . . . made her think she needed him.

And then, when she'd been certain of their future and her love, he'd taken it away. Without warning, without care. With a few simple words that shook her faith and her love.

He'd surely been pretending all along. Their brief marriage had been as much a charade as the masked ball. Only instead of black leather he'd worn a much more complete mask. The mask of a caring and tender man. A mask of love and longing.

He was an actor, like his mother. A very good one to be able to pretend so well. At least she had the comfort of having never confessed her true feelings. Ash would never know how much she'd come to love him.

Perhaps one day she'd be able to pretend herself. To pretend that she hadn't hoped for so very much from this unexpected marriage. To pretend that her heart and her soul weren't irrevocably crushed. Maybe she'd even be able to fool herself . . . but she doubted it.

The knock on the door was so soft she thought for a moment she'd imagined it. As she turned away from the window it came again. She didn't want to see or speak to anyone, not tonight.

"Charmaine, dear, are you awake?" Howard's whisper was hoarse and soft.

She didn't answer. Surely if he thought she was asleep he'd go away. Anything he had to say to her would wait until morning.

"Charmaine?" he called again, and the doorknob rattled slightly. Fortunately, it was locked.

She took a silent step closer to the door. What on earth was he thinking, coming to her room at this time of night? It was highly inappropriate and very unlike the Howard Stillwell she knew.

But then, the man she'd faced in the study was very unlike the Howard she remembered. Desperate, angry, insistent.

"Don't worry, my poor dear Charmaine. I'll take care of you," he whispered. "You have my word on that." The doorknob moved, ever so slightly, as if he were checking again to make sure it was locked.

There was a slight brushing sound, as if he ran his hands over the door or leaned against

337

it. She didn't move, afraid that if he heard her he wouldn't go away.

"We don't need them," he said softly, after the passing of a few silent minutes. Surely he thought her to be asleep. She hadn't said a word, hadn't made so much as a sound. "We have . . . each other."

Charmaine hugged her arms to herself, warding off the sudden chill that had nothing to do with the night air. There was something very wrong with Howard whispering so intimately at her door. *We don't need them.* Them, of course, being Felicity and Ash.

That in itself was disturbing, but was not nearly as troublesome as those whispered words *each other.* As if they were a team or a . . . a couple.

No matter what Ash said, she was not returning to Boston with Howard. The very idea was suddenly more than distressing. It was revolting. She'd been blind to the real Howard just as surely as she'd been blind, for so long, to the real Ash.

No one could be trusted.

There was the sound of a soft footfall in the hallway, as Howard finally moved away from her door. Charmaine sighed with relief, and vowed with a shudder to lock her door every night until he left.

Chapter Twenty-one

Her things were left on the doorstep sometime before dawn, in a trunk that had been neatly packed and quietly delivered. It was a final blow, a dismal reminder that her marriage was over.

A marriage she'd never wanted, a marriage she'd sworn from the beginning to leave behind.

Charmaine spent most of the morning Monday hiding in her room and unpacking her clothes. She didn't want to face Howard. She didn't want to face *anyone*.

She tried to keep her mind on the simple tasks at hand. Hanging the dresses in her wardrobe, folding her blouses and skirts and underthings and placing them in the proper drawers in the massive chest against one wall. She noted a blouse that needed to be mended, and a skirt that she might as well dispose of, it was so tattered at the hem. But her mind invariably wandered to Ash and the farm, and she even found herself wondering what he was eating and if he was sleeping.

She didn't care, she told herself again and again. *Any* woman would do, she reminded herself.

When the knock on her door came, her heart lurched into her throat. She didn't want to speak to Howard, not after that odd whisper at her door last night. But the door swung slowly open and Jeanette slipped into the room, closing the door behind her.

"Are you all right?" Jeanette appeared to be truly concerned, with a frown on her pretty face and hands clenched tightly at her waist.

"Of course," Charmaine said in her most reasonable voice. "Why wouldn't I be?"

The answer seemed to satisfy Jeanette, for the moment.

"Why are you unpacking all these clothes?" Jeanette took a skirt from the bottom of the trunk and shook it out to loose the wrinkles. "You should take out what you'll need for the week and choose a traveling outfit and leave the rest packed," she said as she refolded the skirt neatly.

"I'm not leaving."

Jeanette stopped, and held the folded skirt to her chest. "Well then, what are you going to do? Howard said you'd be traveling with us."

Howard. She had a feeling he had more to do with this than she knew. "I haven't told him yet that I've decided definitely to stay in Salley Creek. When we spoke about it last I did say that perhaps something could be arranged, but . . . but it was a lie. I had no intention, even before . . . of leaving."

Jeanette sat on the edge of the bed, the skirt now a wadded ball in her hands. "You're staying."

"Mother will need my help," Charmaine said sensibly, "and besides . . . there's nothing in Boston for me, not really."

"What about your seminars and lectures with Howard?"

She couldn't tell Jeanette about the odd whisper at her door last night, or how Howard's words sent unpleasant chills up her spine. "I'm needed here."

She waited for a speech on how she would be wasting her life in this tiny town . . . but Jeanette simply sighed. "I wish I were staying."

"You do?"

"Not without Robert, of course, but . . . I do miss home, terribly some days."

Charmaine sat cross-legged on the floor and faced her sister. "I thought you loved the city."

"I did, at first," Jeanette practically pouted. "But I've seen everything there is to see there, and now it's simply tiresome. Some days I long for a home where everyone knows everyone else, and you don't have to go to such lengths to impress people who pretend to be your friends but really aren't."

"I know what you mean."

"But Robert's job is in Philadelphia, and he loves what he does, most of the time. And I love him, so there I'll stay." She sighed again. "Maybe things will be different after the baby's born."

Charmaine couldn't tell Jeanette how she envied her the child she carried. It would reveal too much.

"I have to finish unpacking these things," she said, rocking up onto her knees and peering into the trunk. What she saw there stilled her heartbeat and brought a fresh tear to her eyes. There, at the bottom of the almost empty trunk, was her mask, the white and peach creation with pearls dripping from the edge. Ash had kept it, all this time, but now he had no interest in hanging on to it. He was getting rid of everything, evidently.

Most especially, he was getting rid of *her*.

His head ached, and the field before him tilted ever so slightly in his distorted view. Ash closed his eyes for a moment. The winter wheat

342

was doing well, with the temperate weather and the goodly amount of rain they'd had lately, and would be well established before the first frost. Next year would be a good one.

Next year would be a lonely one.

The two hours of sleep he'd gotten last night had come on the floor in front of the fireplace. He probably wouldn't have slept at all, but the whiskey had made him finally drop off there. When he woke he was sore from sleeping on the hard floor and had one hell of a headache that was still with him.

In that moment, a moment of pure panic as he'd lifted his head from the floor, he wondered what he'd done—but a moment later he remembered that he'd only done what was best for Charmaine.

By that time her trunk was already packed and sitting by the door. He'd placed her belongings in that trunk as soon as he'd returned home from the Haley house, making damn sure he didn't linger over this dress or that, or hold her hairbrush too long in his hands.

He'd pulled out well before dawn to deliver that trunk, to get that chore done while he still could. There had been a moment of doubt as he'd placed that trunk carefully on the Haley front porch, a moment when he'd considered walking through that door and up the stairs and knocking on door after door until he found Charmaine's room.

He didn't do any such thing, of course. After returning to the farm he'd found enough work to keep him busy all morning, hard physical labor that wouldn't give him time to think. It almost worked.

The worst of it was coming into the house for the noon meal. He was all alone, and there was no warm and welcoming fire, no waiting dinner or the smells filling the house, no laughter or kiss or hug. . . .

This was what he'd always wanted, wasn't it? To work and live on this farm alone, to have peace and quiet. To be his own man. When the time came he'd take another wife. Hell, he was no martyr who'd live out his days as a hermit and moan about what he had almost had. He'd marry, one day, and fill the house with children and be a good husband and father—but he'd never love another woman the way he loved Charmaine.

Walking back to the house, he passed the pond. They'd never had a chance to skate there. They'd never had a chance to do a lot of things. . . .

The confrontation was inevitable. Charmaine had successfully avoided Howard all day, but before supper he found her in the parlor. Alone, as her mother had excused herself with an untimely bout of nausea and Jeanette's sympathetic reaction had sent her scurrying from the room a moment later.

"There you are."

Howard's cheerful greeting from the doorway startled her, and she spun to face him warily. "Good evening, Howard," she said formally.

He swept into the room with a falsely concerned frown on his face. "How are you, my dear?" He took both of her hands in his own and leaned much too close.

"I'm afraid I'm not feeling well," she said, slipping her hands from his and backing away. "I really should rest before supper." She tried to walk past him, but he sidestepped into her path.

"You'll feel better when we get to Boston," he said lowly, and then he placed his hand on her arm. "I promise you that."

She took a step back and his arm fell away. "Howard, I'm not going back to Boston. I'm staying here."

The expression on his face frightened her. Pure rage flitted briefly across his features. "You can't mean that."

"I do," she said firmly. "I'm going to stay here and help my mother, and . . . and . . ." And try to win Ash back? Was it possible? No. If he'd wanted her he never would have left her here and talked so calmly about choosing another wife. "And besides, it wouldn't be proper for me to stay with you with Felicity out of the house."

"But I need you," he reached forward and

345

grabbed her arm, his hand a tight vise at her elbow. "The lectures are not as well attended when you're not there, and donations to my fund suffered while you were away. With the scandal of Felicity's betrayal shadowing my every move, I need you to stand beside me and support me, Charmaine. Don't desert me now."

"I can't, Howard. Let me go," she insisted, squirming ineffectively. The grip at her elbow held fast.

Howard leaned closer, so near she could feel his breath against her face. "And as for propriety, when your divorce and mine are final, we can marry."

"What?"

"If I'd met you before I married Felicity, I would have done everything in my power to make you my wife." His lips brushed her cheek. "We are meant to be, Charmaine. I knew it the first moment I saw you. Surely you felt it, too."

"Howard!" She leaned away from those cold lips. "Don't be ridiculous. Stop this nonsense and release me!"

He gripped her chin in his hand and forced her to be still while he laid his lips on hers. It was revolting, cold and wet and repulsive. She pressed her lips tightly together and struggled against his greater strength.

Finally, he lifted his mouth from hers to whisper. "You must come to Boston with me."

Charmaine stilled her struggling, which was

to no avail in any case, and lifted her face to stare coldly into Howard's gray eyes. "If you so much as touch me again, I'll have my father shoot you. He will, you know, and I won't have to ask twice." She kept her voice calm. "He shot Ash for kissing me, and I was a very willing participant in that kiss. What do you think he will do to you when I tell him you molested me?"

"I certainly did not molest you," Howard said as he released her. He was afraid of her father, afraid of this unrefined world he couldn't control. She could see that in his eyes and in the sudden change in his demeanor. "This was mentioned yesterday, I believe. Stuart actually shot your, ummm . . . husband?"

"In the leg," she said, stepping quickly to the door to make her escape. "He was trying to kill him, of course, but Ash was quite a distance away." She turned in the doorway, wanting to watch this little man squirm. "How fast can you run, Howard?"

She didn't wait for an answer, but left Howard to grapple with his limited imagination.

The open window let in a cold wind that filled every corner of the dark room. It washed over his body, reminding him that no matter how dead he felt, he was still alive.

He'd likely never sleep again. Ash lay on his back in the bed he'd shared—for a while—with Charmaine. She was still here, even though everything that belonged to her, everything that reminded him of her, was gone. He could feel her in the air, smell her on the bed, and there was a piece of her heart that remained in his. It would fade with time, he was sure, diminish a little every day until she was truly gone. And if it didn't . . . God help him.

He'd survived a full day without her, if you could call this misery surviving. If he loved Charmaine a little less he'd make his way to the Haley house and claim his wife and bring her home. He'd make her sacrifice everything she wanted to be his wife. To sleep in this bed with him every night, to have his children and fill this empty house with love. To be his family.

There would be no sleep tonight, nothing but the snatches of restless dreams his body claimed when exhaustion took over.

He wished he loved her a little less.

Tuesday afternoon, as Charmaine was discussing baby names over tea in the parlor with her mother and Jeanette, someone pounded furiously on the door. Her first thought was *Ash has come to his senses*, but it was a hope that died quickly, well before Jane opened the front door.

Felicity appeared at the parlor door, wide eyed and travel weary, and a moment later Tavish was behind her; he was a full head taller and had Felicity's daughter Hester, cradled easily in his large arms.

A darker head appeared beside and slightly below Tavish's red one, and Jeanette came up in a shot.

"Robert!"

Felicity and Tavish stepped aside so Jeanette's husband could enter the room. He was such a handsome gentleman, well groomed and well dressed, with a face almost perfectly proportioned and eyes the color of black coffee.

"What are you doing here?" Jeanette said as he took her hands in his. "Oh, something must be terribly wrong."

"This telegram came after you left." He reached into an inside pocket of his jacket and withdrew a crumpled piece of paper. "It seemed important."

"You could have sent a telegram yourself," Jeanette said as her husband handed her the paper. "There was no need to come all this way." She unfolded the paper in her hand, read it quickly, and gave Charmaine a pitying glance. "Oh, I'm so sorry."

Charmaine reached out and took the telegram from Jeanette. Without reviewing the words, she folded the paper twice.

"But still," Jeanette said to her husband. "You didn't have to come all this way. What about your important case?"

Robert gave his wife a quick kiss. "I've left the

firm," he said without further preamble.

"Oh, Robert," Jeanette whispered.

"It's been a long time coming, darling. You know that."

They sat silently side by side on the sofa.

"He left," Felicity said softly, "because they objected to him handling my divorce." She continued to stand in the doorway, perhaps afraid to come in and find out what sort of reception she would receive. "They said it was distasteful and scandalous, and they would not have their firm associated with such a case."

Charmaine watched her mother step quickly to the door to wrap her arms around Felicity in a welcoming hug. Relief flooded Felicity's face, and her eyes filled with tears.

"He's here, isn't he?" she whispered. "Howard's here, that's what Robert said."

Tavish got a disapproving glare from Maureen, who lowered her gaze to her granddaughter with a wide smile and a "gootchy-goo." She started to take the tot from Tavish, but Charmaine was there before she could.

"You shouldn't, Mother," Charmaine said as she scooped Hester into her arms. "She's much heavier than she looks."

"Nonsense. I'm perfectly capable of holding my granddaughter." Charmaine had no choice but to place Hester in her grandmother's arms.

"Charmaine," her mother said as she sat with Hester cradled in her arms, "tell Jane we'll be eight for dinner tonight." She glimpsed briefly and sharply at Tavish. "Though I imagine we'll have to eat in shifts to avoid unpleasant scenes."

Tavish said nothing, had not said a word since stepping into the Haley house. Maureen Haley, usually so proper and sweet, would have none of that.

"Well? What do you have to say for yourself, young man?" she asked sharply.

Tavish stepped just past Felicity to face Maureen Haley bravely. He was bigger even than Ash, a good six-foot-three with a broad chest and massive arms, and there was nothing pretty or gentle about his face. That face was rugged, as if it had been battered and weathered for all its time on this earth.

Tavish wasn't dressed in a fine suit of clothes, as Robert was, but sported a well-worn shirt and brown twill pants and a heavy coat. "All I have to say for myself, ma'am," he said in a deep Scottish brogue, "is that I love your daughter, and I love her daughter as well, and I couldna stand to see them treated as they were. No man, no matter how important or rich or educated, should be allowed to strike a woman when it takes his fancy."

"Tavish!" Felicity hissed.

He took Felicity's hand in his and turned a loving face her way, and in that moment he was beautiful. "They love you too, and they have a right to know the truth, no matter how painful it might be."

Charmaine had never seen her mother look like she could do anyone physical harm—until this very moment.

"Close the door, Charmaine," she ordered. "And hold off on informing Jane on the number we'll be for dinner. I think we all need to have a nice long talk first."

Burned bacon, eggs that were half-scrambled and half-fried, and a slice of leftover apple pie. Ash played with his supper. If he was going to have to cook for himself for a while, and it looked as if he would, he'd have to stock up on beans, some canned vegetables, and maybe a loaf of that bread Eula sold at her mercantile.

Of course, restocking the kitchen would have to wait. He wouldn't take the chance of running into Charmaine in town, so there was no way he could make the trip before Friday. If he saw her he was likely to toss her over his shoulder and carry her home, just as he had on their wedding day.

He hadn't expected to miss her so much it hurt, but he did. From the beginning . . . from the first dance, the first kiss, the impulse that had commanded him to throw her over his shoulder and carry her home . . . he'd known she wouldn't stay, that she would never be happy here.

So why was he feeling so goddamned sorry for himself?

He hadn't expected a quiet house to grate on his nerves the way it did. He could almost—*almost*—wish for Elmo's whining and Oswald's complaints and Verna's nagging to fill the silence. Maybe then he wouldn't be so certain he'd made the mistake of his life in sending Charmaine away.

Howard never had a chance.

He came downstairs expecting a quiet dinner for five, and was greeted well short of the dining room door by an impenetrable wall of outraged Haleys and their chosen mates.

It gave Stuart great pleasure to step forward and confront the pompous ass.

Howard's eyes went past Stuart to Felicity and the towering Tavish. "What are you doing here?" Not a word about the exhausted child who was sleeping in Jane's arms in the kitchen. No *Where's my daughter?* or *Is Hester here?*

"Stillwell," Stuart said softly, commanding the man's attention. "Did you hit my daughter?"

He sputtered, turned red, and mumbled a "well I never" and something about unfair odds.

"A coherent answer, if you please," Stuart demanded.

It took Howard a moment to gather his composure. "There were occasions where I felt it necessary to reprimand Felicity. She has an unnecessarily flighty side to her nature, as you well know. As her husband, it was my right to discipline her."

"How could you?" Charmaine stepped forward to plant herself defiantly at Stuart's side. Her hands were balled fists, her eyes blazed. "All your talk about equality and honesty and—"

"Charmaine," Stuart interrupted. "Go stand with your sisters." Amazingly enough, she obeyed.

Stuart faced Stillwell, alone but with the strength of his family behind him. "As Felicity's father, it's my right to kick your scrawny butt out of my house and tell you never to darken my door again. It's also my right to advise you not to show your face around town before the Thursday train. Word spreads fast in Salley Creek, and we don't take to wife-beating here."

"It was hardly wife-beating," Howard defended himself with a roll of his eyes. "An occasional scolding, that's all."

"An occasional scolding with a riding crop, from the look of her back." Tavish said with quiet menace. He took a single step forward, and Howard took a couple of quick steps backwards. "Mr. Haley," the big man continued. "It would be my great honor to assist Mr. Stillwell from your home. With your permission, of course."

"Permission granted."

In the blink of an eye Tavish had Howard in

his grasp, an arm around his neck, another around his waist as he lifted the little man from his feet.

"I can't believe I was ever associated with this family!" Howard shouted, his voice reverberating with Tavish's steps. "You're all demented, and . . . and you breed like rabbits!"

"I'll have your things delivered to the hotel," Stuart called out as Tavish carried Howard to the front door. He followed, then gleefully stepped ahead of Tavish to open the front door. With a mighty heave, Howard Stillwell was tossed onto the front porch.

The slamming of the door was like a gunshot.

"Thank you, sir," Tavish said softly. "I've been wanting to do that for a long time."

Stuart had to look up to see the man's face. A Scot, for God's sake.

Tavish returned to Felicity's side, and Charmaine hurried to her father. The look on her face was not a happy one.

"I needed to handle this myself, and that's why I shooed you back," he began, explaining away his actions before she had a chance to lambast him.

"That's not why I'm so angry," she snapped. "You pull a gun on Ash at the drop of a hat, even blacken his eye. Howard is guilty of a heinous offense, and you don't so much as raise a hand."

He placed an arm around his youngest daughter's shoulder. "I would've killed him, if

I'd raised a gun. I would've beat him to death if I'd raised a hand." It was the truth.

"I can't believe I never saw, that Felicity never told me what was happening. I thought I knew Howard, that he was a good and decent person, but I was blind." There was a forlorn quality in Charmaine's voice, the kind of pain that would break any father's heart. "I thought I was so darn smart, but I didn't see anything clearly. I didn't know people the way I thought I did. Not at all."

He stopped her there in the hallway and placed both hands on her shoulders. "Are you terribly disappointed that you won't be returning to Boston right away?"

She shook her head, and her eyes filled with tears. "I can't go back there. Even before I found out what kind of man Howard was, I knew I couldn't return to Boston and simply take up where I left off. It's not what I want anymore."

"What do you want?"

A single tear ran down her face. "I want Ash."

"Then you'll have him," he declared with finality.

Charmaine shook her head quickly. "No. He doesn't love me, he doesn't want me, and I won't have you interfering this time. I don't want him back at gunpoint!"

His daughters would have what they wanted. The best clothes, the best education . . . huge Scots, city-bred lawyers, even sodbusters.

Maybe in this case the truth was a more effective weapon than a six-shooter. "I don't know if you realize it or not, but Howard said some pretty strong words to Ash on Sunday afternoon."

"Like what?" she snapped, her tears drying quickly.

"That you were too bright and beautiful to be stuck on a farm for the rest of your life. That you were . . . wasted here, and you deserved better."

"You didn't *stop* him?"

Stuart tightened his fingers. "Maybe in my heart I agreed with him. After all I've done to keep you here . . ."

In spite of the tight grip on her shoulders, Charmaine backed away. "This is the worst thing you've ever done to me," she accused. "How can I ever forgive you?"

"Charmaine . . ."

She turned from him and ran to the stairs, hurried up the steps with her skirt held in both hands, and disappeared into the upstairs hallway. A moment later, the door to her room slammed with as much force as the front door had slammed shut on Howard minutes earlier.

Chapter Twenty-two

Morning light made her dreary world seem horribly bright and warm. The remaining red leaves on the maple tree outside her window danced playfully in the wind, brushing the windowpanes and calling to Charmaine, reminding her that life was rich and beautiful and forever changing.

She unfolded the telegram in her hand and read once again. As she'd read it by candlelight last night and by the rays of the rising sun this morning.

Disregard previous telegram. I seem to be falling in love with my husband!

If Ash had seen this telegram when he'd seen

the other, would he have forgiven her? If she showed it to him now, would it make a difference? Perhaps, perhaps not. It all depended on whether or not he loved her, too. She believed, in some hopeful moments, that he did love her. She'd seen it in his eyes, felt it in his touch . . . no one was that good an actor.

Her heart lurched when the knock came at the door, and then she remembered that Howard was gone from this house and wouldn't dare to return.

"Come in."

The door swung open, and Felicity poked her head into the room. "Are you sure?"

Charmaine folded the telegram and set it on her bedside table. She went to the door, took Felicity's hand, and pulled her sister gently into the room. "Of course I'm sure."

They hadn't had a moment alone since Felicity's arrival. Last night Charmaine had stayed in her room, and Felicity had surely retired early after her long trip. There was so much to be said.

"Why did you never tell me?" Charmaine asked. She accompanied her question with a hug Felicity responded to.

"How could I? I was so ashamed." Felicity placed her head on Charmaine's shoulder. "And you adored Howard so."

"I didn't adore him, I admired him," Charmaine said sternly. "And I certainly wouldn't have felt a smidgen of admiration for him if I'd known what was going on, if I'd had any inkling of the kind of man he was." Felicity didn't need to know about Howard's advances, his foolish declaration that they were meant to be together. She set herself back and looked Felicity squarely in her deep brown eyes. "You should have come to me."

Felicity sniffled. "That's what Tavish says, what he said all along."

"Tavish," Charmaine said, her hands on her hips. "Now that's another surprise. I had no idea—"

"You were so caught up with Howard's work," Felicity interrupted. "I couldn't very well admit to you that I'd fallen in love with another man. A man more tender than Howard will ever be, a gentle and loving man who made me realize that there's more to love than sacrifice and pain."

"He's good to you, is he?"

Felicity's eyes were suddenly bright. "He is. Tavish saved me, Charmaine."

"I have to know," Charmaine said sternly. "Is Tavish his first name or his last?"

That got a smile from Felicity. "His first. Tavish Alexander Ewan Dougald MacCullen."

"That's a mouthful," Charmaine said with a smile of her own.

"Daddy's making him sleep in the bunkhouse," Felicity confided. "I imagine he'll either shoot him or put him to work before the week is out."

"Daddy shot Ash."

Felicity paled and her smile disappeared. "He did? I was just kidding. . . ."

"It was just a scratch," Charmaine amended. "And he didn't know it was Ash at the time."

That news didn't console Felicity at all. "I have to warn Tavish."

The door opened, and Jeanette slipped into the room and closed the door behind her. "What are you two talking about? I was headed down for breakfast and I heard these little voices chattering away."

"Nothing important," Felicity said quickly. "I have to run. . . ."

"Wait." Jeanette came to them and placed an arm over each sister's shoulder. "I have news."

"More news?" Charmaine said lightly. "I don't know that I can take more news for at least a few days."

Jeanette ignored her. "We're staying!" she said gleefully. "Robert and I discussed it last night, and then Robert talked to Daddy bright and early this morning, and we're going to stay!"

"Robert's not going to take up ranching, is he?" Charmaine asked dubiously. She couldn't imagine the refined man living her father's lifestyle.

"Of course not," Jeanette said sensibly.

"Small towns need lawyers too, you know."

"We're staying, too," Felicity said softly, "if Daddy doesn't shoot Tavish," she added forlornly.

They put their heads together, the way they had as little girls. Charmaine was still the runt, the little one, the baby. Right now that didn't seem so bad.

"Just imagine it," she said. "The three of us, here in Salley Creek again."

"We'll turn this town on its ear," Jeanette whispered.

"They'll never know what hit them," Felicity said with a smile.

"And what are we going to do about Ash?" Jeanette asked in a no-nonsense voice.

"Nothing." Charmaine drew away slightly. "We're going to do absolutely nothing."

She was pinned between her sisters, and they gave her matching devilish smiles.

"Nothing?" Felicity repeated. "Think again, Runt."

Tomorrow Charmaine would be gone. Ash paced in front of the fire, half-crazy with lack of sleep and missing his wife.

Principle was all well and good, but just how much sacrifice was a man supposed to make in the name of what was right? And . . . a horrible thought . . . what if he was wrong? What if Charmaine was pacing her room in the Haley house, packed and ready to go to Boston and missing him as much as he was missing her?

He'd never expected her to stay, in spite of her promise of forever. Science, right? Magnetism.

He knelt on one knee and threw back the rug to reveal the Montgomery treasure hiding place. The box was small, but it held so much of his mother and what he remembered of her. He brought the box up and placed it close to the fire, where he could see more clearly.

Opening the Bible, he settled himself comfortably on the floor. His name was the last entry in the book. He had been so certain that Charmaine's stay in his life was a temporary one that he had never entered her name and the date of their marriage. And she'd never asked him to.

He barely glanced at the Montgomery blessing. One true love to cherish for all time was not a concept he could deal with right now.

The book of poems was at the very bottom. Somewhere in this book was the poem his mother had made him memorize. It had been years ago, before she got sick. All he could remember was that his name was in there, somewhere.

It was a slim volume of poems by Thomas Campion, and as he picked it up the pages fell open to a well-used page. His poem.

Thrice toss these oaken ashes in the air;

Thrice sit thou mute in this enchanted chair;
Then thrice three times tie up this true love's
* knot,*
And murmur soft: "She will, or she will not."

There was more, but this one verse was enough to make him doubt everything he'd done.

He hadn't given Charmaine a choice. He'd made it for her, thinking it was for the best, certain he had to sacrifice his happiness for what was best for her. But he hadn't given her a choice.

Charmaine Haley, who flouted convention and spoke her mind and preached on the rights of women from her very heart . . . that woman wouldn't have stayed with him after their bizarre wedding unless somewhere deep inside she had wanted to. She could've run, she could've disappeared, she could've made his life hell, instead of heaven.

She will, or she will not.

How could he let her go without knowing for sure? He'd spend the rest of his life wondering. . . .

It was late, but he couldn't sit here and do nothing. Would she, or would she not?

He delayed only long enough to take an ink pen and write Charmaine's name next to his, along with the date of their shotgun wedding.

*   *   *

Everything was in place. Charmaine paced in front of the window and fiddled with the ribbons at the cuff of her nightdress. Eula had assured her that Ash always did his shopping at her mercantile, and that wouldn't change no matter what. When she finally saw him and told him that Charmaine was planning to stay here in Salley Creek and marry the first man who asked her, after their divorce was final, he'd have to do something—wouldn't he?

What if he didn't?

Then at least she'd know that his reason for sending her away had nothing to do with what was best for her.

Felicity and Jeanette were convinced that it would work. And if it didn't they planned to show him the second telegram. Charmaine hadn't agreed to that part of the plan, not yet. It was too much like begging, and she would not beg.

What if Ash had decided, in these days apart, that he didn't need her after all? What would she do then? She could just see herself, a spinster living here with her parents for the rest of her life. It was a sad, sad picture she conjured in her mind.

At least tomorrow Howard would be gone and out of their lives for good. He'd signed Robert's papers without a word of protest, not even asking about Hester, and then he'd taken Stuart Haley's advice about lying low. He was closeted in his room at the boarding house, hiding from Tavish and the Haleys, no doubt. He was such a coward, a coward who had hit his wife.

In her mind she went over the discussion she'd had with Felicity that morning, and wished again that she had seen what was going on in the Stillwell household. She'd been so blindly naive. So utterly stupid.

Charmaine wondered if she really appeared so unforgiving that Felicity was afraid to tell her the truth. Did she appear to be so harsh that there was no sympathy in her heart?

She'd done her best for a very long time to ignore the workings of her heart, at least until Ash had come along.

Felicity was fortunate to have found a man who loved her and Hester so completely. Tavish seemed perfectly content, even though Daddy was making him sleep in the bunkhouse. At least he hadn't pulled a gun on the Scot. Yet.

It looked as if Robert and Jeanette really would be settling in Salley Creek, at least for a while. There was only one lawyer in town, and he was nearing retirement. Once Stuart Haley had promised to throw what business he could Robert's way, they'd made their decision.

Everything was falling into place. Now, if she could only bring Ash around. . . .

There was a sudden plinking sound at her window. Sleet? It was cold enough, but it hadn't looked like rain earlier, and the moon was lighting her room brightly, without a blanket of clouds masking its brilliance. Then all was silent again. Surely it wasn't her imagination . . .

The plinking sounds came again, a little harder this time, and Charmaine went to the window. No sleet after all, just a man standing in the shadows of the maple tree under her window. Probably Tavish, looking for Felicity's room. Goodness, he was on the wrong side of the house. One window over and he would have been tossing pebbles at the master bedroom.

She lifted the panes slowly and silently. "Are you completely insane?" she hissed.

"I think I must be."

Her heart stopped. It wasn't Tavish at all. It was Ash.

"What are you doing here?"

With a leap off the ground, he took a tree limb in both hands and hoisted himself up and closer to her open window. "I came to talk to you."

"To *talk* to me?" Her heart lurched with hope, and terror that her hope was useless. "After what you said to me the last time I talked to you, what makes you think I might possibly be interested in continuing *that* conversation?"

He sat on the limb and leaned against the tree. Leaves ruffled in the wind and again as he pushed them aside to give her a full view of his face.

"I was thinking of starting a whole new conversation, if you don't mind."

"Have you been talking to Eula?" So soon?

"No. Why?"

"Never mind," she snapped. "Well, what do you want? I don't suppose you've come to apologize for your atrocious behavior."

He stood on the limb and grabbed another, one that would bring him even closer. A small limb cracked and fell, and she held her breath, but Ash was perfectly steady as he raised himself a few feet higher.

"I came," he said testily, "to ask you to sacrifice everything you are and everything you want for yourself because I love you. To ask you to come home with me and be my wife. To be my one true love to cherish for all time. That's what I should apologize for," he said harshly, "that I dare to ask for so much . . ."

"You love me?" she whispered.

"Of course I love you." He stood too quickly and one foot slipped off the limb. He teetered for a moment, and Charmaine held her breath.

"Be careful," she hissed.

He reached out and grabbed a limb for support, and it crackled slightly. "I haven't climbed a tree in fifteen years," he confessed, "but I couldn't wait another minute to do this. I didn't get the chance to ask you to marry me, but I'm asking you now to be my wife."

She had to pull Stuart down to lie beside her. "You stay where you are and keep quiet."

"Maybe you should tell Ash Coleman that," he hissed. "I've never heard so much racket in all my life."

In the dark, she smiled. Everything was going to work out for the best, she was certain. "He isn't exactly cat-footed, is he? At least any fears you might have had about Ash being a burglar are put to rest."

"There's sure as hell no Indian blood in the Coleman family," he grumbled. "That boy couldn't sneak up on a deaf man."

"We won't have to worry about him stealing up on you during Sunday visits and startling you out of your wits."

"Sunday visits," he whispered. Outside his window, another limb cracked loudly. "It's what Charmaine wants, isn't it? Ash and that farm."

"Ash wherever he is, I think. I imagine tomorrow Charmaine will be packing her things and moving back to the Coleman farm."

"If Ash doesn't kill himself playing Romeo," Stuart grumbled.

They could hear whispered words, the clatter of leaves and limbs, a gust of wind.

"It's hard," Stuart whispered. "Harder than I ever imagined."

"Having children?" she asked with a smile in the dark.

Stuart sighed. "No. Hell, even Howard Stillwell can make a baby. Having them is easy. *Loving* them is what makes everything so damn hard." He placed a wide and rough hand over her gently rounded stomach. "And here we are starting all over again."

"Are you sorry?"

He turned a grinning face to her. "Sorry? Hell no. I can't wait."

A gust of cold wind grabbed him and he had to clutch at a limb to keep from falling to the ground.

"You'd better come in," Charmaine whispered, and she opened the window wide and offered her hand.

He climbed a bit farther, and then took her hand and threw one leg over the windowsill.

"Your hands are like ice," she said as she tugged gently at his hand. He slipped into Charmaine's darkened room, and she closed the window behind him. "I can't believe you. . . ."

With the hand she held, he pulled her gently into his arms for the kiss he'd been dreaming about for days. "I do love you," he whispered against her warm lips. "More than anything. If you just have to go to Boston, if you can't live without it, I'll sell the farm and come with you. Because I can't live without you."

It was the simplest solution, and he knew it as the words fell from his mouth. He would live anywhere to be with Charmaine. The idea had come to him as he'd circled the house . . . three times . . . looking for a sign. And then she'd passed in front of the window and he'd known what he had to do.

"What do you think?" he whispered.

She stood squarely in front of him and grasped the front of his shirt as if she needed the support or else was afraid he'd walk away. Lifting her head slowly, she looked him boldly in the eye. When she gazed at him this way his senses left him, and he was filled with the foolish notion that no matter what they faced, it wouldn't break them.

"I've always been very honest about what I think, and it's come very easy to me. I can freely say what I think, no matter how outrageous or shocking, but when it comes to how I feel it's much harder."

He would give her an easy way out, it was the least he could do. "If you don't want to stay, and you don't want me to go with you, I'll understand. I won't like it—" A quickly raised finger against his lips silenced him.

"I love you," she breathed softly. Her eyes shone with unshed tears, and he couldn't help but wrap his arms around her and hold her close.

When his arms were securely around her, she laughed lightly and a single tear ran down her cheek. "You know, I've been in love with you all my life. I used to think it was a curse that I thought about you so much while I was away. Childish memories, that's all they were, and yet they came to me again and again while I was at school and then living with Felicity and Howard."

He kissed her damp cheek.

"And then I came home and found out that I love you so much more as a woman than I did as a child. I love the way you laugh. I love your kind heart and your gentle soul. I love knowing that you've never taken any woman to your bed but me, that you waited for me just as I waited for you." She lifted her face to him, and in the moonlight he saw new tears join the first, rolling down. And still she smiled. "I love your eyes, the way they light when they meet mine at the end of the day, the way they tell me when you want me. I love you in more ways than I can possibly tell you, and if you don't take me home soon my heart will be forever broken."

"You love me," he whispered.

"Yes, and I have no intention of going back to Boston," she said softly. "I want our children to grow up here. I want them to have grandparents and cousins and aunts and uncles close by."

"Our girls are *not* going off to school," he insisted, and as he spoke he took a step toward the bed with Charmaine secure in his arms.

"Of course not," she agreed easily.

"Are you sure you won't miss it?" Another step toward the bed. "The seminars and the manuals, the shocking discussions."

Her moonlit smile was positively devilish. "Why, I won't miss it at all."

The backs of Charmaine's legs were against the mattress. "What's that supposed to mean?"

"They use the schoolhouse for community meetings, so I was pretty sure they'd agree to let me use the building on occasion. Mayor Hildreth agreed with only a *few* reservations." She sat on the edge of the bed and without taking her eyes from his began to work at his belt buckle. "Seth Brand, at the newspaper, was very enthusiastic about cooperating with me in the printing and sale of informational manuals."

As the belt buckle fell loose, he took Charmaine's hand and pulled her to her feet. "When did you set this up?" He loosened the ties at her neck and pulled the nightgown over her head.

"Today," she said as the nightgown cleared her head. "Really, Ash," she started unbuttoning his shirt. "You didn't think I would give up on you so easily, did you?"

His clothes joined her nightgown on the floor, and together they slipped under the fat quilt that was bright in the moonlight.

"I missed you," she whispered as she pressed her body to his and kissed him deeply. "More than you know, more than I thought I could ever miss anyone."

"I missed you, too," he confessed. He wanted her, now, but he kissed her mouth and her throat and then her rosy nipples, and when she moaned and arched against him he parted her thighs with his knee and slipped his hand between her legs to touch her feminine core.

She was wet for him, already, warm and inviting and calling out to him with every subtle rock of her body against his, with every breath he took for her, with her.

When he rolled Charmaine onto her back and towered above her, she parted her thighs and took his manhood in her hand. "One true love for all time," she whispered, and then she guided his hard shaft to her welcoming body.

He filled her, and at the same time she somehow filled him. Heart and soul, with a spirit and a joy beyond his comprehension. He loved her, with his heart and his body, until *she* was all he knew.

And outside this warm haven, in the distant chill of the night, the town clock struck twelve.

Epilogue

The Annual Haley Masked Ball, 1900

Charmaine and Ash always looked forward to the masked ball, but this one was special. This year's party fell on their fifth wedding anniversary, and everyone was here.

She loved dancing with Ash, who managed to grow more handsome with every passing year. At the moment there was a crowd of little ones dancing at their feet. To their right, Hester, now a beautiful seven years old, was trying patiently to dance with her cousin Montgomery, who at four was the very picture of his father. Green eyes, dark hair, black mask. To the left their two-year-old Nate was dancing with Tavish and Felicity's Megan, who was also a feisty two years old. Her brother Connor, who was four years old and a full head taller than Montgomery, was dancing clumsily just behind Ash with Jeanette and Robert's Alice.

The babies, their own Lila, Tavish and Felicity's Bonnie and William, and Jeanette and Robert's James, were in the nursery upstairs. After another song or two the other children would join them, and the adults would be able to dance without fear of stepping on their sons and daughters, nieces and nephews.

Tavish, tall as he was, was particularly afraid of stepping on one of the *bairns*, as he called them. While he and Felicity danced, he continually glanced down and around. Who would have thought, when he'd arrived in Salley Creek, that he'd become such a good foreman for the Haley ranch?

Jeanette and Robert were a lovely couple still, even though he was turning gray and she was, at this moment, well along with their third child. Robert, though he always had an air of the city about him, was a fine Salley Creek lawyer. Just last year he'd built Jeanette a house almost as large as this one.

Charmaine watched her parents dance, for a moment, smiling at the heartening sight. Her father, rough and tumble cowboy at heart that he was, loved nothing more than having a house full of family. He openly delighted in his children and his grandchildren. Sundays were a circus in the Haley house, and through the commotion, the laughter and the tears and the occasional crisis, Stuart Haley grinned from ear to ear.

The entire town was here, dancers mingling with the large family. Eula and Winston, who'd wisely left their five children at home; Delia and her husband of three years; the new Mayor; Reverend Howell, who'd performed that memorable marriage ceremony five years ago—everyone.

Nathan and Oswald had made the trip this year, and Oswald was presently surrounded by an assembly of giggling young girls who found the well-known actor fascinating. The stage agreed with Oswald more than anyone had ever expected. He was successful and much sought after—and loved it.

Nathan was on top again, with Oswald as his leading man. Five years of success hadn't changed him a bit. Pumpkin was getting on in years, though, and when Nathan left Salley Creek this time he would be leaving the mare on the Coleman farm.

Verna wasn't here, thank heavens. She was comfortably settled in San Francisco with the husband she'd taken four months after leaving Salley Creek. Elmo and Ruth had made the trip, though. They'd been married two years now, had one little boy who was a chubby replica of his father, and Elmo had become quite successful as a geologist. As a matter of fact, his trip to Kansas had nothing to do with the masked ball or the anniversary.

Charmaine glanced around but didn't see them anywhere. "Where are Elmo and Ruth?" she asked as the music stopped. "They said they'd be here."

Ash was unconcerned. "You know Elmo. Always late, and these days he's much more interested in rocks than in people."

"Except for Ruth and Bink."

His grin was bright. "Except for Ruth and Bink. Who names a kid Bink, anyway?"

Before she could chastise him for being rude, little Stu was tugging on his pants leg. "Ash," he said in his most grown-up voice. "I don't want to go upstairs with the children. I want to stay up all night like my sisters."

Ash explained in a very patient voice how dull the party would be once the children left, and how much fun they'd have at their own little party upstairs, and without another word of protest Stu left with the other little ones.

Everyone but Charmaine thought it was odd that Stu listened to Ash better than he did anyone else. Ash could reason with him when no one else could, and the child ran to him for comfort and hugs and occasionally to dry his tears on a sleeve. Of course, Ash was more than Stu's brother-in-law. He was also his godfather.

Charmaine was thankful for so much in her life. Ash and their children, the farm that continued to do well, having her family close by . . . even though her father and Ash still butted heads on occasion. Stuart Haley insisted every year on giving Ash cattle, and every year Ash refused. Just to irritate his father-in-law, she'd decided.

She gave regular lectures at the schoolhouse, usually the second Tuesday evening of every month, and printed corresponding manuals to distribute. There were those who were dismayed, of course, but she looked at those narrow-minded people as challenges to be met and conquered. She was almost always successful.

Her seminars on family planning were the most scandalous, and the most well attended.

When the music began again, a waltz, Ash gave her his full attention. There were no children to watch out for, no little hands tugging at their clothing.

"When it gets too warm for you," he said softly, "we'll take a stroll out to the gazebo and rest a while."

Goodness, they never got a moment's rest in the gazebo, but this had become a yearly ritual.

"I don't know," she whispered. "How do I

know you won't attempt to dally with me once we're alone?"

Oh, she loved that smile, so bright it grabbed her heart and wouldn't let go. "You can be assured I will," he promised.

"Ash! Dammit Ash, where are you?"

Ash closed his eyes and his smile faded. Elmo's distraught cry came from the main entrance, and all heads turned in that direction. The music came to a gradual halt.

Elmo was wide eyed and red faced and . . . and absolutely filthy. He was covered in black smears from his head to his boots. In fact, he was tracking some of the mess onto the carpet.

The crowd gave him a wide berth as he spotted Ash and hurried across the room. A few women squealed when he came too close to their expensive gowns.

"What happened to you?" Ash placed his hands on his hips and glared down at his stepbrother.

"I found it, I knew it was there and I was right!" Elmo's grin was white in contrast to a near-black face.

"You found what?" Ash asked patiently.

"Oil, in that ridge I've been drilling on all week." Elmo was so excited he was near breathless. "Oil." He waited for a reaction and was disappointed. "Ash," he said with a despairing moan. "You're rich!"

Ash stared at his stepbrother for a moment as

the news sunk in. "Well, that's nice," he said calmly. "Now, you go clean up and bring Ruth to the party and we'll celebrate."

Elmo left, the crowd murmured and stared, and the orchestra didn't begin to play until Ash turned to them with a wave of his hand and a demand for another waltz.

Charmaine and Ash began to dance first, and eventually the rest of the crowd joined in.

"We'll have a hell of a time slipping away now," Ash whispered. "Everybody's watching." He leaned close, so that his mouth was near her ear. "We'll have to distract them, somehow."

"Didn't you hear what Elmo said?" she asked as he pulled slightly away. "You're rich."

He stopped dancing, in the middle of the waltz, in the middle of the room. The dance went on, brightly lit and brightly clothed friends and relatives circling around them in time to the music. Ash ignored them all, placing a hand beneath her chin and lifting her face to his for a brief and tender kiss.

"I know," he whispered. "I know."

And they lived, for the most part, happily ever after.

Read on for a preview

of Linda Jones's upcoming

Legendary Lovers romance,

The Indigo Blade

available in Spring 1999

from Love Spell!

The prisoner would be delivered into Chadwick's hands well before dark, and in a matter of days the troublemaker would serve as an example to the damned rebels who were making this job so bloody difficult.

Captain Bradford Thurman considered himself to be a good soldier. Better than most, to be honest. But he preferred fighting the French to playing nursemaid to a bunch of ungrateful colonials. Where would they be without the British Army? Suffering at the hands of savages or fighting off French settlers, that's where.

Bradford glanced over his shoulder to check on the prisoner and the four guards who flanked the unfortunate colonial. The rebel wasn't much of a troublemaker at the moment, thanks to the beating he'd received just that morning. An unkempt head hung defeatedly, so that a fall of greasy hair shielded the rebel's face. His shoulders were slumped as if he knew he was traveling to his death. The insolent colonial would think twice before arguing with a soldier in the British Army again, if he had the opportunity in his few remaining hours on this earth.

The rebel had committed his third, and final, act of sedition. Twenty lashes on the first offense hadn't dissuaded him, nor had the fifty that had followed a few months later. This third transgression had sealed his fate. Tomorrow the dissident would hang.

These damned colonials were like children, according to Bradford's logic. Rowdy, whiny children who didn't know a good thing when they had it. A goodly amount of excellent tea had been wasted in a fit of pique by grown men not-so-cleverly disguised as natives! If that was not a childish act, what was?

Perhaps when they saw one of their own swinging on a gallows they'd think twice about the preposterous concept of independence.

The January afternoon was nippy and the damp chill penetrated Bradford's uniform in a most unpleasant way. South Carolina was certainly not as cold as the northern colonies, but humid air made the chill all but unbearable. The road they traveled was narrow and lined with a thick growth of trees, bare-branched hardwoods and evergreens growing together and intertwining their boughs so that in spite of the blue sky above, Bradford felt as if he were passing through a long, winding tunnel. Wilderness, that's all this blasted country was . . . mile after mile of trees and water and more trees. How he longed for London. . . .

He saw the overturned wagon as he came around a bend in the path, and cursed beneath his breath as he lifted a hand to still the soldiers to his rear. An old man with unruly gray hair and clothing that resembled a collection of sacks draped around his body was kneeling by the wagon, his back to the soldiers as he muttered loudly.

"Make way," Bradford ordered. The wagon, a number of scattered baskets, the old man, and the skirted body he knelt over blocked the path completely.

The man jumped, obviously surprised, and as he spun his stooped body around, the left sleeve of his crude garment swung free. He raised his one hand in greeting. "Praise be. The Lord has answered my prayers and sent these kind soldiers to assist me."

"We've not come to assist you, old man," Bradford said sternly. "Clear this road immediately. We must pass."

The codger appeared to be puzzled for a moment, wrinkling his nose and peering up through narrowed eyes. Eyes that were topped by dominating dark eyebrows that were stark on a too-pale face. The man's skin was, in fact, more gray than was normal for a healthy man of any age, and was marked in several places. Good heavens, the fellow was probably diseased.

"I see," the old man muttered in a gratingly coarse voice. "I'd better get busy, then.

He turned his attention to the woman on the ground. "Rebecca," he said in a softened voice. "Open your eyes now, your poor old grandfather needs you." He knelt beside her again, lowering his body with obvious effort, and gently patted her face. "Wake up, dear."

The old man looked back at the squad of soldiers. "I don't think she's badly hurt," he said, as if they might have a care for the injured woman. "There's no blood, but she's got a lump on her head the size of an egg."

The woman he so fondly called Rebecca stirred, and a long strand of dark hair fell from her face. What a homely one she was! Long face, long nose, large mouth . . . but as she rolled onto her back she revealed an admirable, shapely figure.

"That's right, Rebecca, we must move the wagon so these fine soldiers can pass."

There was no way a one-armed old man and a wounded girl would be able to right that wagon and move it to the side of the road, so Bradford grudgingly ordered two of his troopers to dismount and assist. The other two moved close to the prisoner, in case the rebel was foolish enough to think his reduced guard offered a chance for escape.

Bradford himself dismounted, eager to get moving again and to deliver the prisoner to Charles Town and Victor Chadwick.

The old man tried valiantly to assist the soldiers in righting the wagon, while the dazed girl sat forlornly in the middle of the road. She rubbed the side of her head, moaned softly, and played with a strand of hair that fell past her full breasts.

"Out of the way," Bradford ordered as he moved the one-armed man aside to take his place. He had no desire to rub elbows with a diseased peasant. The old-timer mumbled his thanks, moved clumsily aside, and asked gruffly after his granddaughter. Bradford gave all his strength and attention to the chore at hand, heaving until his muscles strained and an unpleasant sweat broke out beneath his heavy uniform. It was hard work, but he had the help of his soldiers. With a final mighty surge of effort the wagon was righted.

"Thank you, sir, thank you," the old man said, and Bradford turned to find the man and his granddaughter, who had come to her feet and was amazingly tall, standing very near . . . and pointing a variety of weapons in his direction. The old man held a dagger with a wooden grip and a long, thin, well-honed sword, and the young woman had a .67-caliber pistol in each of her large, roughened hands. The miscreants were close and the weapons were steady; Bradford decided it would not be prudent to reach for his own.

"Common wayside bandits," he spat. "You're fools if you think you can take on soldiers of the British Army and get away with it. Threaten me if you like, but you're headed for disaster. My troopers will take care of you."

"These troopers?" With a wavering hand the old man pointed his dagger at the wide-eyed men who flanked their captain.

"Those troopers," Bradford said grandly, pointing toward the men who guarded the rebel who was traveling to his death.

The old man turned his head slowly, and seemingly without a care. "What troopers would that be? Surely you don't mean those two unfortunate lads."

Reluctantly, Bradford turned his head and looked to the spot where his troopers and the prisoner had been waiting patiently and securely moments earlier. His soldiers had dismounted, been stripped of their weapons, and they had been quite efficiently bound and gagged. They sat, wide eyed, with their backs against the trunk of a young tree. The prisoner was gone.

"How dare you—" Before he could finish they came without warning from the woods, five gray-haired old men dressed as the thief before him was, in baggy and torn clothing and soft moccasins. They came with ropes and strips of cloth, and in a matter of minutes he found himself and the remainder of his contingent stripped of weapons and securely bound.

The one-armed man knelt before him, and that dagger danced wickedly, cutting the air and coming awfully close to Bradford's heart.

"Perhaps I should do to you what you had

planned for the young man you were transporting to Charles Town. What was his fate to be? Hanging? Firing squad?"

Suddenly Bradford was afraid. These weren't ordinary bandits, and it wasn't chance that brought him and his troopers to this meeting. These were revolutionaries, madmen, hotheaded rebels.

"I was delivering my prisoner to Victor Chadwick, who is an important member of the Governor's Council. What Mr. Chadwick had planned for him, I wouldn't know." Bradford lied, and prayed as he had never prayed before that he lied well.

The man smiled, revealing blackened teeth. "Is that right?"

Bradford nodded.

"I want you to deliver a message for me," the man whispered, and Bradford felt a surge of relief. He would survive this encounter. After all, he couldn't deliver a message if he were dead.

"Certainly."

The old-timer swung his arm and the dagger forward, swiftly, with great power, and the sharp-edged metal was embedded in the road not two inches from Bradford's crotch. The shaking began, uncontrollable, deep trembling that started in his legs and traveled quickly up and through his entire body.

"Tell him to watch his back." Colorless eyes flashed, strong and powerful in a white-gray and oddly weathered face. "Tell him not to sleep too deeply at night, nor relax his vigilance when he thinks himself among friends, nor trust that his King and his soldiers will keep him safe."

Bradford nodded

"Tell him," the old man whispered, "the Indigo Blade is coming."

The Snow Queen
ANNE AVERY

When Boston-bred Hetty Malone arrives at the Colorado Springs train station, she is full of hope that she will soon marry her childhood sweetheart and live happily ever after. Yet life amid the ice-capped Rockies has changed Michael Ryan. No longer the hot-blooded suitor Hetty remembers, the young doctor has grown as cold and distant as the snowy mountain peaks. Determined to revive Michael's passionate longing, Hetty quickly realizes that no modern medicine can cure what ails him. But in the enchanted splendor of her new home, she dares to administer the only remedy that might melt his frozen heart: a dose of good old-fashioned loving.

_52151-2 $5.99 US/$6.99 CAN

Dorchester Publishing Co., Inc.
P.O. Box 6640
Wayne, PA 19087-8640

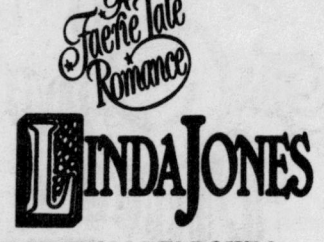

Someone's Been Sleeping In My Bed

A Faerie Tale Romance

Linda Jones

WHO'S BEEN EATING FROM MY BOWL?
IS SHE A BEAUTY IN BOTH HEART AND SOUL?
WHO'S BEEN SITTING IN MY CHAIR?
IS SHE PRETTY OF FACE AND FAIR OF HAIR?
WHO'S BEEN SLEEPING IN MY BED?
IS SHE THE DAMSEL I WILL WED?

The golden-haired woman barely escapes from a stagecoach robbery before she gets lost in the Wyoming mountains. Hungry, harried, and out of hope, she stumbles on a rude cabin, the home of three brothers, great bears of men who nearly frighten her out of her wits. But Maddalyn Kelly is no Goldilocks; she is a feisty beauty who can fend for herself. Still, how can she ever guess that the Barrett boys will bare their souls to her—or that one of them will share with her an ecstasy so exquisite it is almost unbearable?

_52094-X $5.99 US/$6.99 CAN

Big Bad Wolf by Linda Jones. Big and wide and strong, Wolf Trevelyan's shoulders are just right for his powerful physique—and Molly Kincaid wonders what his arms would feel like wrapped tightly around her. Molly knows she should be scared of the dark stranger. She's been warned of Wolf's questionable past. But there's something compelling in his gaze, something tantalizing in his touch—something about Wolf that leaves Molly willing to throw caution, and her grandmother's concerns, to the wind to see if love won't find the best way home.

_52179-2 $5.50 US/$6.50 CAN

The Emperor's New Clothes by Victoria Alexander. Cardsharp Ophelia Kendrake is mistaken for the Countess of Bridgewater and plans to strip Dead End, Wyoming, of its fortunes before escaping into the sunset. But the free-spirited beauty almost swallows her script when she meets Tyler Matthews, the town's virile young mayor. Tyler simply wants to settle down and enjoy the simplicity of ranching. But his aunt and uncle are set on making a silk purse out of Dead End, and Tyler is going to be the new mayor. It's a job he accepts with little relish—until he catches a glimpse of the village's newest visitor.

_52159-8 $5.50 US/$6.50 CAN

Dorchester Publishing Co., Inc.
P.O. Box 6640
Wayne, PA 19087-8640

Please add $1.75 for shipping and handling for the first book and $.50 for each book thereafter. NY, NYC, and PA residents, please add appropriate sales tax. No cash, stamps, or C.O.D.s. All orders shipped within 6 weeks via postal service book rate. Canadian orders require $2.00 extra postage and must be paid in U.S. dollars through a U.S. banking facility.

Name_____

Address_____

City_____State_____Zip_____

I have enclosed $_____ in payment for the checked book(s).

Payment <u>must</u> accompany all orders. ❏ Please send a free catalog.

Desperado's Gold
Linda Jones

Jilted at the altar and stranded in the Arizona desert by a blown gasket in her Mustang convertible, Catalina Lane hopes only for a tow truck and a lift to the nearest gas station. She certainly doesn't expect a real live desperado. But suddenly, catapulted back in time to the days of the Old West, Catalina is transported into a world of blazing six-guns and ladies of the evening.

When Jackson Cady, the infamous gunslinger known as "Kid Creede," returns to Baxter, it's to kill a man and earn a reward, not to use his gold to rescue a naive librarian from the clutches of a greedy madam. He never would have dreamed that the beauty who babbled so incoherently about the twentieth century would have such an impact on him. But the longer he spends time with her, the more he finds himself captivated by her tender touch and luscious body—and when he looks deep into her amber eyes, he knows that the passion that smolders between them is a treasure more precious than any desperado's gold.

_52140-7 $5.50 US/$6.50 CAN

Dorchester Publishing Co., Inc.
P.O. Box 6640
Wayne, PA 19087-8640

Please add $1.75 for shipping and handling for the first book and $.50 for each book thereafter. NY, NYC, and PA residents, please add appropriate sales tax. No cash, stamps, or C.O.D.s. All orders shipped within 6 weeks via postal service book rate. Canadian orders require $2.00 extra postage and must be paid in U.S. dollars through a U.S. banking facility.

Name_____
Address_____
City_____ State_____ Zip_____
I have enclosed $_____ in payment for the checked book(s).
Payment <u>must</u> accompany all orders. ❑ Please send a free catalog.

NO ANGEL'S GRACE

LINDA WINSTEAD

From the moment Dillon feasts his eyes on the raven-haired beauty, Grace Cavanaugh, he knows she is trouble. Sharp-tongued and stubborn, with a flawless complexion and a priceless wardrobe, Grace certainly doesn't belong on a Western ranch. But that's what Dillon calls home, and as long as the lovely orphan is his charge, that's where they'll stay.

But Grace Cavanaugh has learned the hard way that men can't be trusted. Not for all the diamonds and rubies in England will she give herself to any man. But when Dillon walks into her life he changes all the rules. Suddenly the unapproachable ice princess finds herself melting at his simplest touch, and wondering what she'll have to do to convince him that their love is the most precious gem of all.

_4223-1 $5.50 US/$6.50 CAN

A Faerie Tale Romance

Prince of Kisses

Colleen Shannon

Daughter of wealth and privilege, lovely Charlaine Kimball is known to Victorian society as the Ice Princess. But when a brash intruder dares to take a king's ransom in jewels from her private safe, indignation burns away her usual cool reserve. And when the handsome rogue presumes to steal a kiss from her untouched lips, forbidden longing sets her soul ablaze.

Illegitimate son of a penniless Frenchwoman, Devlin Rhodes is nothing but a lowly bounder to the British aristocrats who snub him. But his leapfrogging ambition engages him in a dangerous game. Now he will have to win Charlaine's hand in marriage–and have her begging for the kiss that will awaken his heart and transform him into the man he was always meant to be.

—52200-4 $5.99 US/$6.99 CAN

Dorchester Publishing Co., Inc.
P.O. Box 6640
Wayne, PA 19087-8640

The Gentle Beast

COLLEEN SHANNON

GIVE YOUR HEART TO THE GENTLE BEAST AND FOREVER SHARE LOVE'S SWEET FEAST

Raised amid a milieu of bountiful wealth and enlightened ideas, Callista Raleigh is more than a match for the radicals, rakes, and reprobates who rail against England's King George III. Then a sudden reversal of fortune brings into her life a veritable brute who craves revenge against her family almost as much as he hungers for her kiss. And even though her passionate foe conceals his face behind a hideous mask, Callista believes that he is merely a man, with a man's strengths and appetites. But when the love-starved stranger sweeps her away to his secret lair, Callista realizes that wits and reason aren't enough to conquer him—she'll need a desire both satisfying and true if beauty is to tame the beast.

_52143-1 $5.99 US/$6.99 CAN

Dorchester Publishing Co., Inc.
P.O. Box 6640
Wayne, PA 19087-8640